The
Paradise
Trees

Linda Huber

Legend ▊ Press

Legend Press Ltd, 2 London Wall Buildings, London EC2M 5UU
info@legend-paperbooks.co.uk www.legendpress.co.uk

Contents © Linda Huber 2013

The right of the above author to be identified as the author of this work has been asserted in accordance with the Copyright, Designs and Patent Act 1988. British Library Cataloguing in Publication Data available.

ISBN 978-1-9095935-7-2

Set in Times
Printed by Lightning Source

Cover design by Gudrun Jobst www.yotedesign.com

Linda Huber was raised in Glasgow and trained in physiotherapy. Her writing is heavily influenced by her experience learning about methods of behaviour and how different people react and deal with stressful situations.

Linda now lives in Arbon, Switzerland where she works as a language teacher, based at a school in a 12th century castle. Linda has had over 50 short stories and articles published.

The Paradise Trees is Linda's debut novel.

Acknowledgements

A huge 'thank you' to the many people who have helped and encouraged me with this book.

Special thanks go to Ann Durnford for reading *The Paradise Trees* first, and believing in it.

Also to the team at Legend Press for all your hard work and for making the whole thing such a positive experience.

And to Christine Grant and Johnny Gwynne for answering my questions about police procedure; I hope I've got it right.

And not least to my sons for their invaluable IT support, couldn't have done it without you guys!

To Matthias and Pascal

Chapter One
Friday, 7th July

He had found exactly the right spot in the woods. A little clearing, green and dim, encircled by tall trees. A magical, mystery place. He would bring his lovely Helen here, and no-one would ever find them. No-one would hear her when she screamed and begged for mercy, and no-one would come running to rescue her, like they'd tried to with the first Helen. This time it was going to be perfect. A sacrament - something holy. He was looking forward to it so much.

He'd first noticed her in the village shop last weekend. She was buying bread and fruit, and he'd even helped her when she dropped an orange and it rolled down the aisle towards him. He'd picked it up and handed it back to her, and just for a second their eyes had met. In that brief moment he'd known. He had found another Helen. She had Helen's brown eyes, Helen's long dark hair; even the shape of her body was Helen. Slim, but with delicious curves in all the right places.

Of course he hadn't said anything then, just 'you're welcome' when she smiled a quick 'thank you'. Her eyes were dark and troubled, and a sudden rush of sweat prickled all over his body. He went and hung around behind the shelf with the soap powder until she'd paid and left, and then he asked old Mrs Mullen at the check-out who she was. Mrs Mullen was the biggest gossip in Lower Banford, and usually he was very careful not to start her off. He didn't want to be seen chit-chatting about the village people in their local shop. Now, however, he listened gratefully as she prattled on.

'That's Alicia Bryson, Bob Logan's daughter. She's up for the day to see poor Bob after that last little stroke he had, his fifth one I hear and he's not doing so well. Margaret Cairns – his sister, you know, she looks after Bob but it's getting too much for her, she's nearly seventy herself after all – was saying yesterday that Alicia and her little girl were coming for the summer too. I suppose... '

He hadn't listened any more. Alicia Bryson? No, she was Helen... his Helen. And she'd be in Lower Banford all summer, that was all that mattered. He would find her and make her his own darling love. And there was a child, too, another Helen? Little Helen? How perfect.

And now it was Friday and the sun was setting behind his beautiful woods. Most schools had broken up today, so his Helens might be packing now, getting ready for their journey even as he was thinking about them. Mrs Mullen would know when they were due; he would go and find out first thing tomorrow. And then, whenever it was, he'd be waiting for them. Big Helen and little Helen, and very soon they'd be on their way to join his first Helen, in Paradise.

He would do it all in a beautiful ceremony at the holy place in the woods, and surely then he'd be able to lay the ghost of his own special darling to rest. Helen, haunting him from Paradise.

She wouldn't be alone for much longer.

Chapter Two
Sunday, 9th July

Alicia

Alicia Bryson eased her elderly VW back into fifth gear after what seemed like the hundredth lot of road works, and glanced across at her daughter. Eight-year-old Jenny was dozing in the passenger seat, dark hair already escaping from her precious pigtails – Pippi Longstocking was the latest craze – and a selection of soft toys on her lap. Poor kid. This wasn't the best start to the holidays for her, a long, boring drive up the motorway when she could have been out celebrating the start of the summer holidays with all of her friends in Bedford.

Alicia grimaced. This was so not what she wanted to be doing today. Just exactly how was she supposed to give her daughter a fun-filled summer holiday in a tiny Yorkshire village where they knew no-one except her father and Margaret and there wasn't as much as a swing park?

And now they were stuck behind a smelly white van, hell, even on Sunday everyone and his dog was travelling up the M1. Tight-lipped, Alicia pulled out to overtake. Lower Banford here we come.

You're going back to the bad place.

The thought came into her head as clearly as if her childhood self had spoken aloud, and Alicia winced. Other kids had had loving homes. She'd had 'the bad place', the house where her father still lived, and it was even coming back as a ghost in her head now.

It just hadn't seemed fair. How she'd longed for parents like her friends had: friendly, strict only when they had to be, and caring. Instead she'd had family prayers for hours every evening, listening to her father's rants about God and the good life and lectures about the devil and all his works. The devil's works included things like women wearing trousers, novels, all music except hymns and psalms... As a child Alicia had been afraid of her father, and when childhood gave way to puberty the accompanying hormones and tantrums had turned life into a nightmare. The climax came when she was fourteen and her punishment for sneaking off to the cinema with a boy was the loss of her hair, hacked off by her father in a sickening fit of self-righteousness.

Remembering her teenage angst brought tears to Alicia's eyes, and she blinked repeatedly. The fast lane of the M1 wasn't a good place to start bawling about something that had happened half a lifetime ago. How lonely she had been back then. Mum had been no help at all; she had prided herself on being obedient and submissive right up to her death. Alicia had been left to fight her own battles.

'Bo-ring. Are we nearly there?' said Jenny, sitting up and pouting out of the window.

'We are, and you're being very good,' said Alicia, patting Jenny's jeans-clad leg. It wasn't all doom and gloom, Jen was here too. Time to put stars into her daughter's eyes.

'You know what? Aunt Margaret's got a dog now. We kept it a secret to surprise you. His name's Conker and he's huge, he's a Newfoundlander. Chocolate-brown colour. You'll love him.'

Jenny stared, her face lit up like Christmas and Easter rolled into one, stuffed animals clutched to her chest. 'Did you hear *that*?' she whispered. 'A new friend. Conker.' Eyes shining, she gazed back out of the window, and Alicia smiled to herself. Oh, how very much she loved Jen. Her dreamer.

'Why did we never go to Grandpa's for the holidays before?' said Jenny, turning back so quickly Alicia jumped. 'Tam goes to her Grandma's all the time.'

'Just a sec,' said Alicia, thankful that a speeding motorcyclist halfway up her exhaust was giving her a couple of minutes' thinking time. What could she say to that? That 'Grandpa' had been a terrible father and she had run away to Margaret the day after her sixteenth birthday and could count on the fingers of one hand the number of times she'd been back in Lower Banford since?

Hardly. She didn't want to shatter Jen's illusions about her one remaining grandparent who was going to die soon anyway. And how awful did that sound?

'Well, Grandpa hasn't been well for a few years now,' she said. 'And before that you were just a baby.'

And the whole purpose of this 'holiday' was to find another solution for her father, she thought grimly. A care home was going to be the best option, and as his next of kin – as uncomfortable as that felt – Alicia knew that she was the person to organise it.

A road sign loomed above them and Alicia flipped on the indicator. At last, here was their exit. She swung off the motorway, her shoulders up to her ears with tension.

Here was Merton, first place on the road back home and nearest big town. The fateful cinema was still here. Alicia glared at it as they passed, then grinned. It had got her a free haircut, hadn't it? Better just practise the irony, she'd need it again before the summer was over, she could see that coming a mile off.

After Merton came the Banfords, a trio of villages along the River Ban. Her old secondary school was in Upper Banford, with memories of French homework done on the bus, and agonising over boys and spots. And always being the outsider, the only one who didn't have eyeliner or jangly bangles or whatever the latest fashion was. Then came tiny Middle Banford whose one claim to fame was the ambiguously-named Ban Theatre Festival; four weekends each June when the South Yorkshire Drama Club performed whatever it was they'd spent the past several months rehearsing. This year it had been *A Midsummer Night's Dream*, and the press reviews for once had been favourable.

Two miles on was Lower Banford, nestling between the river and the wooded hillside, quiet and peaceful. *The bad place.*

'Lower Banford!' said Jenny, sitting up straight as they passed the road sign. 'Mummy, we've arrived!'

'We have indeed,' said Alicia. Her voice came out a hoarse whisper, and she cleared her throat a little too hard, aware that Jenny was still looking at her.

The village street was deserted. Apparently shops still closed on Sundays here. It was a yesterday kind of place, old houses with old people living in them. Her father's house was right at the back of the village, the garden bordering on the woods that crept round the hillside. A pretty place that held dark memories.

Alicia turned up the narrow lane, inching past the row of cars parked along one side, and then through the gateway to pull up under the Scotch pine in front of the house. Two storeys of crumbling red brick covered in green ivy, a weed-and-gravel driveway leading round to the long back garden. Home sweet home. Or something.

This is the bad place. You've come back to the bad place.

The young voice was tinged with fear now, a haunting little whisper in her head. Where were these thoughts coming from? Panic fluttering in her throat, Alicia stared up at her father's bedroom window. Was the voice her childhood self? A sudden wave of nausea made her gut spasm and her legs shake. Bile rose right into her mouth and she swallowed, desperately trying not to retch. This was the bad place and for the first time since the night of her sixteenth birthday she was actually going to sleep under this roof. For six long weeks there would be no escaping this house and the parent she had run from.

The nausea passed as suddenly as it had come. Knuckles still white on the steering wheel, Alicia took a deep breath, cold sweat on her forehead. She needed to get a grip. All that was left of her father was a frail, old man, and she was an adult now. She could do this. Jenny was staring at her, puzzlement all over her small face.

'Mummy?'

To Alicia's relief, Margaret opening the front door created the necessary diversion, for as soon as Jenny saw Conker prancing about the hallway she was off, soft toys forgotten for once.

Resignedly, Alicia turned and lifted her handbag from the back seat, knowing that all she wanted to do was grab her daughter and drive away and pretend that everything was all right. But grown-ups didn't do things like that. They faced reality.

She fixed a brave smile on her face and opened the car door.

The Stranger

His vigil started just after lunchtime. He had been quite unable to stop himself. The thought of Helen coming to Lower Banford, driving along the village street and then up Woodside Lane... he had to be there to see it. An early-morning visit to the shop yesterday and a casual remark about summer visitors had set Mrs Mullen off, he'd listened to a long monologue about tourists before she provided him with the only detail he was interested in: Alicia Bryson and her daughter were expected on Sunday afternoon.

At twelve on the dot he stationed his car near the bottom of Woodside Lane, and settled down to wait for Helen. He had an excuse ready, in case anyone saw him and tapped on the window. One of the houses further up the lane was empty, and he was going up to have a quick look round, wasn't he? After all, his own place was nothing special. Looking at property was a perfectly natural thing to be doing.

Nobody noticed him so he didn't need his excuse. There was nothing he could do except sit and wait, but the thought of Helen driving towards him, getting closer by the minute, nearer and nearer... how wonderfully exciting that was, an amazing feeling, almost orgasmic. It made his entire body tremble and the sweat, never far off, soaked through his shirt yet again. He was waiting for Helen... he didn't want it to end.

And then suddenly, they were here. Fortunately the lane was narrow, so you had to slow right down when you turned in from the main road. Helen's car crawled past him and there she was, and oh, she was just as perfect as he remembered, with such a beautiful worried expression on her face. If only he could hold her and kiss that frown away.

An instant later he saw the little girl and knew straightaway that here was another true love, an even greater love, if such a thing was possible. Little Helen, gazing out of the passenger seat window, and oh! – she'd seen him, she had looked straight at him – what had she thought? Did she realise that here was the man who was going to send her to Paradise? No, of course not.

But send her he would. And soon. What a wonderful time he would have, planning his ceremony, making sure that the road to Paradise was smooth.

His Helens had arrived.

Alicia

'Aunt Margaret! Is that Conker? Can I pat him?'

Margaret was still clutching the front door, and Alicia noticed that her aunt looked as distraught as she herself was feeling. Margaret's thin face was pale, and the strain was apparent in her voice.

'Hello darling. Yes, of course, he loves children. Why don't you go and play with him round the back? I'll shout when tea's ready and you can come in and see Grandpa.'

Jenny's face clouded at the mention of her grandfather, but she trotted off obediently with Conker at her heels. Alicia hugged Margaret. However bad she felt about coming here, help was definitely needed.

'Margaret, are you okay? How is - he?'

As usual, it was difficult to say her father's name. She hadn't called him 'Dad' since she'd been a very young child, in fact she didn't call him anything at all if she could help it.

'Hello, lovey, he's not so good - oh, Alicia, it's as if there's less of him every day.'

Alicia allowed herself to be led into the gloominess of the living room. Her parents had preferred to keep the place frozen in the 1930's when the house had been built - or maybe modern fittings and light were part of the devil's works too. The furniture was mahogany, dark and heavy; the thick brown curtains were worn stiff with time, and even the paintwork was brown, providing a muted contrast to the walls, where the wallpaper was a nondescript beige flowery pattern that had possibly looked fresh just after World War Two.

Her father was sitting by the fireplace, at first glance a distinguished old man… except he wasn't old, not by today's standards. And as for distinguished...

'Hello,' said Alicia, bending down until her face was level with his. His eyes lifted slightly but didn't quite meet hers, and his face remained expressionless as his gaze slid round towards the television. Like many stroke patients, his arm was more badly affected than his leg, and his right hand lay stiff and useless on his lap. Alicia bit her lip. She hadn't expected him to say anything; the first stroke four years ago had robbed him of his speech as well as the use of his arm, but even last Saturday there had been some kind of recognition, acknowledgment that someone was there. Today there was nothing.

Margaret pulled her over to the window and they stood watching Jenny and Conker running round the neglected garden.

'He's been like this since he woke up,' said Margaret in a low voice. 'The doctor's been, he said it might have been another ministroke in the night. He's coming back tomorrow. I don't know what to do, poor Bob – he can still walk alright but his arm's stiffer than it was and – it's as if he doesn't know me anymore.'

Alicia looked back at her father, sitting sucking his teeth, blank-faced. A tyrant no longer, in fact he seemed little more than a vegetable now. What a terrible way for anyone to end their life. Even him. The devil's works again…

She blew her nose. 'Margaret, we'll have to find a place for him somewhere. He can't stay here like this.'

Margaret drew herself up. 'Alicia, he can. It's only his mind. He's still quite alright on his feet and it's so much better for stroke patients to be in their own familiar surroundings. You know that yourself, you're a nurse for heaven's sake. I won't consider him going into a home.'

She swept out to the kitchen, presumably to make tea, and Alicia stared glumly after her. Championing her baby brother was the habit of a lifetime for Margaret. She had never stopped idolising him, not even when his 'religion' had led him to break away from the rest of the family. But what was Margaret expecting now? Did she think Alicia was about to move in for the duration and care for him like a dutiful daughter? Well, she wasn't. He'd been no kind of father and

Alicia was going to get him into a place where he'd be looked after by professionals. It was more than he deserved.

She flopped down on the sofa and sat staring at her father, whose eyes were fixed on the blank TV screen. They'd been older parents, him and Mum, both nearly forty when she was born. Now he was simply a wretched old man, broken in body and mind yet still managing to make his family unhappy. She almost felt like a teenager again, rebelling against his restrictions, his righteousness, and his... punishments... and...

Why had that little voice, that *very young* little voice, come into her head today, talking about 'the bad place'? The events she'd been remembering during the long drive north had all taken place in her teenage years, but the little voice in her head had been much, much younger. What other bad things had happened here? Something she'd been too young to remember? But if it had been so bad, surely she wouldn't have forgotten?

Or maybe it was better to forget.

The Stranger

They were here, his darlings, and he had seen them. Helen would have unpacked by now, they might even be having tea. Or maybe his wonderful girls were snuggled up on the sofa, whispering and exchanging sweet little kisses. How he would love to snuggle and kiss with them.

Soon he would have to make a difficult choice. Big Helen or little Helen, which of them should he take first? The little girl was wonderful: long dark hair, and such a sweet face, so very like his first Helen. He would never have thought he could love a child this way. His own Helen as he had never known her. How lucky he was to have her now.

He would make plans carefully. He would meet them around the village first, talk to them and gain their friendship, maybe make occasional visits. Then one by one he would take them to the special place in the woods and send them off to Paradise where they belonged. Little Helen first, yes, that would be best, because then big Helen would turn to him, her friend, in her grief. He would comfort her, hold her close to his heart and feel how trusting she was and how grateful, and she would hold him too, moaning in her distress and oh, how good it would feel, and then he would tell her gently that he was sending her to join little Helen in Paradise. She'd be pleased, of course, but afraid, too, and the very thought of it was making him shiver and sweat all over again. It would be so perfect, so holy, yes, truly something sacred. Soon he would have three Helens in Paradise.

He was going to be rich.

Of course the first Helen had been a mistake. He hadn't meant for her to go to Paradise, she should still be here, with him, on earth. But accidents happen and Helen had died, and in a strange kind of way it was better like this, otherwise he'd never have known how sweet it was to have an angel in Paradise. Ever since then he'd been searching for another Helen. Many times he'd thought he'd found one, only to be disappointed. Now he had two at once. And when it was all over, surely then he would have some sort of peace again, because the thought of darling Helen alone in Paradise was just too unbearably sad. Helen needed company, a sister and a little daughter. Soon now she would have them. How happy they would be.

Chapter Three
Monday, 10th July

Alicia

'Mummy? What did Aunt Margaret mean last night when she said there were too many strangers in the village?'

Alicia smiled, brushing out Jenny's tangled curls. Trust Jen. She had ears like an aerial, constantly picking up signals not necessarily meant for her. Margaret had been speaking generally, but the bottom line was she didn't approve of the fact that villages were for commuting from nowadays, which meant people moving in and out. Change and strangers all over the place in what had once been an intimate, stable community.

And her aunt must know, deep down, that big changes concerning her own life in this house would be inevitable soon. But none of this was explainable to an eight-year-old. Alicia reached for Jen's hair slides.

'Nothing really. A lot of new people have moved into the village this year, that's all.'

'So they're not bad strangers?' Jenny's eyes were still troubled, and Alicia shook her head.

'Nope. Just people,' she said firmly. 'But the rules here are the same as at home, never go anywhere with someone you don't know. Okay, that's you.'

Jenny ran to the window and waved down to Conker who was sniffing about the grass below. Alicia smiled ironically. At least her daughter was going to have better memories of Lower Banford than she herself had. And actually, she was beginning to realise just how few memories she had of her pre-teen self in this house. Years and years of life and almost no memory of them. Was that normal?

It was horrible, living here again. Twice that night she'd wakened, her heart pounding. And that same lingering feeling that she had been afraid like this before, a long time ago when she was even younger than Jenny. She'd been so vulnerable back then, so afraid of… of what? Was that one of the blanked-out memories? Or maybe it was just the whole situation with her father that was making her so uneasy now.

Jenny grabbed her sandals, as yet unworn. 'Woohoo, summer holidays and new sandals! Can we go to the river today? And the woods?'

Alicia nodded, trying to smile. This 'holiday' was going to turn into a constant battle to keep Jen happy, and at the same time sort out things that had to be sorted. Margaret was obviously going to need a considerable amount of persuasion about the whole care home idea, and Jen would want to be here, there and everywhere. Diplomacy would have to be the name of the game and there was no time like the present to start.

'Grandpa's doctor is coming after breakfast, and I want to see him first,' she said, shaking out the duvet. 'Then afterwards we'll do something together. Alright?'

'S'pose. But I do want to go and see the river today, okay?'

Jenny raced downstairs, and Alicia sighed. The river they would manage, but oh for some eight-year-old energy. All the same, having fun here with her daughter might help her lay some ghosts to rest.

She finished tidying the room and stepped across the landing, taking care to avoid the creaky floorboard in case it woke her father. She could hear his breath rattling as he snored away, and realised that she felt no emotion towards him whatsoever. Except contempt. Hell, was it normal to still resent your father at her age?

His bedroom door was half open, and Alicia glanced in. The old iron crucifix was still hanging above the bed, stark against the whiteness of the wall, and she could feel her heart thump as she stared at it. Something here really was giving her the creeps, a horrible sense of unease was crawling over her skin. And yet she had lived here for years… she had been born in that bedroom, and apart from a few days spent with Margaret every summer she had slept in this house every night of her life until she was sixteen. There had been no escaping the bad place for little Alicia. Thank God she'd be able to talk to the doctor today and set the ball rolling about finding a place for her father.

'What time's Doctor Morton coming?' she asked Margaret after breakfast.

'Half past ten,' said Margaret. 'But it's Doctor Carter now, he's taking over Doctor Morton's practice. Frank Carter, you might remember him, his family lived here way back before they moved down south. His wife died in some kind of accident a few years ago apparently.'

Alicia stared. 'Frank Carter? Yes, I do remember him. His sister was one of my friends at primary school. Sonja. They left just before we went to secondary school.'

And just after her father had been so mad at them both… She hadn't thought about it for years. They'd been about twelve, her and Sonja, and they'd spent an evening secretly making Valentine's cards in Alicia's room. Unknown to Alicia, her father had been standing outside the door listening to all their girly talk about boys and who fancied who. He had stormed into the room, sent Sonja home and then dragged Alicia down to the kitchen where he'd made her stand reading the bible aloud. For two solid hours he'd sat there, his eyes fixed on her as she stumbled through the Old Testament. She had loathed him then and the feeling had probably been mutual.

Margaret sniffed. 'Well, Frank's back. I don't know why on earth he wanted to come back to a little place like this.'

'Maybe because he has happy memories here?' suggested Alicia gently. 'It must have been tough for him, losing his wife like that.'

She looked at her aunt, concerned. Margaret was rinsing round the sink and blinking back tears.

She really does hate change, realised Alicia. But things couldn't go on like this, Margaret must see that. Her beloved Bob's condition was only going to deteriorate.

A dull thud upstairs sent Margaret scuttling to the door. 'That's

Bob. I'll help him dress and you make fresh tea. I expect the doctor'll take a cup too.'

She was gone before Alicia could draw breath. Grimly, she put the kettle on. Being independent was fine and good, but Margaret was overdoing it. At this rate she'd have a stroke too if she wasn't careful. Anyway, her father wouldn't realise if he was here at home, or somewhere else *in* a home. Or would he?

Something to ask the doctor about, she thought, hearing a car door slam outside.

Frank Carter was in the hallway before she got to the door, and Alicia blinked. She would never have recognised him. He was slight, only a few inches taller than she was, with overlong dark hair and a thin, lined face. Had the lines come when his wife died? A mere divorce had just about doubled her own tally of frown lines. What must it be like to lose the person you loved most of all, just like that? Please God she would never find out. He smiled, showing not unattractively crooked teeth, and held out his hand.

'Hello, Alicia,' he said. 'You've changed. I saw you in the village last Saturday and I have to confess I didn't recognise you at first. You've grown up since we last met.'

The hand gripping hers was warm, and Alicia felt comforted. This was her old friend's brother, and he'd been a part of her world back then. He was a few years older, too, he might remember things she couldn't. They could jog down memory lane together and maybe he could help her dig up some of the forgotten memories.

She wrinkled her nose. 'Well, it wasn't exactly yesterday.'

Frank laughed. 'Mrs Mullen, ah… reminded me all about you,' he said, leaning against the cutlery drawer. 'She even remembered how you and Sonja once let down the tyres on my bike while I was in buying sweets. I suppose you had your reasons but I can't remember at all what I'd done to deserve such… such wrath.'

Alicia grinned at him. He seemed nervous, but that was ridiculous. Maybe he was shy, or possibly it was awkward, having your sister's old school friend's parent as a patient.

'I expect we were just being brats. What's Sonja up to these days?'

He pulled a face and grinned. 'Sonja's an architect, married to an ambassador, three small boys and at the moment they're living in Paris. Posh dinner parties all the time.'

Alicia laughed. 'Not much like life in Lower Banford, then.'

'You could say that. They'll be here in a couple of weeks, actually, passing through on the way up north to John's mother in St Andrews first of all, and then staying with me the first two weeks in August on their way back. You'll still be here then, won't you?'

Alicia took a deep breath. Wow. Something to look forward to. Summer in Lower Banford might be more fun than she'd anticipated. But first they had to sort her father out. She smiled her most persuasive smile at Frank Carter.

'I'm glad you're here. I could use some support to convince Margaret about a care home for my father. It's getting too much for her here.'

He looked at her sympathetically. 'I know, but she's adamant about keeping Bob at home. And of course she's right about him still being able to get up the stairs and so on, but that could change any time and in all other areas he does need a lot of care. I think you'll have to ride gently for a bit but hopefully she'll agree in the end. I suppose you're only here for the holidays?'

Alicia suppressed a shudder. 'Only' for the holidays... six weeks in Lower Banford sounded like eternity. She nodded at Frank and he leaned back against the table.

'Right. With your say-so I'll put him on the list for St. Joseph's, the geriatric hospital in Middle Banford. It's an excellent place, Alicia. They have a new chief of nursing now, Doug Patton, and he's really keen. We can try to get Margaret over there for a visit one day this week, let her see the place for herself.'

Alicia looked at him appreciatively. At last, someone who was going to help her. 'Sounds good. I'll talk to her and get back to you.'

She handed over a mug of tea, noticing the threadbare cuffs on his jacket and the purple tie that was screaming at the fawn checked shirt. Didn't he notice what he was putting on in the morning?

Margaret appeared in the hallway with Bob shuffling beside her, not looking at any of them. Alicia saw stubbornness written right across her aunt's face, and felt her own jaw tighten as she poured tea for her father. The sooner they got this situation sorted, the better.

Frank followed her into the living room. 'Let Alicia take over for a bit here, Margaret,' he said firmly. 'You should have a complete break, you're tired and you deserve it. Does - '

'Aaaaah!' The wheezy, guttural sound was coming from deep in the old man's throat. Alicia stepped back. Her father's eyes were fixed on hers and his mouth was open.

Margaret bent over to hug him. 'Yes, dear, it's Alicia, back home from Bedford! Isn't that nice?' She turned to Alicia, beaming. 'He knows you, lovey! Isn't that wonderful?'

'Aaah ha ha ha,' said Bob, his eyes never leaving Alicia's. It almost sounded as if he was laughing.

'That's right, dear. Alicia. She's home now. Look, here's your tea.'

Margaret helped him with the mug, and Alicia rubbed her face. Shit and hell. As far as she knew her father had never tried to speak to her since the first stroke... but then she had never been living here, before. *Had* he been laughing just now? It was a horrible thought, and there was no way to tell. She forced her attention back to Margaret and Frank, who were discussing Bob's medication. Alicia drew breath to help Frank convince Margaret that sleeping pills were a good idea, then froze at the sound of Jenny's high, agitated voice outside.

'Mummy! Aunt Margaret, come *quick*, it's hurt, its back leg's all blood... ' She crashed into the room and pulled at Alicia's arm.

'Jenny, darling what's hurt?'

'It's a kitty, out in the lane, I think it's been run over, oh, come quick!'

Frank lifted his bag. 'Show me where it is and I'll see what I can do.'

Jenny looked at him, her eyes wide. 'Are you a stranger?' she asked, and Alicia hugged her daughter.

'It's okay, Jen, this is Doctor Frank Carter, he's here to see Grandpa. I was at school with him when we were children.'

Jenny's face brightened immediately. 'Can you help animals too?' she said, stepping towards him.

'I'll try. Let's have a look.'

Margaret handed Bob's mug to Alicia. 'I'll come too. It might be the Donovan's cat.'

She followed Frank and Jenny outside and the room fell silent. Alicia turned back to her father.

'More tea?' Again, she couldn't bring herself to call him 'Dad'. With immense discomfort, she held the mug to his lips and then wiped away the dribble after he'd taken a loud slurp. Hell, she was a nurse, and before she'd taken her present job as school nurse she'd even worked with geriatrics for God's sake and she still couldn't cope with this, she literally couldn't stand having to touch her father. Trembling, she put the mug down on the mantelpiece. Six weeks of this would kill her.

Her father coughed, then cleared his throat and leaned back in the armchair, his eyes fixed on her again. His mouth stretched to one side and she couldn't tell if he was smiling or leering at her. Alicia managed a quick grin in return, watching his face as he chuckled away to himself. This was quite appalling, and there was no way to tell what he was thinking, sitting there in his chair. Did he know who she was? The first stroke had put an end to his ability to communicate; the speech therapist had tried various non-verbal methods but he had been uncooperative and the end opinion was that his understanding of the world was very limited.

She had never been so glad to see Margaret come back into the room.

'It isn't the Donovan's cat and it isn't badly hurt, just a scrape and a fright,' she said. 'Frank suggested taking it to Kenneth Taylor at the pet shop and Jenny wants to go too. I'll stay with Bob.'

Jenny was standing beside Frank's car, cradling a half-grown tiger-striped kitten wrapped in a green cloth, presumably from Frank's bag. Alicia could see that the cat wasn't the only one who'd had a fright.

'Doctor Frank said the man at the pet shop might know whose kitty it is,' said Jenny, looking up with wide eyes. 'And if he doesn't know, can we keep it? Please, Mummy?'

Alicia let out a small sigh. Jenny had always wanted a cat, but up until now Alicia had managed to banish it into 'someday'. But if no-one claimed this poor creature, 'someday' might just have come. There was her father, and Jen, and Margaret – not to mention Conker – and now a kitten. It was too much.

Linda Huber

'We'll see,' she said.

Jenny settled into the front seat of Frank's car, clutching the kitten tenderly on her lap. Frank chatted away to her about animals in the village, and the little girl answered, her fright forgotten again. Alicia thought sadly that conversations with adult men were all too rare in her daughter's world.

But at least now she had a break, a thirty-minute breather away from her father's house.

Had he been laughing at her?

Chapter Four

Alicia

The pet shop was new, housed in what had previously been the dry cleaners on the High Street, and a faint scent of chemicals still hung around, mingling strangely with the animal smells of the latest inhabitants. The front shop was empty, and Frank walked round the back.

'Kenneth! We need help here!'

There was an answering mumble from above and a few moments later Kenneth Taylor appeared. Alicia stared. The pet shop owner must have been about the same age as she was, but he certainly wasn't doing much to fight off approaching middle-age. He was overweight, obese almost, with thinning, dark blonde hair, and the expression in his blue eyes didn't quite match the smile on his fat shiny face. Even his clothes looked greasy, with several suspicious stains down the legs of his jeans and a t-shirt that looked as if he'd been sleeping in it. But his large fingers were gentle as he examined the kitten while Frank explained what had happened.

'Okay. He can stay here in the meantime and I'll make inquiries.' There was a faint Scottish burr in his high-pitched voice.

'If nobody wants him then maybe we do,' said Jenny bravely, and Alicia sighed again. Please, puss, have a lovely home and a concerned owner waiting for you, please.

'I'll be in touch, then,' said Kenneth Taylor, smiling unattractively at them. 'Mrs Bryson, isn't it?'

'Yes,' said Alicia, surprised. In the rush of explaining about the kitten Frank hadn't actually introduced her by name. Kenneth Taylor smiled again.

'Word gets round fast here,' he said, and Alicia shrugged. He was right, the village was a terrible place for gossip. Harmless, of course, but still…

Outside, Frank turned to her, a hopeful expression on his face.

'Why don't we swing past St. Joe's before you go home, let you see it from the outside. We'd be there and back in twenty minutes, and it would give you a first impression of the place.'

'Alright,' said Alicia, surprised. 'If you've time.' He was being very obliging, and vaguely she wondered why. Or had she just got used to the large town mentality? Country people *were* more helpful. Look at how Kenneth Taylor had taken on the kitten when he could so easily have given it back to Jenny while he made his inquiries.

Frank drove swiftly along the Harrogate road towards Middle Banford and a few minutes later they pulled up in front of black iron gates, opening onto a long driveway. Alicia stared at the house. St. Joe's was a relic from Victorian times, a tall red sandstone manor set in the middle of an enormous garden with a duck pond. It had been one of those country house hotels when Alicia was a child and seen from the road it still looked exactly the same.

'Sixty beds,' said Frank. 'It's split into three wards inside and it is more 'hospital' than 'home', but that's what your father needs. One of us local doctors is always on call, and the nursing staff are great.'

Alicia sighed. St. Joe's really did sound like the answer to all their problems.

'It sounds ideal,' she said. 'But I do want Margaret to agree too, if possible. I'll get her over to see the place this week, and if she's okay with it, we could have him admitted as soon as a bed's available.'

She turned and smiled reassuringly at Jenny as she spoke. Would her daughter have the same problem with her one day? What a horrible thought. Even more horrible was the fact that the high blood pressure that had caused her father's strokes often ran in families. Was disaster slumbering in the depths of her own brain, in Jenny's? It didn't bear thinking about.

Frank Carter turned the engine on again. 'Try to arrange for

Margaret to meet Doug Patton while you're there, he's great with the patients and their relatives. Another idea might be to talk to Derek Thorpe, the charge nurse on the admissions ward. He was a local boy too and he's brilliant with geriatrics - he knows how to get them active even when they're confused.'

Alicia nodded. 'Doug Patton and/or Derek Thorpe. Right.'

Frank grinned. 'Derek's really funny. He jogs here from Lower Banford every day, rain or shine. I think he was married once but he keeps quiet about that, he seems to have spent the last few years lurching from one unsuitable relationship to the next but he can always laugh at himself. Great bloke.'

He drove them home and left, promising to be in touch soon. Alicia went inside. Her father was on his feet, lumbering around the living room, his right arm dangling by his side. She watched as he lifted her mother's photo from the mantelpiece and placed it sideways on top of the television. There was no expression on his face.

'Mummy,' said Jenny, and Alicia jumped. She hadn't realised that Jenny had followed her inside. The little girl came and pressed herself against Alicia's side, staring unhappily at her grandfather and whispering urgently. 'What's wrong with Grandpa? When will he get better?'

Her face was troubled, and Alicia stroked the windswept hair. It was time for plain speaking.

'Come on, lovey,' she said. 'Let's go out to the garden and have a little chat before lunch, you and me.'

The Stranger

Work over for the afternoon, he stood at his kitchen window, basking in the sunlight and gazing across to the woods. The special place was up there, waiting. It was so wonderful having Little Helen to think about, sweet child, with her long dark hair and innocent young face. If only he could take her up to the circle of trees and show her where she would very soon be starting her trip to Paradise. What was she doing right now, his little angel? It was a beautiful day, most likely she'd be outside. In the woods already, perhaps, or playing in old Bob's garden. He could go there and see. The idea made him shiver with delight.

Quickly, he pushed his feet into trainers and trotted off through the village. The lane behind the pub brought him to the trail up through the woods. This had been one of his childhood haunts. A long time ago. He slowed down, the track was steep in places and muddy too, after all the rain that week.

Soon he was walking through the circle of trees, perfect leafy sunshine flickering down on him. The stillness here was positively healing. There was no sound at all apart from the tree tops rustling and his own feet padding softly on the mossy ground. And... was that a shout?

It sounded like a young girl. Was it his little Helen? Surely it must be, the direction was right. He had come up through the woods from the other side so if he continued straight downhill he would come to Bob Logan's place. He jogged on, his breath catching painfully and his t-shirt damp with sweat that had nothing to do with physical activity.

And there she was, running around in the garden, playing with that enormous dog they had. How happy she looked! He'd never had a dog so he didn't know what that felt like, but for a little while he'd had Snugglepuss and that had been just as good. At first. And thank God, little Helen had no dreadful pigtails today. Her hair was literally blowing in the wind. All he wanted was to sweep her into his arms and hold her close and never let her go till she was safe in Paradise with Helen.

But he still had to make his plans about that. Today he could only watch her and dream. He stood by the remains of a dry-stone wall separating the garden from the woods, pleasurably aware of the greed in his soul, for she was so lovely and she was going to be his. Little Helen was oblivious to his presence, she was immersed in her game and laughing, it made him want to laugh too. Maybe he could touch her? He drew breath to call her name, but before he could utter a sound another summons came.

'Jenny! Ice cream!'

And in an instant she was gone, little Helen, running towards the house and ice cream. Slowly, he turned back to the woods.

It was time to start making plans.

Alicia

Alicia stood at the bottom of the garden filling a bowl with fresh raspberries, grinning when she saw how many berries had already disappeared from the canes. Jen, presumably. She herself had loved doing exactly the same thing as a kid, but of course she hadn't been allowed to. She'd had to be subtle, just a few berries every day. Jen didn't have to worry about that. Now, some cream would be nice with these and there was still the dinner to think about too. Alicia strode back to the kitchen, surprised to see her father standing by the sink.

He stared at the bowl in her hand.

I'm sorry Daddy!

The child's voice echoed through Alicia's head, tearful and afraid. What had she been sorry about? 'Stealing' fruit, that was what, she had arrived at the back door one day with a handful of rasps to wash because she'd found a bug in one, and her father had been there. He'd given her a clip round the ear and sent her upstairs and that had been the end of food for the day as far as she was concerned.

Alicia glared at her father. 'I remember you punishing me for eating rasps, you know. What a miserable old git you were.'

It was out before she'd thought twice. Thank God Margaret and Jenny hadn't heard her.

And it was horrible but he started to laugh, wheezing and chortling away as if she'd said something hilarious. Alicia clutched the nearest chair. He had understood that. He had. Quite definitely. And his laughter wasn't with her, it was at her. Not trusting herself to speak, she dumped the bowl down beside the sink, and hallelujah, here was Margaret. She could get out of here for a bit.

'I'll do the shopping, shall I? Jenny! Do you want to come to Mrs Mullen's? I'm leaving now.'

She would just get stuff for tonight's meal, than she'd have a good excuse for a longer outing to the supermarket in Merton tomorrow.

Jenny came running up. 'Does Mrs Mullen still have her bag of sweeties at the till?' she asked hopefully, and Alicia pushed the rasps memory to the back of her mind. In the grand scheme of things, it wasn't important. Nothing she couldn't live with, anyway.

'Chocolate caramels,' she said reminiscently. 'Yup, I think she does.'

Fortunately Mrs Mullen did have a bag of sweeties and Jenny was soon chewing happily. Alicia wandered around the cramped little shop, filling her basket with ingredients for a lasagna, and then joined the conversation queue at the checkout. Good grief, Mrs Mullen could gab for England, she really could. Jenny soon lost interest and went outside to sit beside Conker, and Alicia started planning how, exactly, to approach her aunt with the St. Joe's plan. She would need to present the home in the most positive light possible, make Margaret see that it was a much better option for the old man than living at home. Not an easy task, she would -

'Mummy? There's a car out there with dark windows and I think it's looking at me.'

Alicia sighed. Drat the whole strangers conversation that morning, she really didn't want to turn her over-imaginative daughter into a nervous wreck worrying about something that was never going to happen.

'Oh Jen darling, please don't worry so much, you can't go through life avoiding people you don't know. As long as you don't actually go away with a stranger, everything'll be fine. Okay?'

The child nodded slowly.

'Hello again, Alicia. And I'm sure Jenny can manage another sweetie.'

Mrs Mullen was ready for them at last, and Jenny accepted a second caramel, her face dreamy and contented again. Alicia grinned.

That was one problem out of the way. If only the rest could be solved so easily.

The Stranger

It was wonderful. His girls were here, living in Lower Banford, part of village life and on the verge of becoming a big part of his life too. He'd pulled up at the shop for milk that afternoon and there was little Helen, sitting outside on the pavement hugging the dog. Big Helen was obviously inside. He'd waited in the car, taking small snippets of pleasure in the way that the child kept looking across at him, such a sweet, worried expression on her face. The tinted windows had prevented her seeing who he was, of course, and his shirt soaked up the usual sweat as he feasted his eyes. She was glorious. After a bit she'd gone inside to big Helen, but soon they were both out on the pavement again, little Helen the very picture of happiness as she skipped along towards home, talking animatedly to her mother all the while. Watching them now reminded him oh, so painfully how he'd felt about Mummy, and the hurt he had buried back then was no less today than it had been when he was a boy.

He had loved Mummy so much. For a long time his favourite game had been knights in shining armour, he'd had a little plastic sword and a hobby horse and he'd galloped around saving Mummy from all sorts of danger. It was a bittersweet memory, because Mummy hadn't played back. She'd been too busy, he could see that now, she'd been tired all the time, looking after her children and the house. And of course she already had her knight in shining armour. Stupid Dad had been by far the most important person in Mummy's life. That had hurt.

Then, when he was older and out of the knight in shining armour stage, he'd wanted to help Mummy more, but somehow he was always getting things wrong and Mummy would press her lips together and turn away from him. That had hurt too, it had hurt terribly, and he'd had no idea what more he could do to please her.

His father had worried about him, he knew. Worried that at twelve he was such a Mummy's boy. A wimp, Dad had called him, but he'd ignored that as he ignored almost everything about the man. It had been Dad's stupid idea to get him a dog for his birthday, 'a man's dog', he'd said, one of those dreadful bull terriers. Fortunately Mummy hadn't wanted a dog either, in fact she and his sister had always wanted a cat, so she'd bought him the white kitten instead.

Such a darling soft little thing it was! His sister had promptly christened it Snowball, and Mummy had laughed and agreed, but he'd always called it Snugglepuss. After all, it was his cat. How he'd loved running his fingers through the warm white fur, rubbing his face in it, listening to the purrs, amazingly loud for such a small creature.

For a couple of weeks he'd revelled in being a cat owner. He would rush home from school every day to play games with Snugglepuss, chasing round the living room, pouncing on pieces of string, cuddling up on the sofa together.

Only gradually had he noticed that Snugglepuss was enjoying their games less and less. For a while he didn't believe that the kitten could have turned against him. He was the official owner of Snugglepuss/Snowball, the animal must know that, surely. It was Snugglepuss' *duty* to love him best. But it became increasingly obvious that Snugglepuss preferred the company of everyone else in the house. When his sister came home, Snugglepuss would run up and wind himself round her legs. When they were all watching TV, it was Mummy's lap that Snugglepuss chose to lie on and woe betide anyone who tried to interfere with that. Snugglepuss had sharp little claws and wasn't shy of using them. And even when stupid Dad appeared with one of the disgusting bacon sandwiches he was always eating in the evenings, Snugglepuss would be right there beside him, waiting for a treat.

When the family noticed that he was out of favour with his own cat, how they'd laughed. Every evening. Laughed and laughed and said things like 'Animals always know, don't they?' to each other in loud voices just to annoy him. Yet more hurt.

He'd got his revenge, of course. He arrived home from school one Tuesday to find the house deserted; stupid Dad was at work of course, Mummy was out shopping and his sister was at her piano lesson. Snugglepuss had tried to streak past him and escape through the back door but he had scooped it up and held it at arm's length, rage flooding through him. Snugglepuss/Snowball/Devil-in-disguise had struggled and he had tightened his grip. He literally couldn't stand the sight of the creature now. In the space of just a few weeks his love had turned to hatred. Hatred fuelled by rejection.

How well he remembered the feeling of power and triumph as he looked down at the gasping creature in his hands. *Now* stupid fickle Snowball would realise who was important, who was the strong one here. Who it should have loved. The rage inside him started to build, and without making any conscious decision about exactly what he was doing, he squeezed ever harder while the kitten mewed pitifully, its small pink mouth opening in distress, panic-stricken green eyes widening. Bones crunched audibly beneath his fingers and the cat's little face distorted in pain, bloody froth dripping from its mouth now and splattering on the kitchen floor as he changed his grip and wrenched at the soft furry white neck, and – *crack* – Snowball's head hung limply. He knew that his cat was dead.

For a moment he stared at the still-warm bundle in his hands. The end of a dream. The second unrequited love in his life. Well, he'd got rid of this one. He stuffed the body into a plastic bag, ran down to the weir and tossed his pet into the murky water.

That evening they'd all gone out searching for Snowball/Snugglepuss, and he'd cried real tears – to his father's disgust – because his cat was gone. But underneath the tears part of him was laughing. He'd shown Snugglepuss how dangerous it was not to love him as he deserved.

He'd never had another cat, and he'd never again felt anger like that against an animal.

Next time, it had been Mummy.

Chapter Five
Tuesday, 11th July

Alicia

Alicia forced her legs out of bed. Shit, she hadn't felt this knackered since Jenny was a baby and broken nights had been the norm. There was no baby now, though, just an old man whose mind had gone, and the hard truth was he had been up three times in the night. Each time she'd had to persuade him back to bed and then sit with him, seething with impatience until he'd fallen asleep again. They simply couldn't go on like this, she was exhausted already and they'd only been here five minutes. She would ask Frank for stronger sleeping pills for him and make an appointment for her and Margaret to see round St. Joe's at the earliest possibility.

Her aunt was scrambling eggs when she went downstairs, and a trail of Coco-pops on the floor revealed that Jenny had already had breakfast. Alicia hesitated in the doorway. It felt a bit odd, living with Margaret again. The two years in Edinburgh after she'd run away from here seemed like a very long time ago now. Margaret and Jeff had been great, keeping Alicia while she attended a final year of school and then a year at college before starting her nursing training in Glasgow. Margaret had tried at first to patch things up between her and her parents, but had given that up very quickly. Her father had been adamant and so had teenage Alicia. A slight reconciliation had occurred years later when Jenny was born – nothing like a new baby to mend family rifts – but when Alicia and Paul divorced, her father was incensed and the devil triumphant. Good Christian people didn't divorce. So the contact had ended again, and it had stayed that way all through Mum's death and her father's series of strokes. Alicia had gone to her mother's funeral, of course, been righteously ignored by her father and had subsequently left him to it. Margaret had coped well and willingly with things here. Up until now.

'Morning, lovey,' said Margaret. 'The eggs are just ready.'

Alicia wasn't fond of scrambled eggs but it seemed churlish to say so. It was going to be difficult enough to persuade Margaret that finding a care home was the logical, fairly urgent next step for them to take. A squabble about the breakfast menu would benefit no-one.

'Lovely. Margaret, I'd like to go and have a look round St. Joe's today,' she said impulsively. 'It would be interesting to see it from the inside. Frank Carter said it's a good place.'

Margaret stirred sweetener into her tea, staring at the mug. Alicia could see she was organizing her argument.

'You're giving up too easily, Alicia,' she said at last. 'Your father's a sick man now, but he wouldn't have wanted to end his days in an old folk's home. I know the two of you have never been close, but he's never asked you for anything either. Until now. So let's you and me do this last thing, lovey. For Bob.'

Alicia was silent. So Margaret wasn't above using emotional blackmail. *Why* was it so important to her to keep him here? There was no stigma attached to having a member of your family go into a care home nowadays, was there? Or was it maybe that her aunt was afraid she'd lose her home here if he was in care? Surely not, Margaret moving in after the first stroke had been as much about her having a purpose in life after Uncle Jeff had died so suddenly. And whatever happened, they mustn't fall out over this, because then her father and the devil would have won not only the battle but the entire war as well.

'I'm only here for six weeks,' she said gently. 'I have a job back home, and Jenny has school. We can't stay indefinitely. And Margaret, looking after him 24/7 is more than one person's job.'

Margaret tutted impatiently out of the room and Alicia sighed. Maybe she should get Frank Carter and Douglas Patton over here for a talk, as it was obviously going to be next to impossible to get

Margaret anywhere near St. Joe's. And she would phone David in York and ask him to have a word too. He might be able to make his mother see sense where a mere niece couldn't.

Alone in the kitchen, she opened the back door to get rid of the egg smell. The whole garden, stretching towards the hillside and merging into the woods, had become terribly unkempt. Whatever had happened to Mr Johnston who used to come every week to mow the lawn and tidy up? The grass was more or less civilised, but the summerhouse in the middle was wild with overgrown brambles and beyond that again it was an absolute jungle. And where on earth was Jenny?

'Jen!' she called, sudden apprehension making her voice catch.

'Here I am!' Her daughter ran round the side of the house, and Alicia relaxed. 'Mummy, can I go and ask at the pet shop how the little kitty is? Please? It isn't far and I can take Conker with me.'

Alicia bit her lip as she remembered Kenneth Taylor's shining, round face, and the way he had known her name.

'Not today, sweetheart,' she said. 'Mr Taylor said he would get in touch and I'm sure he will if no-one claims the kitty. But we don't want to make a nuisance of ourselves. After all you don't really know him, do you?'

How mean she was, playing on Jenny's nervousness about strangers like that. After everything she had said yesterday too. But she did *not* want Jen visiting the pet shop owner by herself.

'Oh!' said Jenny, pouting. 'Well, alright. Then can I take Conker up into the woods and play? We won't go far.'

Mother's dilemma, thought Alicia wryly. You can't say 'no' all the time, even her own mother hadn't. She could remember playing in the woods with Cathal O'Brian next door, and wow, what a rarity, a good memory of her childhood. It just felt different now when it was her own daughter about to vanish into the undergrowth. But the woods literally were an extension of the garden, Jen would be within shouting – well, yelling – distance all the time. She nodded, and Jenny whooped.

Alicia watched unhappily as her daughter and Conker raced into the jungle behind the summerhouse and were gone. Margaret had gone to see a neighbour, and it was time she got her father up.

She ran upstairs and paused at the threshold to her father's room, pushing the door ajar to see if he was awake yet.

This is the bad room.

The young voice was brittle with panic. Alicia held her breath as another wave of nausea swept through her, even stronger this time. She stood there retching, quite unable to control her gut.

Oh God. What did it *mean*, 'the bad room'? The bad room in the bad place? Shivering, she took a deep breath. What was this little voice in her head trying to tell her? She leaned her head against the wall and closed her eyes.

The bad room. Her father's room. Why should the child's voice – her own voice? – warn her so insistently that her father's room was bad? What had happened in this room? Something a whole lot worse than bible-reading or no dinner? Worse than having her hair hacked off, something so 'bad' it had literally made her retch, all these years later? But she couldn't remember, she just couldn't remember.

A bang from inside the room brought her back to here and now.

Her father was wandering about in urine-soaked pyjamas. He didn't look at her. Alicia stood in the doorway staring at the spot on the floor where she'd lain - no, where he'd held her down while he cut off her hair. Why hadn't she told a teacher what had happened? She hadn't been able to admit that she'd needed help, that was why. She'd laughed at herself with the 'pixie' cut – Mum had evened it out a bit – and everyone had laughed with her. They hadn't seen the hurt because she'd hidden it very carefully, and anyway by the time she arrived at school the next day she'd already decided to leave home just as soon as she could.

Stepping into the room, Alicia grasped her father's arm and stared into his face. He still wouldn't meet her eye. God, what use was all this soul-searching? He was a demented old thing now, old before his time, there was nothing of him left to be accountable for what he had or hadn't done.

'You cut my hair off right here on the floor,' she said. 'Remember that, do you? I was terrified.'

He gave no indication of even having heard her, sitting passively on the bed while she removed his pyjamas and took out clean clothes. There he was, naked and vulnerable, and for the first time she was the superior one, the one in control.

Forcing the uncomfortable thoughts away, Alicia showered him and took him downstairs, where he wandered round after her like a lost sheep before eventually settling into his chair by the fireplace. Now at least she didn't have to touch him for a while.

'I *was* a good child, you know,' she said, speaking before she had even thought. He stared at her, making eye contact for the first time that morning, then the one-sided grin spread over his face and he wheezed his horrible Aaaah-ha-ha-ha, his eyes never leaving hers.

Alicia swallowed. Did he see how difficult this was for her? Was he behaving like this to taunt her? Was he thinking about the day he cut her hair off? They would have to find out exactly what he could understand. It was a long time since the last speech assessment; a good therapist might be able to help them now. If his mind really was gone Alicia knew she would feel a whole lot better about having to care for him. Illogical but true.

She bent towards him in his chair. 'Do you understand? Can you give me a sign? Yes? No?'

No Daddy no! The child's voice again and she was crying hysterically.

It was like a waking dream, a long-forgotten memory slowly rising towards the surface.

What the hell had he done to her?

Sickening thoughts of abuse, rape and paedophilia flashed through her mind. But surely nothing like that... This was her religious father she was thinking about, she was being melodramatic. Maybe the child's voice was simply her own reluctance to deal with the situation that had developed here. Her father had been a terrible parent and with perfect justification she had broken off contact. Now circumstances were forcing her not only to live in this house again, but also attend to her father's intimate care. That was all. Not easy even for someone with nursing training, but it would pass. Things would get better.

Her mobile rang in the kitchen while she was still helping her father with his breakfast. She set the mug of tea on the mantelpiece where he couldn't reach it, and gave him the slice of toast in his good hand. He might eat it if he was holding it.

'Hello?' It was difficult not to sound harassed.

'Hi, Alicia, it's Paul. How are things with you?'

'Paul?' She repeated the name stupidly.

'Your ex-husband? The father of your child? Don't tell me you've forgotten all about me?'

Alicia sank onto a hard kitchen chair. Hell, this was the last thing she needed. Paul hadn't been in touch for nearly a year and that suited her just fine.

'Paul. We're… okay. Visiting Lower Banford just now. How are you?' There was no point going into details he wasn't interested in hearing.

'Very well indeed. I'm in England on business at the moment. Home's in Singapore now, as you know, and, actually, Alicia, I remarried at Easter. A wonderful girl from China. Siu-pen. So Jenny has a stepmum.'

'Oh - congratulations. Jen's not here at the moment, she's um, out with a friend.'

'Never mind. Alicia, I want Jen in Singapore for a holiday in the autumn. I want her to get to know her stepmother.'

'No,' said Alicia immediately. It was another gut reaction. 'You have a *nerve*, Paul. She doesn't even know you properly and that's because you've never bothered with her. No way am I letting you take her to Singapore.'

'We'll see about that. I have a stable home to offer her now, with a stay-at-home mum and a new little brother or sister expected at Christmas. I could get custody. Think about that, Alicia.'

The connection ended abruptly, and Alicia stared at her phone. He could never get custody, surely. Even if his wife was everything Jenny could wish for in a stepmother, that wouldn't undo the years of neglect that Paul had inflicted on his daughter. He'd been a useless father right from the start, leaving when Jen was less than a year old. Alicia had scrimped and saved by herself ever since; the irregular and inadequate sums of money Paul sent them would barely have financed a cat, never mind a growing child.

A crash from the next room jolted her attention back to the present and she ran back to her father. He was standing by the fireplace, looking down at the remains of the mug he'd obviously managed to reach after all. The rug and his slippers were soaked with tea. Tired tears of frustration welled up in Alicia's eyes, then she tilted her chin determinedly. If Paul sued for custody she might have to prove soon exactly what a super-mum she was, so she would just start right now.

Chapter Six

Alicia

She was pegging out the washing when Frank arrived, emerging from the back door with Bob following behind.

'He was wandering around in the hall,' said Frank, and Alicia sighed. She should be keeping a better eye on him, she knew that. He could open the front door and walk off into the sunset if he put his mind to it. Christ, if only he would. She watched as Frank lowered the old man onto the wooden bench by the back door. He sat there, clutching his cloth cap in his good hand and sucking on his teeth.

Frank straightened and stepped closer, concern on his face. 'You're tired,' he said.

Alicia shrugged. Not the best way to make a girl feel great. But then he was a doctor, he was allowed to say things like that and the mirror had told her exactly the same thing anyway.

'Tired? I'm half dead,' she said, hearing the gloominess in her own voice. 'My father spent half the night trying to go walkabout and then he wet the bed, plus it's almost impossible to get him to eat a respectable amount of anything. Then my ghastly ex phoned, he's threatening to fight for custody of Jen and take her to Singapore. He's married again and thinks he has a 'stable home' to offer her. And Margaret just *will not* see that my father would be better off in St. Joe's.'

Frank was silent for a moment, then he reached out and patted her shoulder awkwardly.

Alicia almost jumped, embarrassed by her sudden outburst.

'Right. I'll give you different pills for Bob. And I'll talk to Margaret again, but you know you don't actually *need* her consent to put your father into St. Joe's. You're his next of kin and I'll back you up about this. And Alicia, for heaven's sake, there's no way your ex would get custody of Jenny, is there? Not in *Singapore*?'

'I don't know,' she admitted. 'I don't think so. It's just so horrible he's threatening me like this. Imagine if I lost Jen, she - hell, where is she? She's been gone for ages! Jenny?'

Christ, she had been so busy being tired and doing her father's washing that she had forgotten to check on her daughter.

There was no reply from the bottom of the garden, and Alicia yelled again, aware that Frank was staring at her. But thank heavens, after the second shout there was an answering call and a few moments later, Jenny and Conker came careering up the garden.

'Mummy! I found a little fairy clearing, it's almost exactly a round circle of trees, great big high ones. We were playing a game where I'm a fairy princess, and Conker is my trusty unicorn and we went all over the galaxy, and the circle of trees is our palace when we're home and our spaceship when we're travelling.'

In spite of her fright Alicia felt her lips twitching. She glanced at Frank, and they exchanged grins.

'Well, your Highness, it's time for elevenses,' she said. 'You'll have a coffee, won't you, Frank? I promise I won't moan too much. You can tell me more about Sonja, and how you're finding life in Lower Banford.'

'Sonja's having a ball in Paris, she loves the good life,' he said, following her into the kitchen and settling down at the table, his face bright. 'They were in Vancouver before. I'll give you her email address if you like. As for Lower Banford - well, I've just moved into Dave Morton's old place which was last redecorated when Doctor Kildare was a boy, so I've got a mammoth job in front of me. The practice suite is fine but the house is going to be... a challenge. It's about the same era as this one.'

Alicia grinned in sympathy. 'Poor you. Never mind, you can do it little by little.'

'That's the idea,' said Frank. He seemed to be enjoying sitting there drinking coffee with her and Jenny, and Alicia wondered if he had made many friends in the village. When you weren't talking to his doctor persona he was really quite shy; maybe he was finding his new life here lonely.

'Doctor Frank, have you seen Mr Taylor from the pet shop today?' asked Jenny, and Alicia groaned inwardly. Jen wasn't going to forget about that kitten.

'I haven't, but I'm sure he'll let you know about the kitten soon,' said Frank. Alicia managed to catch his eye without Jenny noticing, and pulled a face. He rose to the occasion straightaway, and Alicia relaxed gratefully as he spoke.

'Tell me more about your palace in the woods, Princess Jenny,' he said. 'It sounds like a very special place indeed.'

Jenny was only too happy to chatter on about life amongst the stars, and Alicia poured him a second cup of coffee. He was very patient, she thought, listening as he asked about Kings and Queens and spaceships. Her daughter's face was one big beam, and she stood waving fondly as Frank drove off twenty minutes later.

Alicia had to force herself out of her chair after lunch. There was still the shopping to do, and she was way too tired to face the drive to Merton. Mrs Mullen here I come again.

Jenny chose to stay and help Margaret brush the dog, so Alicia trudged down the lane alone, glad to have a few minutes to herself and resentful that it only was a few minutes and not a couple of hours. Still, at least she was out of the house and the village was a pretty little place when you weren't worrying about sleeping pills and voices in your head. It was a pity she couldn't enjoy being here. There weren't many villages like this left, even Upper Banford had mutated into a small town.

At least Frank was around to give her some support. That was the only good thing, actually. Today she felt as if the whole situation was about to rear up and crash back down, flattening them all. She was working so hard here and nothing was going right. And none of it was her fault.

Her fault. Her mother's voice echoed through Alicia's head. *Stop, Bob. It wasn't her fault.*

Alicia stood still, Margaret's ancient shopping bag clutched in one hand. Something hadn't been her fault, but what? She'd been with Cathal… and yes, it had happened more or less right where she was standing, just outside the house where the O'Brians had lived.

The memory was suddenly crystal clear in her mind. She, her parents and Cathal had been walking along here, Cathal had been going home, and he had clapped her shoulder in a friendly goodbye. Not quite a hug, just a fond gesture from a boy of ten or eleven, which would make her eight or nine. The memories were getting younger.

Her father had been outraged that a boy had touched his daughter. He had grabbed her shoulder and shaken her – that was when Mum spoke – and then he had marched her home and… what? She could remember him dragging her up the lane and how terrified she had been, but the rest was a blank. What had he done to her? Something 'bad', she could feel that in her bones.

There were only a handful of people in the shop, and Alicia wrestled a basket from the pile by the door. Mrs Mullen was busy giving a middle-aged woman a very detailed account of someone else's operation while a man waited patiently, his basket on the floor beside him.

Alicia grabbed a family pizza and a lettuce for tonight's dinner. Maybe tomorrow she'd feel up to an outing to Merton. The man was packing his shopping into an old-fashioned leather shopper not dissimilar to Margaret's when Alicia reached the checkout. By the looks of things he was having pasta with cream and bacon sauce for dinner, and Alicia felt slightly ashamed of her ready-made pizza.

'Right then, Alicia dear,' said Mrs Mullen, jabbing at the old-fashioned cash register. Scanners and bar codes obviously hadn't reached this far north yet. 'How's your Dad today?'

Alicia sighed. 'Alright, I suppose, but things aren't going to change for the better,' she said. 'It's just a case of deciding what's the best way to take care of him.'

The man leaned towards her. 'I'm sorry to interrupt, but am I right that you're Mr Logan's daughter?'

'Yes,' said Alicia, surprised. Gosh, this guy was a real Robert Redford lookalike. Maybe eight years older than she was, he had a full head of red-brown hair and he was tall, towering above her. He was smiling - he looked kind.

'Let me introduce myself, I'm Douglas Patton, the head of St. Joseph's in Middle Banford.'

Alicia felt a broad grin spread over her face. Talk about being in the right place at the right time, this chance encounter in Mrs Mullen's shop might just make things a whole lot easier. She shook his outstretched hand. It was warm, and he was holding onto hers for a few seconds longer than was necessary. Which was very interesting... and quite exciting, too.

'Frank Carter has told me about you and the home,' she said, stuffing her pizza into the shopping bag. 'He thinks my father would be better off in St. Joseph's, and I feel the same way, but my aunt isn't happy about it which is why we haven't been in touch yet.'

He stood holding the shop door open for her, leaving Mrs Mullen staring after them.

'That's better,' he said, when they were standing on the pavement. 'Anything you say in the shop in the course of the afternoon will have reached Upper Banford by tea time. At the latest. Mrs Mullen's contacts, you know.'

Alicia laughed. 'Oh, I do know. I grew up here. Mrs Mullen's been gossip-leader since the invention of the wheel. Not that I've anything to hide. But thanks anyway.'

'Frank put your father on our waiting list this week,' he said. 'Would you like to see round St. Joe's by yourself sometime, just unofficially? I'm off today and tomorrow but I could give you a wee tour on Thursday morning, if you like?'

Alicia stared at him. It was actually a really good idea. She would try very hard to persuade Margaret to come too, but if that didn't work, she would go by herself.

'That would be fantastic. I might be able to convince my aunt to come as well. What time would suit you?'

Was she imagining the look of pleasure that crossed his face?

'Shall we say half past ten? In the entrance hallway?'

He held out his hand again, and Alicia shook, another grin spreading across her face. But maybe she was reading way too much into a couple of handshakes. She didn't get out enough, that was the problem. Well, today she'd had coffee with one man and now she'd made a date – of sorts – with another.

She grasped her bag and turned to go. 'Fantastic. Thanks. See you on Thursday, then.'

He waved, then walked up the street in the opposite direction. Alicia strode homewards, aware that she felt lighter. What an interesting half hour that had been.

The Stranger

The most wonderful thing had happened. He had touched little Helen. A lovely warm shiver ran through him as he recalled the moment.

He switched on the lamp by his armchair and pulled the heavy velvet curtains across the window, shutting the world out. It was beginning to get dark, and here in the stillness of his own home it was safe to think about the miracle that had occurred. With shaking hands he poured himself a glass of red wine, then sat down slowly, cradling the glass in both hands, watching the ruby liquid swirl as he raised it to the light.

Such an amazing thing.

He had gone up through the woods late that afternoon, hoping that little Helen might be playing outside again, and she was. In the woods, at the special place. He had talked to her, he had touched her sweet face, and it had been just the two of them. And oh, she was so lovely. His own Helen herself must have been exactly like that as a little child.

She'd been running round amongst the trees, talking to that stupid enormous dog. He ducked behind a tree to watch her, then crept closer, still carefully concealed, until he could hear her every word. She was pretending to be a princess in a palace. How perfect she was.

'Come and sit on your throne, Unicorn Conker,' she said. 'We have to wait for the King.'

He hadn't been able to help himself. He stepped out in front of her and bowed, a low, old-fashioned bow. The dog growled, then barked twice.

'Your Majesty,' he said. 'I am your humble servant, King Oberon. Permit me to wait upon you and the unicorn Conker.'

'Oh,' she said, and he could see both puzzlement and fascination in her eyes. 'Alright. Be quiet, Conker. You can play too, King Oberon. I'm Princess, um - '

'Queen Titania,' he said, bowing again. The dog had subsided, thank God.

'Oh yes. Queen Titania. And Conker, does he have a special name?'

'The jester, Puck.'

It was that easy, he couldn't believe his luck. She had laughed and chatted and showed him round the 'palace'. Then Big Helen had called from their garden.

'A secret,' he said quickly, bending close and touching a finger to her perfectly formed lips, feeling the warmth from her delicious little body spread right through his own. 'We won't tell anyone, not a soul. This is our secret.'

And of course she agreed straightaway. She was his friend now.

'A secret.' She touched her lips too, then turned and raced down through the woods, the dog loping along behind her. It was a pity about the dog, he would have to get rid of it.

Very soon it would be Paradise time for Little Helen. When he was certain that big Helen trusted him – and that wouldn't be long now – then it would be his hour. His day. And when little Helen was safe with his own Helen, big Helen would turn to him. All his Helens, how lucky he was.

Little Helen in Paradise. It would be easy, she was so sweet and trusting.

The wine glass was empty, and he set it down on the table, smiling gently. The good times were beginning.

Alicia

Alicia said nothing about her encounter with Douglas Patton when she arrived back home. She wanted to get Margaret to help her, see if they could find out more about what, exactly, her father could understand now. There was a big difference between suggesting putting someone who was more or less *compos mentis* into a care home, and sending someone who didn't know if he was coming or going. It would be easier for Margaret if she knew the old man's mind was irreversibly affected by the strokes. And it was - wasn't it? You could see that he was oblivious to the world around him. And yet there was the mystery of his reaction to Alicia herself - what was going on there? The sudden eye contact and inappropriate laughter were reserved for her, he never did that with anyone else. It was impossible to know what he was thinking.

Margaret immediately agreed to try some of the old speech therapy exercises, and Alicia heaved a relieved sigh. Her father was more likely to be cooperative with Margaret around.

They sat down in the living room and tried to engage the old man. He wouldn't look up at first, but eventually Margaret succeeded in attracting his attention and worked with him, trying to get him to sign 'yes' and 'no' with his good hand. Alicia watched in frustration. Bob looked at Margaret when she asked the questions, but his hand stayed limp in her hand.

'It's no use,' said Alicia at last. 'He doesn't understand. He can move that hand perfectly well, he just doesn't know what you want from him.'

Margaret nodded. 'I think you might be right,' she said, patting

Bob's hand and turning to look at Alicia. 'But remember this, lovey, he's still your father.'

She left the room, and Alicia sighed. Somehow that remark didn't bode well for a successful 'let's put Dad in a home' conversation later on. A soft snigger made her look up, and she gasped before backing away. Her father was staring straight at her, with perfect eye contact, and he was laughing quietly, his mouth half-open and his breath wheezing in his chest. A dribble of spit worked its way down his chin.

Fury took hold of Alicia. 'You know exactly what you're doing, don't you,' she said quietly. 'Be careful, old man. You only have one family.'

His gaze left hers but he chortled on as Alicia went out to the kitchen, not trusting herself to stay in the same room as him.

The kettle was boiling when Alicia came down from settling her father for the night. Jen, bless her, was sound asleep already. She'd spent most of the day in the woods with Conker. Alicia smiled, remembering how the little girl had come running into the kitchen at dinner time. Not for the first time her daughter had managed to surprise her.

'Mummy, who's King Oberon?' she asked. 'It's a game I play in the woods but I can't remember who he is. And Titania?'

'Oberon? He's from a Shakespeare play called *A Midsummer Night's Dream* – that was the one they did in Middle Banford this year – Oberon is King of the Fairies, and Titania is his Queen. What made you think about them?'

'Nothing. I was just playing. It's our special game, isn't it, Conker?' And off she'd run back outside, Conker galumphing along behind her.

Alicia reached for the teapot. Thank Christ she'd be able to go to bed soon, this tiredness was horrible, and if her father didn't let her have a better night's sleep tonight she didn't know what she would do.

She poured tea and lifted the mugs. Margaret was sitting out on the bench, lit up from behind by the light from the kitchen window. The garden was in near darkness. It was an almost midsummer night right here, but the dream was more of a nightmare.

'Tea up,' said Alicia, handing over a steaming mug and sinking down beside her aunt. 'Oh, this is just what the doctor ordered. I'm exhausted, Margaret. I don't know how you've been managing here all by yourself.'

Margaret sniffed. 'Perfectly well on the whole. And the doctor's been ordering something else too, I see. I don't approve of sleeping pills, Alicia. It isn't natural.'

'Well, not sleeping isn't natural either. We all need our sleep,' said Alicia mildly. She took a deep breath. 'Margaret, I really would like the two of us to go together and have a look at St. Joe's. Then we could have a proper talk about it, involve Frank Carter too. We'll be able to decide things much better when we've seen exactly what we're deciding about.'

If only she could make Margaret understand. It would be much better if they both went to St. Joe's on Thursday, met Douglas Patton, and saw round the place. Her aunt, however, soon dispelled any illusions she had about that.

'Alicia, there's nothing to decide! I don't want my brother in a home and that's all there is to it. He has family to look after him! It isn't as if he's wheelchair bound. I'm very grateful for your help this summer, and I'll be glad to take things a bit easier while you're here. Then I'll have plenty of energy to cope by myself again when you go back to Bedford.'

Alicia was silent. By the looks of things she would have to go it alone. Frank would help her. And maybe Douglas Patton. But her aunt wasn't finished yet.

'David phoned this morning to invite me to stay with him and Sheila in York for a few days while you're here to hold the fort. I knew you wouldn't mind, so I'm going on Thursday morning. I'm sure when I get back you'll have come round to my way of thinking, Alicia dear. Bob doesn't make much work at all, and looking after him here is something I feel I have to do.' And with that, Margaret stood slowly, and headed back inside.

Left alone in the darkness, Alicia sipped her tea, feeling her courage sag. Brilliant. With Margaret away, not only would she be alone here with her father, but the plan of moving him to the care home would be on hold until Margaret returned. Alicia knew she hadn't reached the point yet where she would go completely against her aunt's wishes. She could still go to St. Joe's on Thursday, of course, but now she would have to find a sitter. She couldn't leave Jenny and her father here together with just Conker looking after them.

She glanced across to the house next door, all but hidden behind tall shrubs.

One of the neighbours would help out for sure, and this way at least she'd get Douglas Patton all to herself for an hour or two.

Which, when you thought about it, was a very big advantage.

Chapter Seven
Wednesday, 12th July

The Stranger

Two afternoons in a row with little Helen, how lucky he was. The memory of his finger brushing over those warm little lips was so, so delicious. He had never touched another person's lips before, except of course for his own Helen's. Or possibly Mummy's too, but he couldn't remember anything definite about that. And now that he had little Helen within grasping distance he didn't want to think about his futile quest to win Mummy's love. Those had truly been years of desperation, starting with the death of Snugglepuss and not ending until Mummy went to hell. It was only afterwards, with the hurt all parcelled away, that he had learned how to live in the world. He had realised that if he was nice to people they were usually nice back, and this had worked splendidly for him until Helen came along. She was such an angel. But she hadn't loved him unconditionally. Just like Snugglepuss and just like Mummy. The anger had returned and that wasn't his fault. He hadn't wanted to hurt Helen, he truly hadn't meant for her to go to Paradise. But now he could make it up to her by giving her the two new Helens. And oh, little Helen… he just had to enjoy her as often as he could in this world before he sent her off to the next.

So he'd gone back to the woods this afternoon, and what a good thing he had, for there she was, and this time when she saw him she waved and laughed.

'King Oberon! You're just in time for a picnic, Mummy gave me some lemon wafers and some grapes, look!'

He bent over the bag she was holding out. 'Food fit for a king,' he pronounced, taking his place on the fallen tree trunk. She busied herself setting the 'table', a paper serviette spread beside him, and he sat there watching her, clasping and unclasping his hands, feeling his body tremble in anticipation. She was here, and his was the power. He could do whatever he wanted with her. He could kill the dog 'by accident' and then comfort little Helen and cuddle her straight off to Paradise today.

But of course he wouldn't. A fairy queen deserved a better plan, a special ceremony. And he deserved more of her, too.

'There!' said little Helen, looking up at him with those sweet, trusting eyes. 'That's the table almost ready, now if you watch that um, Puck doesn't steal the biscuits I'll just pick some flowers.'

'It will be my pleasure,' he said, watching as she crouched down to pick bluebells. How glorious she was. What a pity she wasn't wearing something a little more regal. He would find her something fitting to wear on her journey to Paradise. A golden robe, for instance, or a white one.

She danced back to the tree trunk and spread her handful of bluebells around the grapes. 'We're ready! What would you like, King Oberon?'

'But Madam! Allow me to serve you first. My Queen must eat her fill before her king and humble servant.'

He had lifted a little bunch of five grapes, and slowly, one after the other he placed them in her perfect little mouth, touching her lips every time. She giggled and chewed and swallowed, and then when the fifth grape was gone he took a tissue from his pocket and wiped her lips, holding her face with his other hand. And she had let him. It was so wonderful; it made the sweat start all over again.

'There!' he said. 'Now my Queen has eaten, and *you* may serve *me*!'

She stood in front of him, holding the grapes to his mouth, but some sixth sense had told him that she wasn't quite comfortable doing this so he'd only accepted two before offering her a wafer to eat by herself. Then she had chatted away again, telling him about the dog and her mother and poor Grandpa... she was absolutely enchanting. He would make his plans carefully now, ensure that her passing ceremony was indeed fit for a queen. He would enjoy her again, and much, much more.

And at the end of the enjoyment they would have a beautiful midsummer ceremony before little Helen started her long journey to Paradise. Sunday would be a good day, a holy day, and it would give him time to plan everything perfectly.

And to meet little Helen again, tomorrow and the next day and the next...

Alicia

The ringing of the house phone woke Alicia abruptly and she struggled upright on the elderly sofa, adrenalin rushing through her. She had fallen asleep after dinner, right opposite her father in his chair, and just for a moment on waking she'd been back in this house as a child. It was the same phone, the same ring tone, and her stomach shifted as fear gave way to tiredness. Hell. Another memory, half-disguised as a dream this time. A teacher had caught her and a little group of friends smoking after gym class one day and had threatened to call all their parents. He had, too. How terrified she'd been when the phone rang that evening and her father had answered it. Okay, thirteen-year-olds shouldn't be smoking but it had been the first time, they'd only been trying it out and what kid didn't do that? She had been grounded for a month and made to read some section of the bible, all about sins and vices, every night for an hour. All month. Over and over, her father listening righteously. However, he hadn't touched her, and the punishment would have been fitting if there hadn't been so much of it.

'Mummy? It's a lady for you.'

Jenny put her head round the living room door and Alicia struggled to her feet. After a night chasing after her father every time he'd woken – four times – and then a day spent sorting through some of her mother's old things she was completely knackered.

She took the receiver from Jenny and sat down on the bottom stair.

'Alicia? Hi, honey, it's Sonja. Frank told me you were back in Lower Banford.'

Hot tears of pleasure rushed into Alicia's tired eyes. Sonja. Her old friend. Sonja and Cathal had been the best parts of her life back then.

'Sonja. You sound like… like yourself!' she said. 'It's lovely to hear from you, how are you?'

'Great. We've been in Paris for two years now so the kids can chatter away in French, be a big advantage for them later. We've got a really nice house just up from the Champs Élysée, huge rooms and a fantastic conservatory which is marvellous for all the entertaining we have to do for John's job. And as you can imagine the shops are brilliant. But tell me about you, Frank said your Dad's been ill?'

Alicia grinned to herself. Even as a child Sonja had been keen on the posher side of life and it sounded as if she really was living the dream now. She peered round the bannister to see if Margaret was in the kitchen, but the back door was open and there was her aunt halfway up the garden, heading towards the rasps with a colander in one hand. Good. She could talk openly.

'He's had a few strokes, plus he's got dementia. I'm looking into a home for him but unfortunately Margaret's dead against it. Frank's been great, he's a big support.'

'Oh poor you. How awful. I'm glad Frank is there for you, how is he, do you think he's okay? I was worried when he moved back to Lower Banford, I was afraid he was chasing the past and you know you can't go back. He was distraught when Nell died and I really think he should have made a fresh start in a completely new place.'

Alicia pictured Frank's thin face. 'Well, he's a bit skinny but he seems positive enough. I didn't know him well back then, but if I didn't know about his wife I'd never have guessed he has such a tragedy in his life.'

'It was a dreadful time for him. We were afraid he was going to lose the plot completely and end up in hospital himself. He and Nell were completely devoted to each other, he barely spoke for weeks after she died. Sounds like he's a lot better now so maybe moving back was the right decision for him after all. I'll see you both for myself next week, Alicia, I can't wait to visit!'

Happiness spread warmly through Alicia, an unaccustomed feeling in her father's house. Sonja would soon be here.

'Me too! And you can help me with some odd memories I've been having,' she said impulsively.

Sonja laughed. 'Odd memories? Sounds intriguing. I'm sure your Dad never let anything in the least odd anywhere near you,' she said. 'We'll stroll down memory lane together over a bottle of something, shall we? Alicia, I have to go, Logan has a fencing lesson in half an hour and I'm chauffeur as usual. I'm really looking forward to seeing you! Bye, honey!'

Alicia found herself smiling as she replaced the phone. Sonja hadn't changed, scatty but with a heart of gold nonetheless. She stood up and stretched, glancing through to her father in the living room.

Sonja was wrong about one thing though. There were plenty of odd memories attached to those years. But soon they'd be able to sit down together and have a real talk. So one little thing – big thing, actually – had gone right today.

Counting out her father's evening pills, Alicia thought about Frank. It sounded like he'd been through the wringer when his wife had died. You'd never know it to look at him now, though. And he hadn't mentioned it at all yesterday.

Wasn't that just a little strange?

Chapter Eight
Thursday, 13th July

Alicia

Tripping over her feet in her hurry, Alicia rushed into Jenny's room and gently shook the little girl awake. By the smell of things Margaret was grilling bacon downstairs, and Alicia grabbed clean jeans and a t-shirt from Jen's wardrobe and tossed them onto the bed.

'My alarm didn't go off, we're running late. Get dressed, have breakfast, and *don't go off to play!*' she said, already halfway out the door. 'Your bus leaves at ten, and Margaret won't be pleased if she misses it because you and Conker are out gallivanting in the woods!'

It had been Jenny's own idea to go with Margaret and visit David and Sheila. Alicia had agreed, knowing that Jen would enjoy seeing Sheila preparing for the baby expected in September. The little girl was to come back by herself – with Conker – on the half past six bus. Alicia frowned uneasily. Margaret had assured her that she'd place Jen on the bus herself, and ask the driver to keep an eye on her. The journey took less than an hour, and with so much else to worry about, Alicia felt she needed to trust Margaret on this one. After all, no child needed an overprotective mother.

Staggering around in haste, Alicia grabbed some clothes, anything at all would do in the meantime. Of all the days to sleep in. Now she had little more than an hour to get Jen organised for her trip, as well as get her father up, dressed and fed before Eva Campbell from next door came to sit with him. Tears welled up in her eyes as she scraped her hair back into one of Jenny's scrunchies. She was just so tired. Her father was sleeping a bit better with the new pills but even one nocturnal excursion to his room left her half-dead the next day. The whole situation made her skin crawl, how she loathed being with him in the bedroom that reeked of old man. It was horrible, going in there at night, when it was dark and nobody else was awake... The nausea she'd experienced twice hadn't returned, though, and neither had the young voice warning her about 'the bad room'. Still, the sooner she could get him safely into St. Joe's the happier she would be.

She pushed her father's bedroom door open and knew straightaway that she was in for a bad run. Again. The new pills maybe helped him sleep, but they had the unfortunate side effect of making him doubly incontinent. Determinedly closing her mind to the horrible thing she was doing, Alicia helped the old man out of bed and into the shower. As a nurse she'd dealt with plenty of similar situations, but somehow it was a lot less bearable when it was your own father. Your own father who you didn't love as a daughter was supposed to... but he hadn't loved her either.

She took him downstairs and then raced back up to deal with the bed and open all the windows. When at last she was sitting at the breakfast table with a slice of toast in front of her and the washing machine sloshing the bed linen around, Alicia just felt sick. It was tempting to start ranting to Margaret about St. Joe's being better equipped to deal with incontinent geriatrics, but then her aunt would only say that if he hadn't taken the sleeping pills in the first place they wouldn't have that particular problem, which of course was entirely correct. There was no point in arguing.

To her relief, Margaret took her tea upstairs to see to her bags. Alicia rubbed her face, aware that Jenny was staring at her.

'Mummy, you look funny.' Jenny's brow creased in a worried little frown.

'Thank you, darling, but I don't feel in the least funny. Oh, I'm sorry, Jen, I'm tired because Grandpa wakes up in the night and needs me, that's all. It's nothing for you to worry about.'

Jenny nodded, pushing her chair back and tossing her last bite of toast in the air for Conker to catch. Alicia glanced at her watch.

Eva would be here in twenty minutes. No-one else knew about her visit to St. Joe's. Alicia meant to make her own mind up, then talk to Frank and Margaret. She had phoned David the previous day and he'd promised to try to persuade his mother that the hospital wasn't some kind of medieval torture chamber. But with or without Margaret's approval, Alicia knew she would have to make other arrangements for her father before the end of the summer. Things couldn't go on like this.

'Mummy, I've got a secret,' said Jenny, turning from the kitchen window where she'd been staring up to the woods.

'Have you, darling? Is it a nice one?' Alicia smiled as she carried the plates over to the sink.

Jenny smiled back, her face dreamy, then hesitated. 'Um yes, I think so,' she said vaguely, and Alicia looked at her. At that moment the phone rang, and Jenny ran to answer it.

'Daddy!'

Alicia strode out to the hallway and took the receiver from Jenny. Her ex certainly had timing, she thought dismally.

'What is it, Paul?'

'Dear me, Alicia, how very abrupt you are, someone get out of the wrong side of the bed? I wanted a chat with Jen, to tell her about her new mum and about her visit to Singapore in the autumn.'

'Jenny is not going to Singapore, Paul,' said Alicia, hot fury rising in her gut. 'Not for a visit and definitely not to stay.'

'We'll see. I'm putting my lawyer onto it,' said Paul, and she could hear the sneer in his voice. 'See you in court, Alicia.'

Alicia banged the phone down, and turned to see Jenny staring up at her with huge, frightened eyes.

'Oh, Jen darling,' she began, and Jenny ran into her arms.

'I don't want to go to Singapore without you,' she whispered, and Alicia hugged her, determination flooding through her as Jenny held on tightly. Of course Paul wouldn't get custody. Most likely he didn't even want it, he was just being mean, trying to make her life miserable, and he was probably enjoying it, too. But she was stronger than that, wasn't she? Of course she was.

With a great effort she jollied her daughter back into something resembling good humour, then accompanied the travellers to the bus stop and stood waving as the bus jerked towards the village shop. Right. So far, so good. Sort of.

Eva Campbell joined her at the garden gate, knitting in hand.

'On you go, dear, Bob'll be fine with me for an hour or two,' she said, accompanying Alicia inside where the old man was standing at the living room window, hugging his cloth cap to his chest very much as a child might hug a teddy bear.

'Thanks, Eva. I won't be long. Make yourself a coffee, you know where everything is, and my, um, Bob would probably enjoy a digestive too.'

Alicia ran upstairs and pulled on black linen trousers and a pale green blouse. No point going to St. Joe's looking like someone's poor relation, she thought, applying blusher to her cheekbones. A squirt of perfume and she was almost a new woman.

Alicia stared into the mirror, remembering the touch of Douglas Patton's hand on her own, and the compassion in his eyes. Could he be interested in her? It was years since she'd had anything approaching a serious relationship, but somehow it was easy to picture herself with him. Grinning, she grabbed her bag.

Don't go into the bad room.

This time the child's voice could almost have been real. Alicia stopped dead, level with her father's bedroom. Dear God, *what* had gone on in there? Had they left her in the darkness of her father's bedroom as a punishment? Or had it been more than that?

She stood there thinking. He might have abused her. Maybe not rape but he might well have undressed her, whipped her. Or *had* it been sexual abuse of some kind? In the name of religion? Surely not, and shit, she didn't have time to think about this right now and she didn't want to, either. Time to put the memories – if that was what they were – away. She would mull it all over later.

The phone rang again as she was running downstairs, and for a moment Alicia toyed with the idea of leaving it. Better not, she decided, jumping down the last two steps and grabbing the receiver. If it was Paul again she'd well and truly scare him off. She didn't want him bothering Eva.

For a moment she couldn't place the rather high-pitched male voice, then she realised. It was the pet shop owner.

'Hello again, Mrs Bryson. Just to say the little cat's quite well again, and I haven't found anyone who's lost him. He's not chipped, either. Do you still want him?'

Alicia hesitated and then remembered Jenny's eyes as she'd stroked the kitten. After all, other cats lived in small flats and seemed to thrive quite well. And in a few weeks Jenny would be leaving Conker behind in Lower Banford, so a little cat to take home with her would ease that pain quite considerably.

'I think so, yes. Shall we come and get him? Jenny's away all day unfortunately, would this evening be okay? Around seven?'

'That would be perfect. I live above the shop, just come in and shout. See you both tonight.'

Wondering if she had done the wisest thing, Alicia drove to the care home, consciously relaxing her shoulders. It was wonderful to be by herself for a while, away from her father and all his problems. It wasn't exactly me-time because she was still doing something connected to the old man, but at least she was getting out of the house for a bit.

St. Joe's looked exactly the same as it had done on Saturday when she'd been here with Frank. The same sunshine, the same old people sitting out in the same wheelchairs beside the same rose bushes. The fate of the aged, she thought, pulling up in the visitors' car park in front of the house. Every day was pretty much a carbon copy of the one before.

The front door was propped open, and Alicia walked into a wide hallway where two leather sofas were placed along cream walls with flowery prints hanging at various levels. It didn't look like your usual NHS place, she should find out if any costs were involved here before committing herself to anything. No way could they afford a private home. Right at the back was a desk with a bell on it, but before she reached it, Douglas Patton ran down the stairway and strode towards her, hand outstretched.

'Hello, Mrs Bryson - can I call you Alicia? You know I'm Doug.'

His huge warm hand gripped hers, and Alicia realised that her heart rate had increased. He was obviously delighted to see her, towering over her with a big grin on his face. It was difficult not to feel like 'the little woman' beside him. A lovely flutter of excitement ran through her. She smiled, and regained possession of her hand. It wouldn't do to seem too keen.

'Sure. Well, here I am, and feeling a bit nervous. It's a big decision.'

Doug chatted reassuringly about life at the care home as he led her upstairs and round the admissions ward, seeming to understand exactly what she needed to know.

And really, the whole place seemed ideal. Alicia stood looking round the dayroom where some old people were watching cricket on TV. It was clean and bright, it didn't smell too antiseptic and there was no school-dinner cabbage smell either. The nurses looked cheerful, and it *was* NHS. So maybe something, at last, was going to work out well for her this summer. There was nothing here that Margaret could possibly object to.

'Isn't that Mr French?' she asked, looking at a shrunken old man sitting at the end of the corridor picking a hole in his cardigan.

'Yes, do you know him?'

Alicia smiled rather sadly. Harry French had been caretaker of her secondary school. He could always be depended on to retrieve tennis balls from the roof and he'd kept an eye on the playground games too, in case the footie got too rough. It was sad seeing him here like this, no longer his old vital self.

Doug chuckled. 'He doesn't look it, but he's a bit of a tearaway. His grandsons bring him cans of lager and officially he's allowed one a day. The problem is he has an illicit stash that we're not supposed to know about. Keeps him happy and we try to make sure that he doesn't have more than two a day. We don't always succeed. And the old chap over there's just as bad. Jim Slater. He's forever getting the ladies fighting over something or other. Real characters, both of them.'

Alicia laughed. Jim Slater had been the butcher in Lower Banford, he'd been a real ladies' man in those days too. Her father had disapproved, of course, and poor Mum always had to bike to Middle Banford for meat. It was nice in a way to know that the old people were still able to do their own thing here at St. Joe's.

Doug took her arm, and her heart rate doubled immediately.

'Come and meet Derek Thorpe, he's the charge nurse in this

ward. Derek!'

Derek Thorpe was emerging from a side room further up the ward. He came over, hand outstretched much as Doug's had been and Alicia wondered in amusement if it was some kind of hospital policy.

'Sorry, my hands are like lumps of ice,' said Derek, grinning ruefully. 'I've been rearranging the meds freezer, but don't worry, I'll heat them up before I touch any of the patients. Frank Carter told me about your father the other day. Must be really difficult for you.' He gave her hand a cold squeeze with both of his, his face serious now.

'Well, it is a bit,' said Alicia, surprised. A lot of people had commiserated about her situation but somehow Derek's sympathy seemed more personal. She hadn't said a word to Frank about how much she was hating being here but Derek had obviously seen something of her unhappiness. His next words confirmed this.

'It's hell, isn't it, the whole dependent parent needing care thing,' he said, lowering his voice as two of the patients walked past, zimmer frames clicking on the polished floor. 'Your father's place isn't too far from my flat, so if you ever needed help just give me a call. What do you think of St. Joe's so far?'

Alicia chatted for a few more minutes before Derek was called away. He grinned cheerfully as he said goodbye and Alicia smiled back. What a happy, down-to-earth personality he had, and he was kind, too. He didn't ignore the problems, and that was exactly what was needed in a geriatric hospital.

'Derek's one of the best nurses I've ever met,' said Doug, steering her back to the ward doors. 'He's a real charmer, too, the old folks all love him.'

'I can imagine,' said Alicia. Gales of aged laughter were coming from the room Derek had just entered.

'Would you like to have a coffee and a chat in my office?' said Doug, sounding hopeful.

Alicia glanced at her watch. 'I would, but I'd better not. Mrs Campbell from next door is sitting with my father, so I can't be away too long. Thanks very much, Doug. It's been a really helpful visit.'

He smiled at her, his brown eyes shining. 'My pleasure. And let me know if you have any questions.'

Alicia smiled back. 'Thanks. What a lovely boss you must be. No wonder your staff seem so happy here.'

He laughed. 'Oh, I'm still the new boy in town. Only been here four months. It's working out well, though.'

'I can see that. Okay, I'll be in touch.'

'Good. And Alicia, let's make a point of having that coffee another time, shall we?'

She felt herself blush. 'I'd like that.'

This is what walking on air feels like, she thought, returning to the car. It was ages since a man had asked her out. Well, maybe her luck was about to change.

She arrived home to find her father asleep in his chair and Eva just finishing her second sleeve.

'Quiet as a lamb, he fell asleep soon after you left,' she reported, and Alicia sighed. Sleeping half the day meant her father would be up half the night, pills or no pills. Oh, well. She would leave him until lunchtime and give herself some peace and quiet to think. She had a lot to think about now, and Doug had certainly raised a few forgotten emotions.

Alicia smiled to herself.

The Stranger

After two glorious afternoons in the woods with little Helen he had gone up to the circle of trees expecting her to be there today too. It was fortunate that his job gave him so much freedom. A nine to five job with a boss breathing down his neck wouldn't have done for him at all.

But the clearing was deserted. The trees stood silent, leafy tops waving in the breeze. The only person interrupting the stillness here was himself.

The disappointment was heavy, but there would be other opportunities for play-meetings before little Helen's trip to Paradise on Sunday, he reassured himself. He sat down on the fallen tree trunk to think about his beautiful plan.

The old man was the key player, old Bob. He was going to get lost, wasn't he, and then while big Helen was out searching, he himself would have plenty of time for a game with little Helen. Oh God, playing with little Helen. He might even be able to take her home with him, what a beautiful game they could have together then. The lovely times he'd never had with Mummy would be his to take now with little Helen. And then when they'd played as much as they wanted, off he would send her… like Snugglepuss and Mummy but in quite a different way. There had been rage then. With Snugglepuss the rage had come slowly, he'd held his cat that day and the rage had built and built. With Mummy, it had been sudden. She had ignored him once too often and all the hurt that had piled up inside had exploded. With the Helens there would be no rage, just love and then Paradise, almost like it had been with his own Helen.

Nothing at all like Mummy's death.

That had happened when he was fifteen. He had turned into a tall, lanky youth and the whole family often laughed at his breaking voice and gangly limbs. Just like they'd laughed when Snugglepuss had turned against him. Dad would taunt him about being a Mummy's boy and Mummy herself would say things like 'Oh for God's sake get a grip' when he tried to wheedle her into a good mood.

Then one morning, quite early, he'd been coming out of the bathroom and there was Mummy on the landing, about to go downstairs. He'd smiled at her, good morning Mummy - but she'd looked right through him. Not out of anger or to teach him a lesson, no, in one sickening moment he'd seen that he wasn't even worth a word or a smile. Rejection by indifference.

And all the hurt, accumulated over years and years, had overwhelmed him completely. Before he even thought about it he'd grabbed her arm, I'm *here*, Mummy, Mummy, look at me! He was squeezing her arm with both hands now but it felt nothing like white fur this time. She jerked away from him and the rage took control. As hard as he could he pushed her towards the stairs; she tried to keep her balance but another shove sent her crashing all the way down to the bottom. Her head hit the big wooden knob on the bannister and he heard bones snap as she landed in the hallway.

Silence fell. He crept downstairs and pulled at her shoulder and she let out a weak, breathy groan. She was staring at him now, he couldn't stand it. She was looking at him with desperate eyes and it was just like with Snugglepuss because suddenly he didn't have to think at all about what to do, he simply reached out and held Mummy's nose and mouth closed and watched as the light went out of her eyes and the faltering breathing stopped. She barely struggled. The whole thing had taken seconds.

He'd waited a moment, frozen to the spot and thinking his father would come running, but then stupid Dad always slept deeply. Mummy was dead, she was dead… And the agony now in his head was ten times worse than the hurt. He had to get rid of it, so he parcelled it up and locked it away in the part of his mind he never used. He'd gone back to bed and lain there waiting until his father got up and found Mummy, though of course it was only Mummy's body, for by that time Mummy herself was in hell.

He had vowed then never to love again, that way he would avoid more rejection and more hurt, and this had worked perfectly until he met Helen. She'd been his angel right from the start, his love. Almost like Mummy but so, so different. Then came the dreadful day when he'd pushed her too... He had to make that mistake good again.

Very soon the two new Helens would be safe in Paradise. His loves would all be together. He sighed. Helen was the sweetest name in the world.

The tree trunk was damp and he rose and jogged regretfully down the pathway to the back road, away from the memories and away from the clearing and away from little Helen's home.

It was time to make the final arrangements. Sunday would soon be here.

Alicia

'We can collect him tonight? Oh, how brilliant! Conker, we're going to have a cat!'

Looking down at Jenny's excited face, Alicia felt a spark of enthusiasm return to her. No matter what else was going on, she was giving her daughter a wonderful summer. The little girl had thoroughly enjoyed her day in York, including the solo bus journey back home again, sitting right at the front where the driver could keep an eye on her – Alicia's worry had been needless – and now they were going to pick up a cat. A cat of their own, to take home to Bedford. Life just didn't get better.

Pigtails flying, Jenny danced out to the car. Alicia looked back at her father, sitting staring at the television news. They would only be gone fifteen minutes. It maybe wasn't the best idea to leave him alone like this but he'd be okay. As long as the telly was on he'd stay put, he never moved in the evening.

The village street was deserted as they drove to the pet shop, and Jenny was out of the car before Alicia had switched the engine off. Grabbing her bag, she followed her daughter inside.

'There he is!' The little girl ran to the counter where the cat was sitting, and Kenneth Taylor lumbered over to greet them, a beaming smile on his shiny fat face.

'Hello, hello. Yes, there he is. All better now.'

Alicia made herself smile back. She didn't know what it was about Kenneth that made her feel so uneasy, after all he had been nothing but friendly towards them.

'Thanks, Mr Taylor. Now, Jen and I are what you might call

novices at cat-keeping, so a book might be good, and we'll need some things for him too,' she said, and he reached past her and plucked a book from the stand.

'Right you are. This one's very good, it explains all about cats in a nice easy to read way. And all the extras are over there.' He nodded at the shelves on the other side of the room.

Jenny immediately began gathering bowls and toys together, and Alicia went to help. There seemed to be an unlimited amount of cat accessories available, but at last they had a small selection sitting on the counter. Kenneth added a few packets of food and produced a sturdy carton to double as transport box and sleeping quarters. Alicia couldn't help feeling impressed – surprised, too – when he advised against buying an expensive basket in the meantime, just in case the cat was still claimed.

'Have you got a name for him?' he asked, tickling behind the cat's ears. It arched its back, purring loudly.

'Moritz,' said Jenny. 'Like the cat in my book. He's going to be best friends with Conker, you know. He couldn't come now because he's guarding Grandpa at home.'

Kenneth nodded, pressing his lips together. He was evidently aware of her father's condition and Alicia wondered how he knew. Mrs Mullen, probably, who else?

'Parents can be a problem, can't they,' he said in a low voice while Jenny petted the kitten. 'I know that because my own mum was a bit of a tyrant in her own way. And when she died my Dad just went to pieces, we left the area and went to London where he drank himself into an early grave. I always think the important thing for me now is to make sure I don't end up like either of them.'

'Absolutely,' said Alicia, his sensitivity surprising her again. Avoiding your parents' fate was something she could definitely agree with him about. Kenneth Taylor was maybe worth more than he was selling himself for.

He picked up the cat and kissed its nose before putting it into the box and Alicia smiled to herself. He was a real funny bunny and no mistake…

'Thanks, Mr Taylor. You might find us in quite often at first, needing advice!'

He grinned, and she saw that he was younger than she'd thought. 'Call me Kenneth,' he said. 'I'll look forward to it. You'll have lots of fun with him, I'm sure.' Gently, he pushed the box across the counter to Jenny.

'Thank you - oh, you're bleeding!' The little girl reached past the box and took hold of his thumb, where blood was oozing from under a piece of sticking plaster. He snatched his hand back, a sudden hiss escaping from between his teeth. Jenny jumped, and Alicia put an arm round her.

'Careful, Jen, you shouldn't grab sore hands like that,' she said. 'Are you okay, Mr um, Kenneth?'

'Yes of course, I'm so sorry, I just got a little fright,' he said, smiling and nodding away...

Alicia had to force herself to smile back now. She lifted the bag with the accessories while Jenny held the box with Moritz, looking as if someone had given her the moon. A lump came to Alicia's throat. Jen was having a wonderful summer, and that was the important thing. She drove home, trying not to laugh at the way Jenny was commiserating with the cat about being taped into a box. What with the pet shop owner's antics and now her daughter's, this had turned into one of the most entertaining outings she'd had all summer.

To Alicia's relief her father hadn't budged from his chair. There. Something else had gone well today. Lots of things had, actually. She had seen St. Joe's, and Doug Patton had asked her out. Mr Taylor had been funny and Jenny was happy about her cat... a good day overall. The downside was it might not be over for a bit, collecting cats just before bedtime might not have been the best idea.

After several false starts, Jenny disappeared upstairs with Conker in tow. Alicia took her father up too, and tucked him into his bed as well. And now the rest of the day was her own. Hallelujah.

The grandfather clock in the hallway was striking when she sank down in the corner of the sofa, clutching a gin and tonic. Thinking time at long last. Alicia put her feet on the coffee table and sipped appreciatively. The memories, or lack of them about her childhood were disturbing and she mulled over the different possibilities as to how to deal with them. She should (a) get away from Lower Banford and (b) go for some kind of counselling. She needed distance. She needed perspective. She needed help to unlock the gaping holes in her memory.

She would talk to Frank again. He had so much common sense, and he was part of her past, he didn't feel like one of Jenny's dreaded strangers. Or maybe she could ask Doug Patton for advice. Alicia smiled to herself. He would probably be only too pleased to help her. It felt good, knowing that Doug found her attractive. The little wave of pleasure whenever she thought about him had been missing in her life for a long, long time. Just a little wave, rushing up the beach with a kind of fizzing sound... And it could so easily turn into a positive tsunami, too, and what an exciting thought that was.

The stairs creaked as the old house shifted and settled for the night. Alicia sat in the dimness, sipping her drink.

Living here. Playing spaceships with Cathal... Kids didn't change, in spite of all the technology nowadays. But her childhood was long gone, and what *had* happened, exactly?

A picture flashed abruptly into her mind. Pain. Herself, maybe Jen's age, maybe younger, lying on a bed and crying in the dark. Alicia shivered. There was so much she didn't remember. What had it been like, living here year after year with a religious fanatic for a father, and a meek, submissive mother? It was beginning to look very much as if her childhood hadn't been at all what it should have been, and that was something she really didn't enjoy thinking about. She had been afraid. She had been punished for things that other kids took for granted, like a clap on the shoulder from a friend, and eating a handful of rasps.

Sometimes you read about perverse, religious-motivated abuse that went on. Her father had been careful to spurn the devil at every opportunity... had that involved cruelty towards his own child? Whipping the wickedness out of her, maybe? Or had it been more than that? Would Margaret know? Or Cathal, her best friend, would he remember? She should look him up and ask.

Alicia made herself another drink, a small one this time. Glass in hand, she stood gazing out of the kitchen window. The garden was in near-darkness now, she couldn't see as far as the woods on the hill. How excited Jenny was about her secret place. What had she said this morning? Oh, it was no use. She was much too tired to think. You could do too much soul-searching. It was time to go to bed.

Chapter Nine
Saturday, 15th July

The Stranger

He paced up and down his comfortable, old-fashioned living room, hands balled in frustration and glaring across at the wooded hillside every time he passed the window.

It was so frustrating. He hadn't seen little Helen since Wednesday. Of course, the wet weather hadn't helped. Thankfully the forecast for tomorrow was better, sunny intervals with the odd shower. Dry weather would make his plan so much easier to carry out. Just his luck that rain had stopped play with little Helen these past few days. After being with her in the woods like that, touching her, laughing with her, he'd wanted more, much more. Paradise was beckoning little Helen, and he had so wanted to see her again before her long journey. That wasn't going to happen now. But tomorrow would make up for everything.

He thought back to his last meeting with her. So wonderful, the way she had trusted him, played with him. Had she told her mother about their secret? Surely not. And she couldn't be *afraid* of him, he'd been so careful to be 'nice'. It was something he was rather good at, he played the role of nice man every day: friendly, respectable, always ready with good advice. He hadn't been back in the village long, but Lower Banford had accepted him without question. Once a villager, always a villager.

Why hadn't she come then, poor little Helen? Of course, maybe she had. He had other things to do, he couldn't spend all day patrolling about in the woods. But he was getting anxious. A lot could have happened in three days.

The plan with the old man was a positive stroke of genius. He knew that Margaret was away at the moment – Mrs Mullen had done him proud with that information – so big Helen would have to do all the work herself. It would be easy to put his first plan, Plan A, into action. The old man would most likely end up in St. Joe's, big Helen there with him, guilty at what had happened and concerned, leaving little Helen to be looked after by someone else. By him, for example. He still wasn't sure exactly what big Helen thought about him, but under the circumstances she would certainly trust him to look after her daughter for an hour or two... and that was plenty of time.

Yes, a little care, and he would have his fairy queen right there in his arms, in his power, and he would take her and make her his own sweet darling. That was a promise to himself. Then it would be big Helen's turn. His first Helen in Paradise had been waiting long enough.

And even if Plan A went wrong for some reason, well, he could go straight to Plan B, couldn't he? What a genius he was. Yes, he could relax now, it was all going to be fine.

Sunday... Sunday morning, in fact, how very fitting... A long walk for old Bob, and Paradise for little Helen.

Alicia

'Bath time,' said Alicia, looking thankfully at her watch. 'Come on, Jenny-penny, you can be in the bath while I'm helping Grandpa into his pjs.'

And that way she wouldn't be alone with him, not really, she could chat to Jen in the bath all the time. It was horrible the way her skin crawled whenever she had to touch her father. He was pretty spaced out most of the time. He would get up from his chair and go for a wander, he would lift things up and put them down in different places, but there was obviously no thought process going on behind the actions. And other, appropriate actions often just didn't happen – she had to hold his food to his mouth and wipe away the dribble, not to mention having to take him to the bathroom every couple of hours. It was enough having messy sheets to contend with every morning. But it all meant she had to touch him, trying all the time to control herself so that Jenny wouldn't see the shudders… Christ. Was she just a hateful person, or was her body remembering something her mind had made itself forget?

It took the bribe of a double portion of bubble bath, but eventually Jenny left Moritz in the kitchen and followed on upstairs.

'Pooh, it's a bit stinky in here, isn't it?' she said, standing in her grandfather's doorway. 'Poor old Grandpa.'

Alicia was silent for a moment. How to make your mother feel ashamed in three short words. Trust Jenny to have the empathy to think 'poor old Grandpa' and not 'disgusting old Grandpa'. Maybe her daughter was a nicer person than she was. After all, he was a sick old man now, was she building something in her imagination here, something that hadn't happened? The whole child's voice in her head could be a sign of her own insecurity and not her father's 'abuse'.

No. Alicia stood still, frantically trying to think. He *had* been abusive. She'd been a victim, but like a lot of other victims she had pushed it away. Buried it somewhere, deep down. That happened all the time, according to the news reports.

Unfortunately it was true that the room was smelly. Her father had woken up doubly incontinent almost every day that week, and no matter how long the window was open for, there was still a residual aroma that wasn't pleasant.

The old man sat down on the bed, then looked straight at Jenny and laughed his wheezy laugh.

'Did he understand what I said?' said Jenny, looking from Bob to Alicia and frowning uncertainly.

Alicia shrugged, barely managing to hide how shocked she was. 'I don't know, Jen. I don't think so, don't worry.'

But maybe he had understood. It was the first time he'd reacted to Jen since they'd arrived here. Was it possible that he was using what little sense he had just to be nasty? And maybe he had more sense than they knew about. One thing was clear, from now on she was going to make very sure that Jen was never alone with him. Not that he could physically harm her in his current state, but he might frighten her, and that alone would be intolerable.

The frown on Jenny's face disappeared as soon as she was in the bath, and Alicia kept up an amusing cat conversation while she was sponging her father's hands and face in the bedroom.

The phone rang while she was buttoning his pyjama top. Hell, she should leave it... but if it was Margaret she would worry if nobody answered at this time of day.

Warning Jenny to be careful, Alicia dived downstairs. The communication system in this house was antiquated to say the least. No internet, and the one and only phone had been old-fashioned in the seventies. Add to that the precarious mobile reception and you could almost believe that The Beatles were still on Top of the Pops.

'Hello?'

'Hi, Alicia, it's Frank. How's things?'

'Oh, Frank! Thanks for calling.' He was being very supportive, thought Alicia, stretching the phone cord to the limit so that she could keep an eye on the upstairs landing. He'd called nearly every day to check how things were, or to give her an update on the empty bed situation at St. Joe's. After two deaths earlier in the week there would be room for her father any time, and Alicia knew she didn't want to lose the place for him. They *had* to make Margaret agree, and soon.

'We're okay, I guess. I'm going to reduce the new pills to just the one tablet, he slept all night but he was in a real mess again this morning.' She squatted sideways on the bottom step, wincing. She was stiff, as she and Jen had spent every spare moment for the past two days trying to tame the front garden. There wasn't much else they could do here with her father to look after, and she was discovering muscles she'd never known she had.

'Okay. Give him one tablet for the next three nights, and if that doesn't work out then we'll have another think. You know yourself it can take a bit of trial and error.'

The splashing noises from above had stopped, and Alicia frowned. Time to check that her daughter wasn't treating herself to one of Margaret's expensive face packs.

'Right,' she said. 'I'll have to go, Jen's in the bath and my father is half into his pyjamas. It's like having two kids.'

'Oh, I'd forgotten Margaret's away. I was going to ask if you'd like to come to the pub for an hour or two but I guess you can't.'

His voice was disappointed, and Alicia grinned, secretly pleased that Frank wanted to spend time with her.

'I'd love to, another time,' she said. 'Thanks Frank. I'll see you soon.'

Upstairs, she settled her father for the night then played bubbles with Jenny, happier in herself than she'd been since arriving back in her hometown. Frank was a good friend to have, he would help her convince Margaret about St. Joe's. And in a week or so, Sonja would be here with her family, and that would be great for Jen too. Then with her father in the home she could leave Lower Banford and all the dark memories safely behind her, see a therapist of some kind about her childhood and lay the ghosts to rest. It would be so good to be back in her own place again. Though mind you, she was actually getting a whole lot more opportunities for socialising here than she did in bustling Bedford. In the space of just two days, two men had asked her out. Maybe it hadn't been such a bad idea, spending the summer in her father's house.

Chapter Ten
Sunday, 16th July

Alicia

Sunday morning seemed almost idyllic at first, with her father still asleep and just Alicia and Jenny at the breakfast table.

Church bells for the early service were bim-bamming in through the open window as they sat in the kitchen with the usual Sunday morning bacon and eggs, chatting about how Moritz was going to like town life. Jenny was being enthusiastic, and Alicia was managing to ignore the fact that her daughter was sneaking bits of bacon down to the little cat crouched beneath her chair. Conker, as usual when meat of any kind was on the menu, had been banished to the garden and was whining from behind the back door. His nose must be thoroughly out of joint, thought Alicia, smiling to herself. Jen had spent most of her time since Thursday inside playing with Moritz, who was both more agile and funnier than poor Conker, a typical climbing-the-curtains kitten, in fact, and naturally Jen loved that. But maybe the great outdoors would beckon again; after three days of showers, today was sunny and dry. Her daughter's next words confirmed this.

'Can we have a picnic lunch in the woods afterwards?' asked Jenny, letting Moritz lick her fingers clean. Alicia poured her a glass of milk.

'You wash those hands before you do another thing, my lamb,' she said. A picnic lunch with her father in tow… no way. She smiled her persuasive best at Jenny and continued cautiously.

'Well, we could have a picnic in the garden if you like, but we can't really take Grandpa to the woods.'

Jenny's face fell. 'I wanted to show you my special place now the sun's shining.'

Alicia sighed. Poor scrap, it was a sad day when a simple request like a picnic had to be refused. What Jen needed here was a friend of the two-legged variety. There must be other eight-year-old girls in the village? They could ask Frank, he would know.

'And I'm dying to see it, it sounds brilliant,' she said, pouring herself another coffee. 'But not with Grandpa. Tell you what. I'll make you and Conker a picnic for today. Then when Aunt Margaret gets back, you and me'll have a real day out somewhere – woods, river, swimming pool – whatever you like. You can plan it. Scoot and do your teeth now and I'll make you some peanut butter sandwiches.'

'Yum,' said Jenny, and raced back upstairs with Moritz under her arm. Alicia followed on. Better get her father up before he messed the bed again. He was agitated and uncooperative today, but at least he was clean and dry. She was settling him into his chair in the living room when Jenny called from upstairs.

'Mummy! I can't find Moritz!'

Alicia's lips twitched. 'Find Moritz' was probably going to be the most-played game that summer. She ran upstairs to help before Jenny became frantic. There were only the four bedrooms, but Moritz seemed to have disappeared off the face of the earth. It was ten minutes at least before they discovered him crouched behind the bin in the bathroom.

'Bad kitty!' Jenny scooped him up and covered him with kisses.

Alicia laughed. 'He's been running around avoiding us all this time. Let's get him a collar with a bell on it,' she said, scratching Moritz's ears. He *was* cute. 'Take him downstairs, lovey. I'll just air the rooms while I'm up here.'

She fluffed up pillows and opened windows, listening as Jenny bossed Conker around in the kitchen. Alicia sighed. What was going to happen there? Would Margaret still want a creature like Conker if – when – she wasn't living here anymore? A sudden vision of Conker's large, ungainly form in her own compact two bedroom flat made Alicia shudder, then smile. And now she'd better grill some bacon for her father's roll.

She made Jenny's sandwiches while the bacon was grilling, and waved as the little girl and the big dog loped off together down the garden. Right, breakfast was ready. Carefully, she lifted the loaded tray.

'Here we are at last,' she said, edging round the living room door.

The room was empty. Alicia stood there stupidly.

'Where are you?'

Not in here, anyway, so much was clear, there was no place in this room where a grown man could hide even if he'd wanted to. Alicia glanced up and down the hallway.

'Hello? Bob? Breakfast!' But of course there was no reply. Had he gone back upstairs while she was in the kitchen? She raced up, but the bedrooms were all deserted. Shit, where on earth had he gone?

The Stranger

It had been child's play. And how very gratifying it was too, the way everything worked out straightaway like that. An omen of what was to come, perhaps? He had thought the whole thing through very carefully before setting out. If either of the Helens noticed him he would say that he had just popped by in passing to see how they were managing, alone with old Bob. Big Helen wouldn't have suspected a thing.

He'd jogged through the woods, in case by some miracle little Helen had been at the special place already, and then right up Bob Logan's wilderness of a garden to the back door. The dog was lying in a dejected heap by the step, but it hadn't barked or growled at him today. Not much of a watchdog, then. Good.

He could see through the window that the kitchen was deserted, so he'd let himself in and stood listening. His Helens were talking upstairs, so he crossed the kitchen and stuck his head into the living room.

And there he was in his chair, old Bob, sucking his teeth and staring at nothing at all. Quickly, he'd grasped the old man's hand and pulled him to his feet.

'Come on, Bob. A lovely walk.'

And the old man had followed him outside like a stupid sheep. This was the dangerous bit, if anyone saw them now the plan would be ruined before it even started. He could say he'd found the old man outside, of course, but that would be the end of Plan A. Fortunately the place wasn't overlooked, all those overgrown shrubs and bushes saw to that.

He led the old man round to the front, crossed the lane with him and gave him a shove along the pathway which led down to the river. And Old Bob had trotted off towards the sound of the Ban rushing along to the weir at Middle Banford. It sounded as if it was carrying a lot of water today, all that rain had at least been good for something. As soon as the old man was out of sight he jogged off down the lane.

Well, the plan had started perfectly. Worst case, the old man would be found too soon. Then it would be time for Plan B. Best case, big Helen would have so much to do looking for or after Daddy that she wouldn't even notice how long little Helen had been gone in the woods…

Alicia

'Bob!'

Panic rising inside her, Alicia raced back down to the kitchen and yanked the back door open. No-one. Quickly, she stepped up on the bench by the back door and glared down the garden, but again, no-one in sight. And the driveway was equally deserted.

'Jenny! Jen! Come quick!' There was no point calling after her father, he wouldn't answer even if he was there and he certainly wouldn't come running to see what she wanted.

Jenny, thankfully, was still nearby, and rushed back, hair flying.

'Grandpa's gone – have you seen him – where were you exactly?'

'In the summerhouse. Grandpa's gone? Where Mummy?'

'I've no idea but we have to find him. Take Conker and go up the lane as far as Mrs Watson's. Knock on everyone's door on the way and ask if they've seen him, maybe he's in one of the gardens. I'll drive round the village. He must have gone out when we weren't watching him.'

And she hadn't watched him a lot that morning. Guilt welled up inside Alicia. Looking for Moritz, airing the beds, making sandwiches - she hadn't taken proper care of her father. But then he'd never wandered away before.

Jenny dashed off and Alicia flung herself into the car. Oh God, where was he? How could she not have noticed him leave the house? She should have kept the doors locked, she of all people should have realised something like this could happen... It was one thing wishing him gone, but quite another when he actually was gone and she was to blame.

The village was empty. Sunday morning peace and quiet reigned, the villagers were evidently either still in bed or enjoying leisurely Sunday breakfasts. Alicia drove up and down the main street, peering up lanes and into gardens, realising that it was a hopeless task. She would have to go home and phone the police. Her father could be wandering round someone's back garden and she would never see him from the car. Her heart still thumping under her ribs, she pulled the car round.

Jenny and Conker were trotting back down the lane, the little girl's hand clutching the dog's thick collar. Alicia jerked the car to a halt.

'Any luck?'

'No, but Mr Watson and Mr and Mrs Campbell are out looking in all the gardens and Mr and Mrs Donovan have gone down to the river. Mummy, where is he?'

'Darling, I don't know. I'll have to phone the police.'

Tears welled up in Jenny's eyes and Alicia put one arm round her while she phoned, conscious that her voice as well as her hands were shaking. It was twenty minutes before the police arrived, two uniformed officers from Upper Banford. By this time the village was beginning to gather that old Bob Logan was missing, and quite a search party was forming on the front driveway. The police sergeant listened to Alicia's explanation, and bent over a map of the area with his colleague.

Alicia looked at the people milling around in front of the house. How kind everyone was, coming to search like this. She didn't even know most of them. Oh, she should phone Frank, he would want to help too – and Doug Patton? – but he had said he usually worked weekends. She dialled Frank's number.

'I'm on my way,' he said, when she explained, barely able to keep the tears back. This was all her fault. Where was he? The strokes hadn't affected his leg function much at all, a slight limp, a stumbling gait, that was all... he could be a long way away by this time.

The police were organising the villagers into groups to search the woods, the river pathway, and the village. Alicia stood cuddling Jenny by the front door, apprehension twisting her insides into knots. Frank jogged up the driveway, his face concerned.

'Doctor Carter, good,' said the sergeant, sending the woods group round the back of the house. 'You should go with the river group, if you don't mind, in case… ahm. You stay here and wait, Mrs Bryson. He might well come back on his own and then it's best if you're here for him just as usual.'

Alicia nodded. Her mouth was dry. Why was she feeling this way about a parent she didn't even care about? Was it guilt that all these people were out searching just because *she* hadn't looked after her father?

Frank put a hand on her shoulder and squeezed briefly. 'Try not to worry, Alicia, we'll find him.'

She watched as the river group left the front drive. Be here for him just as usual, the sergeant had said. But there was nothing usual about her being here. She winced. Was that why her father had wandered off? To look for Margaret? And if he had gone down to the river… She knew his life would end one day soon, but dear God, not like this. If he died today it would all be down to her. A dry sob rose in her throat, and Conker whined in sympathy beside her.

'Come on, Mummy. Doctor Frank said it would be okay,' said Jenny, pulling her arm. 'Let's get Grandpa's bed ready for him.'

Now her eight-year-old daughter was taking charge. Alicia swallowed hard. 'Thanks, love,' she whispered, following Jenny upstairs. She smoothed the duvet out over her father's bed, then remembered the hot water bottle in the bathroom. Warmth, he would need warmth. She filled it and placed it on the bed, then stood there stupidly, staring at the dark red rubber bottle against the white sheet.

For a split second she saw herself, a young child, huddled on exactly this bed and crying out in pain.

And there was blood on the sheets.

There was blood on the sheets. Red blood on white sheets.

The picture in her mind vanished almost as suddenly as it had appeared, leaving her nauseated and more frightened than ever before.

The Stranger

He glanced at his watch and nodded in satisfaction. So far, so good. Fortunately the old man hadn't been found yet. Which probably meant he had landed in the river. One thing he hadn't anticipated was that both Helens would stay at the house, he'd thought that big Helen at least would go out searching. But that really didn't matter, the important thing was to keep a close eye on proceedings so that he was ready with his offer of help the minute it was needed. He would be left holding the baby, so to speak, and it wouldn't be his fault when the baby ran off in the woods, would it?

The woods. He thought for a moment, feeling a tight pain start in the middle of his head. His lovely plan had a flaw he hadn't considered until now.

There were dozens of searchers out there in his woods. The thought was unbearable: strangers in little Helen's palace. It was so stupid, too – an old man who wasn't great on his feet wouldn't go uphill into the woods, no, he would go downhill to the river, just as old Bob had done. With a little help.

But now there would be intruders beneath the trees. All those do-gooder feet would be trampling around, stamping out the holiness of the place. He rubbed a hand over his face, feeling the sweat on his forehead. Every bone in his body was telling him to get up there and see for himself what was going on. His woods, the special place, what was happening to it?

And the new Helens, what were they doing now? Were they thinking of him at all? It was so difficult, not being able to watch their every move. He took a deep, shaky breath. It *would* be alright.

Big Helen liked him, he felt that clearly. She would let him help today. When the old man was found, big Helen would be so happy, so glad to have her father back – they would take him to St. Joe's, of course, and she would stay by his bedside like a dutiful daughter should and then – then he would have his time with little Helen. Just the two of them. Very soon now. Yes.

Alicia

There was nothing to do except wait. Alicia paced between the kitchen with its view up the wooded hillside, and the living room where she could see out to the lane. The searchers had vanished and to all intents and purposes this was a normal Sunday morning. Nothing happening in Lower Banford, same as every week.

What on earth was she going to tell Margaret? She would have to phone soon no matter what happened, but it would be so much better if she could say 'He wandered off outside earlier but he's tucked up in bed now... ' Shit, all this concern over a parent that she despised and who certainly didn't love her. She wasn't even sure if he knew who she was any more. Then she thought of the times his eyes had fixed on hers, the way he had laughed his wheezy laugh. He did know. He knew, and he'd been mocking her. Maybe he even knew what had gone on between them in her childhood. What a terrible old man he was, really. A parent to forget.

But now *she* was the parent figure and she was supposed to have been looking after him. Coming back here to do exactly that had been 'the right thing'; such were the ties of duty, the ties of the past. Did they prosecute people for not taking proper care of their invalid parents? But then it wasn't as if he was wheelchair bound, he could walk... He might simply be lost up in the woods, oh, please God he was just wandering about among the trees and not lying hurt somewhere, not fallen in the river. How strange it was to feel such strong disgust for someone, and yet worry frantically if they were okay.

The phone rang, and she sprinted into the hallway, almost

shouting into the receiver. 'Hello?'

'Hi, it's me, Doug. Is there any news yet?'

'Oh, Doug. No, nothing. I just don't understand how he could vanish off the face of the earth like this. The search parties have been gone nearly an hour now, they're down at the river and in the woods as well as the village and... ' A lump rose in her throat and her voice wobbled. His words were warm in her ear.

'Alicia, with all those searchers they'll find him, sooner rather than later I should think. And it's mild today, he won't get cold if he's wandering around. There'll be a bed for him in St. Joe's if he needs it, that wouldn't be a problem.'

Tears came to her eyes. She was surrounded by such kind people, everyone was being so helpful. Look at all those strangers, giving up their Sunday to search for her father. A deep breath steadied her voice.

'I just want him found safe,' she whispered. 'This is all my fault.'

'No, no, accidents happen. I'll be in touch later. Try not to worry more than you have to, I'm sure everything will be fine.'

She replaced the receiver and sank down on the sofa thinking about the conversation she just had. 'Try not to worry' was said quickly, how could she not worry? Supposing he was in the river? Would everyone still be so supportive if her neglect had killed him? Maybe she would go to prison, Jen could end up in Singapore with her father and new mother after all. She took another deep breath.

Jenny came in with both hands clasped round a mug, full to the brim with weak tea.

'I made you a hot drink, Mummy. Who was on the phone? Have they found Grandpa yet?'

Her voice was apprehensive, and Alicia forced herself to sound calm. There was no point in upsetting Jen even more. In fact helping her daughter was the only positive thing she could do at the moment apart from filling hot bottles. She smiled her thanks and sipped at the lukewarm milky tea. How lovely Jenny was to have made it.

'No, sweetie, not yet. It was Mr Patton from the care home.'

Jenny perched on the arm of her grandfather's chair. 'Will Grandpa be going into hospital?'

Alicia swallowed painfully. 'I don't know, Jen. Don't worry, sweetie. They're bound to find him soon.'

She forced the tea down and went upstairs to refill her father's hot water bottle. His pyjamas were still on the chair where she'd dropped them earlier, so she took out clean ones, fresh blue cotton, ironed, even, because Margaret ironed everything, and draped them over the bed.

Maybe he *would* have to go into hospital. If he'd fallen in the woods and broken his hip... The whole problem could be taken out of her hands, and how ironic was that, because all she really wanted right this minute was to have him back here in his own bed. But that was the guilt speaking. Could she have subconsciously neglected her father because deep inside she knew he had harmed her in some way, here in 'the bad room'? Why had there been blood on the sheets? If only she could remember.

It was impossible to sit still. Alicia strode to the bottom of the garden where the woods began. There was neither sight nor sound of the search party and the stillness was almost eerie. Clear summer sunshine danced between green leaves, some descending far enough to touch the mossy ground under her feet, more remaining caught in the tree tops. This was a beautiful place, normally, a tranquil place, full of peace and serenity. No wonder Jenny loved it.

What if her father *was* dead? Would she grieve? Not for him, no, but she would grieve for the past, for the relationship that had gone so horribly wrong. But that had been his fault. And she would have to organise a funeral, sit in the church and listen as an unknown cleric talked about her father, making him sound like a lovely old guy whose family were in bits about his death. Well, Margaret would be, but there was nobody else who would mourn old Bob Logan. But if he was dead she would live the rest of her life knowing that his death had been her fault. Her stomach churned.

A bird crying from a tall tree broke her train of thought, and her shoulders slumped dismally before far-off voices had her spinning round and racing back towards the house.

'Mrs Bryson! He's found!'

The voices came from the front of the house, and Alicia ran. The riverbank searchers were coming down the lane; a stretcher at the front of the group was held by Derek, the charge nurse, and Mr

Donovan. Her father was lying quite still, on top. He must be alright, they were all laughing and talking. Relief flooded through Alicia. He was alive. Frank and the police sergeant flanked the stretcher, and the whole procession halted when she reached them. How small and pathetic her father looked lying there, but he was breathing and his face was warm. The nurse in Alicia reached out and felt for a pulse. It was fast, but steady. Lying here like this, eyes closed, somehow her father looked intelligent, as if he would wake up any moment and speak to them. But of course he wouldn't, she knew he would never speak to her again.

'He's exhausted but otherwise fine,' said Frank.

Alicia's teeth started to chatter. She hadn't killed him, there wouldn't be a funeral. She really could phone Margaret and say that he was tucked up in bed at home. The intensity of her relief surprised her. She nodded at Frank.

'He was in the empty house further up the lane,' he went on. 'The garden has a gate that opens onto the river pathway, we think he must have gone in that way, and then found the back door unlocked. We only looked into the garden on our way down, but then on the way back Kenneth Taylor saw him standing at one of the upstairs windows. He probably couldn't find his way out again but that's just as well under the circumstances.'

The stretcher-bearers manoeuvred up the stairs and deposited her father on his bed where he lay still. Alicia dropped down on the wooden chair by the bed. It was over. She managed to smile at Frank.

'I'm glad it wasn't the river,' she said, and he nodded, glancing at Jenny.

'Jenny, why don't you wait downstairs while your Mum and I give Grandpa a quick check over?'

Jenny gazed beseechingly at Alicia. 'Can we go up to the woods, me and Conker?'

Alicia found her voice. 'Oh, I suppose so. Just for a little while. Take your cardie, it's clouding over.'

She rubbed her face with a cold hand, watching as Frank examined her father. The back door slammed behind Jenny, and Frank glanced up, grinning.

'Kids recover quickly,' he said. 'It's the grown-ups that are left weeping and wobbly.'

'Tell me about it,' said Alicia. 'How is he?'

'His vital signs are fine, but of course we can't know exactly what happened to him,' said Frank, placing his stethoscope in his black bag. 'Alicia, you should take him to St. Joe's. The ambulance is still waiting in the lane. I'm off duty today, but John Hammond would meet you there and admit him officially.'

Alicia was silent. It could be that easy. Take her father to St. Joe's now, and the deed was done. But if it happened like that she would always feel the guilt.

'Frank – unless you think it's absolutely necessary I would prefer to keep him here until I can talk to Margaret again,' she said, hearing the tears in her own voice.

He gazed at her for a moment, his face blank, and then nodded slowly. 'We can do that, if you're sure it's what you want. I'll come back and check him again later,' he said, leading the way downstairs. 'You should have a lie down for an hour or so too, you look knackered. You've had a shock.'

Alicia hesitated. Lying down was the last thing she felt like, and her 'shock' wasn't at all what he thought it was. She should tell him what was going on here. Maybe he would be able to help her with the child's voice in her head and the new, disturbing 'memories'.

'Frank, could we have a chat? There's something I'd like to run by you.'

He was already heading for the front door, but he turned and stared for a moment before following her into the kitchen. 'Of course. Come on, the doctor is ordering a nice cup of tea.'

The Stranger

How could it all have gone so wrong? But then he couldn't possibly have foreseen that the old man would end up in an empty house. So old Bob was safe and sound at home, not in St. Joe's, not in the river and definitely not dead. They were all playing Happy Families and there was nothing to say that big Helen would send him to St. Joe's today.

He really needed to get back up to the woods and see what had been going on there. Had the special place been harmed during the search? Oh God, his trees, his magical place, it mustn't be spoiled. He should have considered that they would search the woods for an old man gone walkabout. Worry gnawed away at his soul in much the same way it had after Mummy died. That had been a terrible time too.

She had died at his hands, like Snugglepuss, but of course he couldn't throw Mummy into the river. And a person was a lot more serious than a cat, he'd known as soon as he'd done it that the police would be involved. Would they notice that he'd held her nose and mouth shut? Had he left bruises, fingermarks on Mummy's skin?

The next two days had been hell, he'd expected that at any moment a policeman would come knocking at the door and arrest him for murder. But apparently no-one had noticed anything. The cause of death was given as multiple fractures and a head injury. There hadn't even been a post-mortem because *fortunately* stupid Dad had said she wouldn't have wanted that. They must have thought the cause of death was obvious, and so thankfully, everything had worked out well. He and his sister had been sent to live with Mummy's aunt so he didn't even have to see much of his stupid father after that.

And now he had little Helen to plan for. His mood lifted when he thought about her, sweet child, what was she playing now that her grandfather had been found safe? Oh God, please, maybe the plan could still be saved. Big Helen would be busy with the old man for the rest of the afternoon, this was actually the ideal time to take little Helen... it might not even matter that big Helen was at home and not St. Joe's.

The problem was that he was uptight now, he was nervous, he wouldn't enjoy playing with little Helen feeling like this.

He would go to the woods anyway, just as soon as he could he would go up to the special place... if he was lucky, little Helen would be there.

Alicia

The phone rang while she was waiting for the kettle to boil.

'Alicia, how's your father now?'

'Doug, I was going to call you. He seems okay, Frank's just examined him and he's going to come back tonight too. Then we'll decide about St. Joe's, but I'm hoping to wait up with that until Margaret gets home.'

His voice was comforting as usual. 'I'm sure your aunt will appreciate what you're doing. Is Frank still there, then?'

Alicia glanced into the kitchen, where Frank was scribbling in a folder at the table, oblivious to everything else.

'He's writing up his notes. Thanks again, Doug, for your support.'

'Wish I could do more. I'll be in touch.'

Alicia filled the teapot with hands that had almost stopped trembling. It was a relief to be doing something as normal as making tea, and the fact that Doug had called again was a good feeling. He definitely cared. And so did Frank. She placed a mug in front of him.

'Great, thanks,' he said, sipping. 'Alicia, I know it's like hitting a man while he's down, but you know yourself that once dementia patients start to wander they tend to keep it up, and it's incredibly difficult then to keep them safe. And while I'm not expecting anything terrible to happen to your father health-wise after his escapade today, the bottom line is we just don't know how he's going to react, and the care and facilities in St. Joe's are better than anything we can offer him here at home.'

Alicia warmed her hands on her mug. How wonderful it would be not to have to take care of her father any more.

'I know,' she said. 'But I do want to talk to Margaret before making the final decision. I'll phone her when I've had my tea.' She smiled wryly. 'Gather my arguments first.'

Frank nodded, looking across at her with an expectant look on his face. Alicia bit her lip. Now for the big confession.

'I… I don't love him,' she blurted out. 'You were gone by then but I left home the minute I was sixteen, I couldn't take any more, he was so… restrictive and so… so mean with it too, it was as if he hated me for trying to be a normal teenager. He… I don't know what he did, Frank, ever since I've been here I've had this child's voice in my head talking about 'the bad room' upstairs and crying and it's scaring me. And today I remembered lying there on his bed and there was blood on the sheets and I don't know where it came from.'

She caught her breath, forcing herself to stay calm. Why had these thoughts and memories never come to her before? And why hadn't she seen his cruelty to her teenage self later on for what it was… abuse? In those days she hadn't been too young to tell someone.

He stared for a second, then stretched out a hand and squeezed her arm on the table. 'Okay, let's talk about this,' he said quietly. 'You said he was mean when you were a teenager, I guess his religion wouldn't let you do a lot of things and you rebelled, right?'

She looked at him and he patted her arm again before leaning back and sipping his tea.

'Okay. I can understand there could still be some unfinished business there. Now tell me about the child's voice and the blood on the sheets.'

Slowly, Alicia explained about the frightened little voice and the nausea, and the sudden, horrifyingly vivid picture of a child crying on a blood-covered bed.

He frowned. 'That sounds like a flashback. You know, the sudden memory of a traumatic experience that's been suppressed.'

Alicia fought back hot tears. 'Oh God. What do you think happened to me?' she whispered.

He shook his head. 'There's no way to tell at the moment. It might not even be a flashback of a real event, it could be a dream you had once, or something scary you saw on TV and couldn't handle at the time. You're afraid that you suffered some kind of abuse at his hands, aren't you?'

She looked a 'yes' at him, cold fingers pressed to her forehead. It was a moment before she could speak.

'He shoved me around when I was a teenager, pulling me upstairs and locking me in my room, pushing me back onto a chair to read the Bible, that kind of thing. But this child in my head's a whole lot younger, and she's really scared about something but I can't remember a thing about it.'

He remained silent for several moments, staring at the table top, and she felt herself grow calmer. He was going to help her. At last he looked up.

'Okay. Alicia, we don't know what happened yet but whatever it was, you survived. That's the thing to hold on to. You survived; you're an adult in charge of your own life. Try not to worry about it, if you relax you might remember more. By today's standards your father was certainly physically abusive. You're afraid there was sexual abuse too, but you'll need time to work through that, maybe in some kind of therapy.'

She exhaled deeply. That all made sense. She was an adult, she could cope with whatever had happened to her as a child. He was right, she *had* survived.

'Thanks, Frank,' she said, realising that she felt lighter within herself now that she had told someone her fears. 'That helps.'

'Don't try to force anything,' he said. 'Memories are funny things, the more you try to bring them to the surface, the further underground they go. Maybe Margaret can tell you something about how your parents treated you back then. And we'll ask Sonja if she remembers anything, you can have a good chat with her when she arrives.'

'I wondered about finding Cathal, too. I played with him a lot, and he was older, he might remember more,' said Alicia.

Frank drained his mug. 'Good idea. We'll get this sorted, but you can't rush it. Have a think and get back to me about it. This makes the whole situation here with your father quite horrible for you, doesn't it? Try to get Margaret to agree to St. Joe's, Alicia. It would be so much better for you all.'

'I know,' said Alicia miserably. She was caught right in the middle here, between her own wishes and Margaret's. And Margaret had been so good to her, giving her a home when she'd left this one. Margaret had been a whole lot more motherly to Alicia than her own mother had been. But if her father stayed here at home…

She imagined the next few weeks caring for him, with no help except Margaret, and Frank popping in. Having uncomfortable, frightening flashbacks about God knows what. The sheer uncertainty was the killer - *was* she a victim, or was she building something in her head, something that had never happened? Was her father simply a sick old man whose religious convictions had made him heavy-handed with his teenage daughter? The voice in her head could be a sign of her own identity crisis, not 'abuse'. But no… look at the way he reacted to her. Even if he no longer knew exactly what had gone on, he knew enough to taunt her.

All at once she knew, with complete certainty, that she couldn't do it. No matter what Margaret's feelings were, she just couldn't do it.

'Frank, I'll bring him to St. Joe's tomorrow morning,' she said quietly.

He didn't try to dissuade her. 'Good decision,' he said, smiling. 'I'll get it organised for you. And I'll talk to Margaret too, when she gets back.'

Alicia felt the tense muscles in her neck relax. It really was as if a huge weight had been lifted from her shoulders. This time tomorrow, someone else would be responsible for her father. And she could concentrate on making the rest of the summer pleasant for Jenny. These might be the last memories Jen would have of her grandfather, it was up to Alicia to make them better memories than her own. And with her father in St. Joe's there would be time to sort herself out, too. Find out what the flashbacks were about.

Frank stood up. 'No thanks, I must go,' he said when she lifted the pot. 'I'll let you know about the arrangements with St Joe's when I come back this evening.'

He hesitated by the door, obviously pondering something, and Alicia waited without speaking. After several seconds of silence, though, he merely grinned at her.

'See you sometime after six,' he said. 'Call me if you're worried.'

Alicia watched as he drove off down the lane, then ran upstairs to check that her father was still asleep. He was, breathing slowly and steadily, thank God. No matter what he had done to her, she hadn't killed him. The relief was indescribable.

She ran downstairs again to the sound of fat raindrops plopping against the windows, and here were Jen and Conker running back up the garden. Heavens, she had almost forgotten about her daughter. Jenny hadn't had anything proper to eat since breakfast. It was time to ignore the guilt about being an undutiful daughter and just be a mum.

The Stranger

It was late afternoon before he got up to the woods. The mess was indescribable. The search party had trodden over everything in its way, and the crushed bushes and trampled undergrowth gave the whole place a ruined, wasted appearance. It was worse than he'd been expecting, and of course little Helen wasn't here, he hadn't really expected to see her after the rain. He walked along looking right and left, dismayed at the destruction. His special woods, they had been stripped brutally of their freshness, their vitality, their very soul. What had his own Helen thought, he wondered, as she watched all those people crashing around here? The only things that still looked the same were the trees themselves, tall trees, birch trees and oaks. Everything else had been soiled.

Of course, these weren't Helen's own trees, and definitely not the tree where she'd died. Helen's own tree was far away, but trees were trees, woods were woods, and the special feeling was here too. But now intrusive feet had stamped over everything, and strangers' eyes had peered into the holiness. Sacrilege. It was hard to believe it had all gone so wrong, and the rage was coming back again, swirling around the edges of his mind, and it was against the two new Helens now and oh, he didn't want that. The rage would send them to hell with Mummy and Snugglepuss and he wanted them in Paradise with Helen.

He came to the beautiful circle of trees and stood still, outrage filling his mind until he could hardly think at all. Even here, even here. You would see at a glance if an old man was wandering about the clearing, but still there were footprints, dozens of them, going from one side to the other and back again. The moss was torn and muddied, and little Helen's woodland flowers had been crushed to death. His sacrificial place had been violated. He had so wanted to send little Helen to Paradise today, but he couldn't have done it in the midst of all this mess even if she had been here. And he hadn't been able to take her to his flat, either. So his plan had worked beautifully as far as getting the old man out of the house was concerned, but the last, the most important part, with little Helen... that hadn't worked at all.

Sudden raindrops pattered down, and he stood there, feeling his hair grow heavy and sodden and watching with grim pleasure as the few raindrops turned into a brisk shower. Gradually, the alien footprints in the clearing ceased to be footprints and became mere mud. He breathed out, a deep, heartfelt sigh of relief.

It was going to be alright. Mother Nature was strong, she would soon rebuild his sacrificial alter. Another few showers would wash the place clean, heal the wounds. He would just have to be patient for a day or two. He would get a second chance.

But he had so wanted to be with little Helen here, today...

Back came the rage, filling his head, tightening round his heart until he could hardly draw breath. His world was turning dark around the edges. What right did anyone have to stop him sending a sweet little Helen to Paradise?

He waited, fighting to regain control. This wasn't good for him, these sudden rages always left him with a headache. Of course he could be patient again, and it would only be a very short time. This time tomorrow, you would probably never know that anything had happened here. It was time for Plan B.

His time *would* come.

Alicia

Much to Alicia's surprise, Margaret didn't argue about the decision to put her father into the care home.

'It's not what I'd wanted for him, Alicia,' she said, her voice sounding resigned and flat. 'But it's your decision. Are you sure I don't need to come home today?'

Well done David, thought Alicia. Her cousin had worked a minor miracle with his mother. Or maybe it was the fact that Margaret was having her first holiday away from this house in years, and realising that in a few weeks' time she was going to be a grandmother. She would want time to visit David and Sheila, help with the baby, enjoy the new addition to the family. Not so easy with a stroke patient at home needing care and attention 24/7.

'Frank said he shouldn't be any the worse, once he's had a good rest,' she said carefully. 'I'm sorry, Margaret. I know this was all my fault, but it just happened out of the situation.'

Back in the kitchen she rinsed the mugs, aware that she was smiling. This time tomorrow her father wouldn't be here anymore. She wouldn't need to shower him, feed him, clean him up, wondering all the while what he had done to her. Tomorrow, she would succeed in what she had come here to do, so at the very worst she would have one more soiled bed to deal with, and then the burden would be gone. Happy thought for the day.

An even more pleasant thought was that with her father in St. Joe's she was bound to see more of Doug, and soon, too. Would he be around tomorrow? It would be very interesting, seeing him again. Would the attraction still be there?

She grinned, aware that on her side at least it certainly would. Humming, she glanced out to the back garden. Sunshine and showers, a typical English summer. And very soon she and Jen could start to enjoy it. Thanks to all the people who had helped find her father safe this morning, which reminded her, she should call Kenneth Taylor to say thank you. He had scurried away as soon as the search party had returned and it was all down to him that they'd found her father in that house.

Kenneth was obviously embarrassed by her call.

'It was nothing, Mrs Bryson, just a coincidence that I was looking the right way at the right time. I hope he's none the worse?'

'He'll be fine, thank God. It was all my fault, I should have watched him better.'

Heavens, why on earth had she said that? She barely knew the man. The sheer relief that her father was okay, and that soon, soon she wouldn't have to look after him any longer – it was making her positively garrulous.

Once again Kenneth surprised her.

'We all do things we regret, Mrs Bryson. I know that myself. But don't worry, there's no harm done.'

His voice sounded strained, and Alicia wondered what on earth a lumbering teddy bear like Kenneth Taylor had done to cause regret. She rang off and shouted for Jenny. Chocolate ice cream sounded like a good idea right now.

Chapter Eleven
Monday, 17th July

Alicia

It wasn't so much a flashback this time as a full-blown nightmare. She was on a bed – impossible to say which bed – consumed with pain, she couldn't move, and she was crying. And it was dark; unidentifiable shadows loomed up wherever she turned her gaze. So it probably wasn't her own bed in her own room. She was alone, and she was terrified. It was difficult to breathe.

Then her arm was being shaken and she struggled to wrench herself away.

'Mummy, wake up!'

Alicia forced her eyes open and saw Jenny standing next to the bed looking scared. What a hellish dream. And she had woken Jen up… shit, had she been talking? Had she said anything in her sleep? The very last thing she wanted to do was give her daughter any inkling of the chaos going on in her head at the moment.

'Oh sweetheart, I'm sorry. I was having a bad dream. Did I wake you up?'

Jenny nodded, gulping. 'I was scared,' she said plaintively. 'You were shouting, Mummy 'no, no!', and 'ah!'. What were you dreaming?'

Alicia looked at the clock. It was ten past two and her nightshirt was sticking to her.

'It was just a horrid dream, Jen. We all have them sometimes.

Come on, let's get you back to bed.'

When the little girl had settled she went back to her own room. Relax, Alicia. Don't think too hard. You're the adult, you're in control, you survived. Her new mantra. She would lie down and go back to sleep. Just thank God her father hadn't woken up.

She did sleep but her rest was still broken by uncomfortable images chasing around her head. When the alarm went off a few hours later her adrenalin level shot skywards before she even opened her eyes. It was an abrupt kind of start to the day, she thought, massaging the tightness from her forehead. Did the dream have anything to do with her flashbacks? What was the difference between a flashback and a dream, anyway – one for being awake, the other for sleep? She would have to ask Frank. Or maybe she had slept so badly because this was the day she was taking her father to the care home.

The house was silent as she paused on the landing. Jenny was still asleep, long dark hair spread untidily over the pillow and one hand cushioning her cheek. Conker thumped his tail on the floor when Alicia looked in, but he didn't get up from his place beside the bed. Alicia left them to it.

Her father was still asleep too, and judging by the lack of smell in the room he was clean this morning. A better day than yesterday.

Frank had appeared just before seven the previous evening and together they had washed and prepared the old man for the night.

'Heat him some soup,' advised Frank. 'And give him his sleeping pill along with it. After a day like today you need a good night's rest as much as he does.'

He hadn't said any more about the flashbacks, and Alicia was grateful. She had heated vegetable soup for her father and taken it upstairs along with coffee for herself and Frank. Jenny came in while they were there and fetched herself a coke and a packet of crisps which she shared round, and they had quite a little picnic in her father's room.

'We could call this 'Bob's Caff'. Almost as good as McDonald's,' Alicia teased Jenny.

'There's a new café in Middle Banford,' Frank said suddenly. 'Why don't we go there sometime? My treat. Not that it could possibly be better than coffee and crisps in Bob's Caff, of course.'

Jenny giggled in delight. 'Do they have huge big ice creams?' she asked, and Frank put on a serious face.

'Mega ones,' he said. 'Bet I can eat more than you!'

Jenny giggled again, and Alicia laughed. 'You haven't seen Jenny eating ice cream,' she said. "Expert' doesn't come into it. My money's on my daughter.'

'In that case I'd better start practising,' said Frank solemnly. He looked at her, the expression in his eyes unfathomable. 'That's a date, then?'

'Lovely,' said Alicia, amused. If he wanted to ask her out again he was making heavy weather of it. Was he afraid she'd say no to ice cream, with her daughter as chaperone? Of course he was the nervous type, and maybe the fact that she hadn't been able to go to the pub that night had been enough to make him feel awkward. She smiled warmly at him and he grinned back before accepting another crisp from Jenny.

Alicia sat sipping her coffee. It was funny, but two men had asked her out for coffee this week. Whatever had happened to posh meals in elegant restaurants? Mind you, Frank and elegant restaurants didn't seem to go together, though Doug would probably be very good at that kind of thing. She could imagine him in a tailored suit, looking through the wine list and ordering something confidently. His coffee invitation had been much more personal too. Of course, she was attracted to Doug, wasn't she, and Frank was... what was he? More than just 'the doctor', of course, he was lovely, he was Sonja's brother... her friend now, too, and there was the difference. The thought of Doug increased her heart rate, whereas Frank was simply an old friend... wasn't he?

But what did it all matter? Today she was going to put her father into a home, and the good night's sleep Frank had recommended hadn't come to much, her nightmare had seen to that.

And an hour or so later, she and Jenny were ushering her father through the big double doors into Ward Two. There was an old lady in the dayroom today, humming away to herself in a cracked, high-pitched old voice, staring at the television where the cricket played on and on. What did they watch in the winter? Cartoons? Would her father still be here in the winter for her to find out? Alicia deposited him in a chair by the door.

'Alicia! And Jenny!' She jumped as Doug Patton strode into the room with Derek Thorpe. 'Hello, Robert, you're looking well.'

'Everyone just calls him Bob,' said Alicia, feeling her palms moisten at the sight of Doug. Did he realise he was having this effect on her? She turned to her father. 'Look, um, this is Douglas Patton, a new friend. And this is… '

'Derek,' he said, squeezing her father's good hand. The old man showed no reaction at all. 'It's all Christian names here. Makes the place more homely, I think.'

'Can I go outside?' said Jenny suddenly, and Alicia looked at her in surprise.

'Don't you want to see Grandpa's room?' she said, but Jenny shook her head, staring at the floor and winding one leg round the other. 'Well, alright then. Don't go too near the pond, okay?'

Jenny ran from the room. Alicia looked after her, concerned. Doug patted her shoulder.

'It's probably all a bit much for her here,' he said in a low voice. 'Leave her be for a while, she'll be fine in the garden.'

Alicia nodded, realising that she should have told Jen more about St. Joe's. Told her that it was full of old, old people who couldn't think anymore. Her Grandpa's strangeness was familiar to Jenny now but the poor old lady singing away over there must seem like a witch to an imaginative eight-year-old. Poor Jen. Well, with her father in here she would have much more time for her daughter. They could go out for a hamburger and have a long chat afterwards and she would explain all about growing old.

Derek led them along the corridor to a two-bedded room with blue and green duvet covers and a lovely view over the garden. Identical ducks were swimming around the pond looking lively. Would her father watch them? Probably not. Jenny was out there too, playing a hopping game on the path beside the rose bed.

'Frank Carter said religion was important to your Dad, so we put him in this room because you can see the church tower from here,' said Derek, leading her father to a chair by the vacant bed.

Christ. What a lovely gesture for a poisonous old man who…

'Aaah! Aaah! Ha ha!'

Her father's eyes were wide open, fixed on her face. He struggled to his feet, his good hand grabbing her wrist in a crushing grip, and Alicia fought to release herself. He had obviously twigged that he was here to stay. Thank God Jenny was outside. Doug came to her rescue and stood there almost cuddling her father while Derek produced a sedative. For a few minutes the old man struck out at anyone close enough to hit, then sank back into the chair, his expression softening and his breathing returning to normal. Alicia closed her eyes in relief.

'What exactly can he understand?' said Derek, leading her to one side.

Alicia bit her lip. 'It's difficult to say. I don't think he understands speech, maybe just the odd word. He doesn't cooperate when you try to communicate with signs, either. But he sometimes has a sort of flash when he seems to understand situations, so I guess he might understand that he's here to stay.'

But of course he understood what was happening to him. He had understood that she was staying in his house again, and he had understood enough to mock her, too. All she wanted to do now was get away from him, get back to the house. Doug put a hand on her shoulder and squeezed.

Derek left then, and Alicia sat watching a nurse called Katy arrange her father's things, appreciating the fact that Doug stayed with her, chatting about some of the activities the patients were involved in until he was called away to deal with some upset in Ward Three.

'He's marvellous with people,' said Katy. 'The patients love him.'

'I can imagine. He makes you feel as if everyone here's part of the family,' said Alicia.

Katy nodded. 'He's really big on helping families. He lost his wife in an accident a few years ago, maybe that's why.'

A little shock ran through Alicia. Poor Doug. She would never have guessed. What tragedies people carry around with them sometimes, and no-one is any the wiser, she thought sadly. Jenny appeared below the window, and Alicia beckoned her in. The little girl seemed more relaxed now, and explored her grandfather's new home while Alicia helped Katy lay him down for a rest. He closed his eyes and slept as soon as he was horizontal, and Alicia stood watching him for a moment.

That was that, then. There was nothing to keep her here now.

Ten minutes later she was walking out of St. Joe's, leaving her father behind. A strange mixture of feelings was churning around in her gut as she drove back to Lower Banford, but if she was honest, the sense of freedom was the greatest.

How strangely silent the house was without her father's throaty breathing in the background. Jenny took Conker and Moritz up to the woods for half an hour, and Alicia walked from room to room, looking at her childhood home with new eyes. It almost felt as if her father had died. What on earth would she do with all this stuff? The grandfather clock? Mum's collection of china birds? They were family things, heirlooms, but she certainly didn't want them.

In the living room she sank down on the sofa and buried her face in her hands. The relief that someone else was responsible for her father now was almost paralysing.

And it was only now, when she didn't have to look after him anymore, that she could allow herself to dwell on the extent of the abuse. Was that what the flashbacks were about? Had he been sexually abusive? Had he touched her? Had he used that to punish her? But wouldn't she remember? Maybe not, her nurse's training told her. But they *would* survive. They would get through this, her and Jen.

If only they were part of a real, big, loving family, she thought. Something like *The Waltons*, where everyone helped everyone else and they all called out goodnight. How wonderful it would be to have someone to care for her like that. Maybe, if she got to know Doug better… that was a very attractive thought, and it might well come to pass, but up until now it had actually been Frank doling out the support. She thought of the two men and her two coffee invites, and smiled faintly before frowning. How strange, both Frank and Doug had lost their wives in accidents. But then, strange and tragic things happened every day. It was a cruel world.

The phone rang, and she jumped to her feet. Kenneth Taylor's high voice greeted her.

'Mrs Bryson, I'm so glad I caught you. I wanted to ask after your father, and apologise too for frightening your little girl the other day when you were collecting the cat and she almost touched my bloody hand. I've been meaning to say sorry for a while now.'

Alicia choked back a laugh. 'Oh, my father's in St. Joe's now, he's fine,' she said. 'And please don't worry about Jenny, she quite understood.'

'Super. And I can assure you that your father will be well taken care of at St. Joe's. My old neighbour's there, I pop by to see her quite often and she's very happy. But that's not why I phoned. Thing is, Mrs Bryson, I've got a new little cat family here, Mum and four kittens just three weeks old, and I wondered if Jenny would like to come and see them sometime?'

'She'd love that,' said Alicia immediately. 'We're on our way out now, and I'm not sure that we'll have time this evening what with visiting my father... how about tomorrow morning?'

Kenneth Taylor agreed gushingly, and they rang off. Alicia shook herself. It had been a kind thought, and although he wasn't Mr Universe he seemed to be a caring person, even visiting a neighbour he couldn't have known long. Of course maybe it was someone he'd known when he was a boy, he'd mentioned once he'd grown up nearby, hadn't he? Yet in spite of the sensitivity he'd shown a couple of times it was difficult to warm to the man. There was something about him she couldn't put her finger on, something odd. And Jenny would probably want to visit him and his wretched cats every single day from now on, and she'd want to go by herself, too. Was she happy with that? No, she thought resignedly. Oh, well, they could fight that battle another day. Right now it was time for lunch and her daughter was running up the garden right on cue. Hamburgers here we come.

The Stranger

So it was going to be Plan B. Plan B was more complicated, but the beautiful thing about it was the control. This time he'd have almost complete control over who was where, when and with whom. He'd be able to fix things so that big Helen – and her aunt if necessary – were called to see the old man, leaving him plenty of time to meet little Helen in the woods... He would put it all into writing that evening, just to make sure he had covered all the bases.

When he was sure the plan was foolproof, he would have to choose what day to put the whole thing into action, and there were two things to think about there. One was the weather, of course, trips to the woods required sunshine, or at the very least no rain. The other thing to consider was timing. Whether the weekend would be better, when more visitors would be milling around at St. Joe's, making it easier for him to do his own thing under cover of all the weekend activity, or during the week, when fewer prying eyes were around. He would have to think about that.

The forecast for the next two days was poor, so he would have to wait anyway. While the waiting was frustrating, in a funny way he was learning to enjoy it, the delicious suspense and anticipation. And the biggest advantage of all about Plan B was the fact that he'd have so much longer to enjoy little Helen before he sent her to Paradise. He could anticipate a lovely long time with her right here at home. And there was something very important he hadn't bought yet, too... a golden, sacrificial robe for his little Queen of Fairies...

His day was still well within grasp. His perfect day.

Alicia

It was nearly three o'clock when they arrived home from Merton, the car full of groceries and Jenny happy with her hamburger lunch and balloon on a stick. She ran through to the living room and stuck it into a copper lustre vase which Alicia knew for a fact was valuable, but what the hell. The vase would be joining the grandfather clock, the china bird collection and a whole lot of other stuff in some kind of second-hand shop. Antique, junk or charity, who knew? Alicia didn't, and she didn't care, either.

'Can we go for a picnic in the woods now?' said Jenny, eyeing a packet of almond slices.

Alicia grinned. At last Jen was having a really good day. Which was only right, she'd been so cooperative about playing by herself in the garden or the woods ever since they'd arrived in Lower Banford. It was lovely to be able to indulge her child at last.

'Of course we can. Then we'll just have fruit and yogurt for tea before we pop back to check Grandpa's okay. And afterwards we'll make pancakes.'

Jenny was fizzing with excitement, and Alicia watched her rootling round the kitchen, packing a selection of treats into Margaret's wicker basket. Had Jen taken in the part about visiting Grandpa? It would just be a quick check so that she could put Margaret's mind at rest, and Jen could stay in the hospital garden again if she wanted to.

'Come on, Mummy! Let's go!'

Amused, Alicia followed on down the garden and up the path into the woods, Jenny pausing only to pick some raspberries for the basket. Conker ran on ahead, closely followed by Jenny. Alicia was hard pushed to keep up.

'We're nearly there, Mummy! The palace is just up here. Oh, Doctor Frank! Look Mummy, it's Doctor Frank!'

Alicia entered the clearing to see Frank sitting on a fallen tree trunk, a black and white collie dog jumping about beside him. He rose to greet them, his face alive with pleasure. The collie bounded over to Conker, and in no time the two animals were barking excitedly and tearing round the trees, Jenny chasing after them.

'Well! Who's your friend, then?' said Alicia, and Frank grimaced.

'You won't believe it but I don't even know the creature's name. He belongs to the woman along the road, I helped them this morning when her two-year-old fell and broke his arm. They've gone to the hospital in Merton and I've been left holding the um, baby, so to speak.'

Alicia settled down beside him on the fallen tree, watching as Jenny tried to keep up with the two dogs. After a couple of rounds of the clearing she darted over to Alicia and Frank.

'Is he your dog? What's his name?' she said, panting, and Alicia laughed aloud at the expression on Frank's face.

'His name's Dog,' he said firmly. 'And no, he's my neighbour's.'

Jenny stared. '*Dog!*' Her mouth was as round as her eyes, and Alicia wiped tears from her eyes, aware that she hadn't laughed like this in Lower Banford since she and Cathal O'Brian had played in this very clearing.

'When I was little, I had a friend and his uncle had a cat called 'Cat',' Jenny said, opening the picnic basket. 'But the vet said they couldn't call it that so they always called it 'Herbie' at the vet's… Would you like some fizzy orange, Doctor Frank?'

'Sounds good, if there's enough,' he said, leaning forward eagerly, and Alicia was suddenly touched by how pleased he was to be with them.

'There's lots. I packed the basket,' said Jenny. 'We're having brilliant food today. We had hamburgers for lunch, you know.'

'Yum, lucky you,' said Frank. 'Did Grandpa settle into St. Joe's alright, then?'

Alicia looked at him and frowned. She didn't want Jenny to hear how her father had grabbed her arm and shouted.

'They, um, gave him a pill and he was fine after that,' she said, and he glanced at her. Jenny ran off with the dogs again, and Alicia continued in a low voice.

'He was quite agitated at first. But it's such a relief, Frank, not having the responsibility. Doug and the staff were marvellous. I'm going in this evening, Margaret will want the latest news when we phone tonight. But I know he'll be fine.'

'I'll see him tomorrow,' said Frank, accepting a plastic cup of fizzy orange. 'But you're right, he'll be really well looked after.'

'Have some apricots,' said Alicia, offering the bag to Frank as Jenny flopped down on the grass at their feet again. 'There's rasps from the garden as well but they were an in-passing decision so they're not washed. And chocolate biscuits and cheesy sticks and almond slices. And I don't want to hear a single word about balanced meals, please.'

He laughed. They sat talking about holiday food and favourite restaurants, even Jenny joining in the conversation, and Alicia felt more carefree than she had since... well, for a very long time. Jenny was feeding both dogs with the snacks she'd brought for Conker, and Alicia noticed Frank smiling as he watched.

'It's kind of part of everyone's life dream, isn't it?' he said as the chasing game continued round the clearing. 'Cats, dogs, kids, partner. Not in that order of importance, of course.'

Alicia pulled a face. 'Well, we're doing okay with the animals. I've got a cat and we both have borrowed dogs. But we only have one kid between us, my marriage was a disaster, and I know you lost your wife. I'm so sorry, Frank, it must have been awful.'

'Nell's been gone a long time,' he said briefly. 'But it's scary how your life can change in just a second like that. I was glad to take the job here but now I keep wondering if I'll be stuck in Lower Banford forever, watching summer after summer go by and turning from 'Doctor Carter' into 'Old Doctor Carter'. It's not what I'd thought would happen.'

Alicia touched his arm quickly. 'I know. None of this here is what I wanted either. I guess you just have to find the good in whatever life throws at you. I'm so glad to be in contact with you and Sonja again, and maybe one day I'll get my past sorted out.'

He smiled at her and she thought what sad eyes he had. The picnic in the woods had turned bittersweet. But maybe that was how life was.

The church clock striking five brought the afternoon to an end.

'Time to go. I want to get the house looking less like a war-zone before we go to St. Joe's,' said Alicia, looking at her watch. To her surprise, Frank patted her on the shoulder furthest away from him. It wasn't quite a hug, but the unexpectedness of it almost made her jump and he stepped back, looking confused.

'Um… maybe… maybe we could, um… go for another walk with the dogs again sometime? They seem to be bosom buddies now.'

Jenny clapped enthusiastically. 'Oh yes! We'll phone you next time we're going, shall we?'

Frank's eyes met Alicia's, and she saw his nervousness. 'It's a great idea, Jen, but let Frank phone us. Doctors are busy people.'

She packed up the remains of the picnic, listening as Jenny chattered away to Frank about all the things they were going to do now that Grandpa was safe in St. Joe's. It was difficult to persuade Conker that Dog lived in the opposite direction, but at last they were off. Alicia turned at the edge of the clearing and looked back. What a forlorn figure Frank looked, standing there talking to a dog whose name he didn't know. He obviously had as much baggage as she did. Poor Frank.

Chapter Twelve

Alicia

The phone rang while Alicia was upstairs putting the washing away, and she waited a moment for Jenny to answer it. But a bark and a glance outside told her that Jenny and Conker were playing football on the front driveway, so she ran downstairs, hoping it wasn't Margaret wanting details of a hospital visit that hadn't yet taken place.

'Hello?'

'Alicia, sorry. It's Doug. Am I interrupting anything?'

'Not at all,' she said warmly. 'I was upstairs putting the house to rights. We've been out all day, Jen and I, hamburgers and shopping in Merton and then a picnic in the woods.'

Doug laughed. 'Sounds like a fun day. I bet Jenny enjoyed having you all to herself.'

'She did, and so did I,' said Alicia. 'My father's alright, I suppose?'

'He's fine. I looked in on him ten minutes ago. There's been no more agitation, in fact he was outside for a bit this afternoon with Katy and some of the other residents, and now they're all in the dayroom watching TV. I wondered if you were coming in this evening?'

'Yes, about sevenish,' she said. 'I'm expecting Margaret to phone tonight, and I want to be able to give her the latest about how he's doing.'

'Great, and how about having that coffee afterwards? I've got a super machine right here in my office, and we could have a chat about anything you want to know about St. Joe's.'

'That would be lovely. I do have some questions, actually. Shall we just come down after visiting?'

'I'll be waiting,' he said, and she thought how warm his voice sounded. Dark brown, like his eyes.

'Bye, then,' she said, breaking the connection. Well. That would make a very pleasant end to the day. It wasn't quite going out for a coffee, but it would still be… interesting. Even with Jen tagging along. And now she'd better go and sort out something to wear, because a pink t-shirt and picnic-in-the-woods jeans weren't quite what she wanted to wear for an almost-date with Doug.

A grey and white V-neck top and her new black jeans fitted the bill rather well, and Alicia walked into the ward aware that she was looking forward to seeing Doug again. Derek Thorpe was sitting at the nurses' station, and he waved her over.

'Your Dad's been fine all day,' he said, closing the file in front of him.

'Good,' said Alicia. 'It's such a relief to have him here, I really feel like a huge weight has been lifted from my shoulders. Thank you all so much.'

'Just doing our job,' said Derek. 'Doug asked if young Jenny here would like to help the nurses while you and he have a talk after visiting. Give you more scope for a proper discussion.' He winked at Jenny.

The little girl was one big beam as they walked down the corridor.

'I think I'll be a nurse when I grow up,' she said, opening the door and looking over to where her grandfather was snoring in his bed. 'What's 'scope', Mummy?'

'Um… possibility,' said Alicia, pulling chairs over to the bed.

And twenty minutes later she was heading back along the corridor, leaving Jenny helping with a tea trolley. The two of them had spent visiting time making plans for the rest of the week – Indiana Jones, Merton swimming pool and raspberry jam-making had figured strongly in the conversation – and her father had slept soundly all the while. None of the other old people seemed to have early-evening visitors, maybe it wasn't such a good idea, coming in when the patients were tired and the nurses were busy organising the ward for the night.

Derek had joined her for the last few minutes. 'Don't beat yourself up,' he said in a low voice, looking at her face as she rose to go. 'It's hard losing your parents no matter what the circumstances are, and in a way you've lost your father while he's still alive.'

Alicia floundered. What should she tell him? Would Frank say anything about her father's treatment of her? No, that would come under patient confidentiality. But then she wasn't Frank's patient.

'We had a very up and down relationship,' she said at last, and he wrinkled his nose.

'Tell me about it. I had one of those with both my parents. Like a lot of people. Bob's fine here, Alicia. You've done the best thing.'

He was right, she thought, running downstairs. In fact he always was about things like that, he seemed to be one of those people who did the right thing automatically. If it hadn't been for the story about his ex-wife and the unsuitable relationships that followed, he would have seemed almost too good to be true. Alicia paused at the bottom of the stairs, aware that she was nervous about her meeting with Doug. At the door to his office she wiped damp palms on her trousers in case he shook hands. He was quite a touchy-feely kind of person, she had noticed that before. The kind who would give you a spontaneous hug if he thought you were looking down.

He didn't exactly hug her, but he put a hand between her shoulder blades as he showed her to a sofa by the window. Alicia looked round, surprised. His room was really nice, quite unlike the usual kind of hospital office space. He even had a little sitting area by the window, with a two-seater sofa and a couple of armchairs grouped round a pine coffee table. The pale green walls and polished wooden floor contributed to the calm atmosphere, and with her back to the office furniture like this she could almost imagine she was visiting him at home.

He bent over her when she was seated, and the whiff of lemony aftershave made her breath catch. 'Here we are. Home from home, as you see. Is Jenny alright upstairs?'

'She's having a ball, and you're right, it's easier to talk about my father without her around.'

Doug nodded. 'And then you can tell her everything later on, in a way she'll understand.'

Alicia relaxed into the depths of the sofa. This was comfy, she'd have to be careful, after all the broken nights she could fall asleep here quite easily. On the other hand, just looking at Doug was more than enough to increase her heart rate, so she wasn't very likely to nod off. She grinned at him, and he went over to the coffee machine in the corner.

'Coffee,' he said firmly. 'My machine here does a very good cappuccino. Or would you prefer espresso?'

'Cappuccino please,' she said, watching as he organised cups and saucers. He seemed quite at ease in the little domestic situation, and Alicia suddenly remembered how Paul hadn't known one end of the coffee machine from the other.

Doug placed an aromatic cup before her. 'Here we are. Help yourself to biscuits. Now, you said you had some questions?'

Alicia sipped her coffee and took a custard cream. 'Nothing vital. Things like who organises haircuts, and the chiropodist. The village chiropodist is due to visit him next week.'

Doug stirred his coffee. 'Right. Our own chiropodist sees the new residents automatically when they come to us, so you can cancel your own appointment. And the hairdresser comes every Wednesday.'

Alicia sighed with relief. By the sound of things she wouldn't need to organise anything at all for her father any more. She really was free.

'Great. I can see he'll be well looked after here. Frank was right to want him in.'

He was smiling at her, and Alicia could feel her own smile widen, like two Cheshire cats…

'We'll do our very best to make sure Bob's happy here,' said Doug warmly. 'You can depend on that. With us here to look after him, you'll have more time free just to love him.'

Alicia felt her smile crack. Well. That was something she was going to have to put straight soon. But this wasn't the time. Doug must have noticed something, because he leaned forward, his expression serious.

'Have a shortbread finger,' he said, taking one himself. 'They're shop ones, I'm afraid. I'm not a baker, though my wife did a lot when... while we were together.'

He was giving her a piece of his past, a piece of himself. Alicia accepted another biscuit and looked at him sympathetically. 'I heard you lost your wife. I'm so sorry. It was a few years ago, wasn't it?'

He stared down at his clasped hands. 'Just over five years ago. We didn't have a long time together, but it was a good time. It took me a while to realise that the love we had has actually turned into a part of me, and I can move on with my own life and still keep that love. And my work helps too, of course.'

She looked at him. She could identify with all of that. 'Do you know, that's what I often feel about my marriage. Paul and I had some really good times before it all went pear-shaped, and in a way they're still with me. And that's important for Jenny, too. But it must have been infinitely more dreadful for you, of course.'

He sat there, fiddling with a teaspoon, obviously struggling to find words that would make her understand.

'It was terrible. And it takes a while to get over something like that, but - ' He smiled at her. ' - time *does* heal all wounds, doesn't it? Here we both are. Who knows what life'll bring us?'

She looked at him soberly. 'You're very good at putting things into words. Most blokes aren't. You're lucky.'

And she was lucky too, she thought suddenly. She had a beautiful daughter, an aunt who loved her, and now the prospect of something more than that, with Doug. But maybe they had said all that needed to be said for now. She lifted her bag from the floor.

'I should go and rescue the nurses, Jen's probably talked them all to death by now. Thank you so much, Doug, for coffee and words of wisdom.'

He walked beside her to the door.

'No problem. And now we've had coffee, how about dinner sometime? You haven't told me the story of *your* life yet. When your aunt comes back we can make a date, can't we?'

Alicia took a deep breath. A date. Dinner. Doug. And maybe one day soon, a real, proper relationship, with giving and taking and being a family and… what? A move back to Lower Banford? No. She was getting way ahead of herself here.

She smiled up at him. 'I'll look forward to that. Thanks, Doug.'

His face was inches from hers, and she could smell his aftershave again. Slowly, she reached out and touched his cheek, and felt his arms go round her as she pulled his face to hers. The kiss was strangely gentle and yet earth-shattering. Surely she had never felt quite like this.

It was Doug who broke away first.

'I'm… not very good at this,' he said, and she heard the emotion in his voice.

'Oh you are, you know,' she said, holding on to the front of his jacket. 'But let's just take our time.'

He kissed her forehead and let her go. 'Yes. We can take all the time we need, can't we?'

Alicia walked upstairs and pushed the ward doors open. Jenny and Derek were at the far end of the corridor and by the looks of things, they were entertaining each other very nicely; slightly surprising when you considered that her daughter had been more than apprehensive at the thought of strangers just a week or two ago. But Jen's face was one big beam now and so was Derek's.

Chapter Thirteen
Tuesday, 18th July

Alicia

Jenny banging around downstairs woke Alicia well before seven on Tuesday morning. She groaned, and then remembered the previous evening and smiled to herself. One kiss and she felt like a different person. Warm. Alive. Not just a single mother with a problem parent. She felt ten years younger at least.

She lay there thinking about everything that had happened yesterday, with her father and Jenny, Conker and Frank, and Doug... and the way she had felt when they'd kissed. The friendship was giving every promise of deepening. It was exciting to say the least. At last, at last she would be one of a pair again.

It was nine o'clock before she arrived down in the kitchen, hair still damp from the shower. She'd had a terrific night's sleep, no worry, no nightmares, just sleep, blessed sleep. Because of the kiss, or because her father was no longer waiting for her attention? A picture of him standing by his bed slid into her mind.

Go away, go away!

It was the child's voice again, whispering through her head, throaty and tearful. Alicia winced. She was going to have to deal with whatever memories were coming to the surface. She should treat the child in her head as she would treat Jenny, or as she would have wanted to be treated herself. She should love this child, because maybe no-one else had.

The thought both comforted and horrified her. She was a mother, of course she could help this little voice trying to tell her about something bad. But where had her own mother been when little Alicia had been so afraid? Why hadn't Mum come to her aid? Or had they both been victims?

Jenny came running in from the garden.

'Mummy, there's a yellow scooter at the back of the garden shed, can I try it? Was it yours?'

A yellow scooter. The wave of nausea this time was the strongest of all. Alicia clapped one hand over her mouth and grabbed the back of the nearest chair with the other, retching violently.

'What is it? Are you sick?' Jenny was looking up at her, apprehension on her small face. Alicia took a deep shaky breath as the nausea receded. 'No, lovey, it's alright. I just… choked. Yes, of course you can try the scooter. It was my birthday present when I was five, I think.'

The yellow scooter… she could remember it all quite clearly now, she'd been right here in the kitchen, standing pretty much where she was standing now, holding a doll, a Barbie doll… but surely she hadn't been allowed a Barbie doll, Barbies had boobs and long legs and definitely belonged to the devil… yet there had been one, a present, yes, a birthday present from Sonja, that was it, she had unwrapped it and she'd been so pleased, such a feeling of delight, a *Barbie*, she had one too now… oh thank you, Sonja… And then Mum had taken her and Sonja out to the lane to play on the scooter, and when she came back inside the Barbie doll had gone and her father was waiting for her with a thick leather belt… and…

'Mummy?'

Alicia made herself breathe calmly and reached out to ruffle the little girl's hair.

'Sorry, lovey. On you go and try out the scooter while I'm having breakfast and we'll leave for Mr Taylor's at ten on the dot,' she said, and Jenny ran outside.

Alicia dropped down on the nearest chair and buried her head in both hands. Her father had beaten her with that belt. On and on, he had beaten her, up in his bedroom, the bad room. On her fifth birthday, because she'd been happy to have a Barbie doll. And Mum hadn't helped her at all. It was the most vivid memory yet.

Five years old. There wouldn't be many younger memories, she knew. Was this all, did she know everything now? Immediately she knew that she didn't, there was something even bigger still locked away in her head with the child. Deep breaths, Alicia. Remember the mantra. You're the adult, you're in control, you survived.

Okay, it had happened and she *had* survived. This wasn't the time to dwell on it, she could do that later with professional help. Sonja should be here tomorrow, she might remember the incident too. And Cathal, she must try to find him. The family had gone back to Bantry about a year before she'd left herself, so that might be the place to start. There couldn't be many Cathal O'Brians around, even in Ireland. Alicia straightened up, squaring her shoulders. She would find an internet café later on and start the search, but right now she was damn well going to make sure that her own child had better memories of Lower Banford than she herself had. Pet shop here we come.

The four black kittens and their mother were in a pen in the front shop, and Jenny dropped to her knees beside it.

'Hello kitties! Mr Taylor, what are their names and how old are they and are they girls or boys and... '

'Whoa, slow down,' said Kenneth Taylor, crouching down beside the kittens' enclosure while Alicia perched on a set of steps. 'Now, these young fellas are three weeks and four days old, all boys except this one here. Mum's name is Cindy but the kits won't have names until they go to homes of their own.'

'Have they got homes yet?' asked Jenny, and Alicia looked apprehensively at Kenneth. His big face beamed at her.

'Two definites and four maybes,' he said, scooping up the smallest kitten and kissing its nose. Alicia smiled to herself. Thank goodness. A little friend for Moritz wasn't really on her shopping list.

Jenny frowned. 'But that's six!'

Kenneth patted her shoulder, then snatched his hand away again. Alicia blinked. What was the man doing? Jenny had noticed nothing, however, she was still intent on matching kittens with prospective families.

Alicia struggled to make conversation with Kenneth while Jenny played with the kittens. It was hard going talking to the man, he was a bag of nerves when he wasn't talking about animals, so she ended up gabbling away about Conker and Moritz until she couldn't think of another thing to say about either of them. It was a relief when she could say truthfully that they had to go.

'You can come back any time and play with them,' Kenneth said to Jenny. 'They like you because you're gentle and quiet with them.'

'Oh! Thank you!' Jenny's face shone with happiness.

Kenneth Taylor stood there wringing his hands when he was saying goodbye, his round face sweating and his eyes sliding away from Alicia's. Why on earth was the man so nervous? Was she really so fearsome, or was there another reason? A sudden thought struck her and she giggled aloud as she unlocked the car. Maybe he fancied her... no, no, that couldn't be. Dear Lord, no.

'Right, Madam,' she said to Jenny as they turned into the lane. 'Fish fingers for lunch. Then after we've visited Grandpa we'll pop along to Merton and get some jam-making equipment. Then back home to meet Margaret off the bus. Okay?'

There would be an internet café somewhere in Merton. And wouldn't it be great if they happened to see Doug while they were 'visiting Grandpa'?

The house phone rang while Alicia was rummaging in the freezer, and Jenny ran to answer it. To Alicia's dismay it was Paul. She rushed through to the hallway where Jenny was standing, phone in hand and red of face.

'I don't know, Daddy, I don't think so,' she said, and Alicia snatched the phone, her hand closing the mouthpiece.

'Thanks, Jen. I'll speak to Daddy,' she said, trying to sound calm. Damn Paul and his insensitivity. Jenny shouldn't have to cope with all this as well, and she shouldn't have to listen to her mother arguing with her father, either.

'Take Conker up to the woods for half an hour before lunch,' she said firmly, pushing the little girl towards the back door. 'On you go.'

'Well, Alicia, you took your time,' said Paul, his voice hurtful and sarcastic in her ear. 'I was just saying to Jenny I want her in Singapore for a holiday at least this year. But we don't have to talk

132

about this over the phone. I'm in York on business this week. I'll come by about four this afternoon to talk to Jen about coming to visit her stepmum and me.'

The line went dead and Alicia found she was trembling. She walked through to the kitchen in an angry daze. How dare Paul command her to be at home at a certain time. And Singapore... What on earth was she going to do?

Just say no, she told herself. Or fob him off, say you'll both visit Singapore next year sometime. And she should check on her legal position too. But be firm.

Drearily, she started cooking lunch. Jenny appeared at the back door as the church clock was striking the half hour, but to Alicia's surprise the little girl didn't ask about Paul's phone call. Her face was flushed, and she ran to the sink to wash her hands without saying a word.

'How was your palace? Bet you're hungry after such a busy morning,' said Alicia, dishing up fish fingers and frozen peas and setting the plates on the table.

'Uh-huh.' Jenny looked up at Alicia, her face suddenly radiant. 'Mummy, there are lots more little blue flowers today, almost like fairy flowers. We played at Kings and Queens again.'

'Did you now? Who was King, then, Conker?'

'No, Oberon was King. And he brought chocolate biscuits but I only had one because I knew it was nearly lunchtime,' said Jenny, fishing in the pocket of her shorts and producing a red and silver biscuit wrapper.

Alicia stared. Wasn't this just a game? But if Oberon had provided biscuits he couldn't be a figment of Jenny's imagination.

'And... um... who's Oberon, exactly?' she said, struggling to keep the rising panic out of her voice. Jenny would never speak to a stranger, would she? Or wasn't Oberon a stranger?

'He's... ' said Jenny, then clapped a hand over her mouth. 'Oops, it's a big secret. I nearly forgot.'

'But, Jen darling, I must know who you were playing with. Is it a grown up, or another child?'

'It's alright, it's a grown-up, and you know him. It's quite alright, Mummy. You would say yes. Really you would. But it's a secret, I can't tell you.' Jenny put her fork down and reached for her glass.

Alicia felt almost breathless. Things seemed to be spiralling right out of control at the moment, there was hassle just everywhere. Her father and Margaret, sleazy Kenneth Taylor and his cats, those bloody flashbacks, Paul, and now Jenny with someone she herself knew who called himself Oberon, played at fairies, and was 'quite alright'. Could she *make* Jenny tell her who this person was?

Oh, for heaven's sake, she thought. It'll be one of the neighbours for sure, who else could it be? John Watson often went mushrooming or herb-gathering in the woods, and he was a retired English teacher... he'd been very involved in the 'Midsummer Night's Dream' production too, according to Eva Campbell... yes, of course. Stop being so neurotic, woman. It wasn't as if she didn't have plenty of other things to worry about right now.

'Mr Watson, bet I'm right,' she said cheerfully, and Jenny looked at her, a little smile on her face.

Feeling more settled about the episode, Alicia pondered what to do about Paul. She had an old school friend who was a lawyer, and she could be sure of straight answers and real help from Louise. But the most important thing was to make sure she took charge of the situation when Paul arrived this afternoon. He really didn't have a leg to stand on. Or did he?

The Stranger

The decision had been made; in fact it had almost made itself. He would put his plan into action on Saturday. At the weekend he would have just that bit more freedom both to control what was going on at St. Joe's, and – most importantly – to persuade little Helen to come back home with him. And then of course he wanted plenty of time to enjoy being with his perfect little almost-angel before sending her off to his own Helen. Then on Sunday, when he already had two angels in Paradise, it would be big Helen's turn.

He had laid the first stone in his plan already. The forecast for the weekend was good, and Little Helen had promised to meet him at the special place on Saturday morning, as soon after breakfast as she could. He had been coy, the promise of a special Saturday surprise had been enough. He had hinted about kittens and that was all that was needed to have her clapping her hands and jumping with excitement. It would definitely be alright, she said, Mummy always did the housework after breakfast.

So now there were things to be bought. Plan B would involve leaving little Helen alone in his flat for an hour or two. Of course it was impossible to know exactly how the various people participating in the plan would react, so he couldn't organise things in as much detail as he would have liked. This meant he had to be prepared for a number of eventualities. Which was why he was standing in the gardening section of Merton's biggest department store.

'Can I help you?' An assistant was looking at him with cow's eyes, big and brown with eyelashes clogged with mascara.

He shuddered. How very much he preferred his three lovely,

natural Helens. 'I'm looking for cord to tie a sapling to a stake,' he told her, surprised and pleased that his brain had worked out such a good answer on the spur of the moment.

Ten minutes later he was heading for the soft furnishings department, a length of beige coloured nylon cord safe in his pocket.

The next assistant was an older lady with a grandmotherly figure and thick glasses. She approached him while he was looking round a confusingly large selection of material, searching for something golden to do duty as a robe. This time, he had his request ready.

'I want something golden to make a throw for my daughter's bed,' he told the assistant. 'She's always playing Kings and Queens.'

'Bless her,' said the woman fondly. 'We have ready-made throws, you might find something there.'

And how incredible, there *was* a golden throw, made of heavy, shiny material. Who would have thought that finding a golden robe would be so simple? It was proof that the whole plan was simply meant to be. He bought the throw, and as the material was rather scratchy he bought a fluffy yellow baby blanket as well, soft and sweet.

Back in his car he examined his purchases carefully. Perfect, perfect. The cord would tie little Helen up safe and sound while he wasn't at home. The fluffy blanket would keep her warm and cosy, and the throw would make the whole occasion regal and dignified. He could cover her with it or they could use it to lie on. Oh, it was going to be so good. The anticipation was delicious.

Tomorrow would be Wednesday. He'd start the other preparations then. There was big Helen to see to as well. And on Saturday, another angel would be winging her way to Paradise, and his own darling Helen would be so, so happy.

Just three days to go.

Alicia

Standing at the bus stop with Jenny and Conker, waiting for Margaret's bus to appear round the corner, Alicia could feel the tension in her neck. She would get a headache if she wasn't careful, what a God-awful afternoon it had turned into, first with Paul's arrogant phone call, and then having to rush back from Merton in time for his visit. There had been no time to look for an internet café. She should have been late; it would have served him right. And poor Jen, she'd been terribly nervous before Paul arrived, though her father hadn't half exerted his charm. Alicia shuddered. What had she ever seen in the man?

The bus drew up, and Jenny jumped up and down excitedly, waiting for Margaret to get off. Conker was bounding around too, anyone looking at them would think they were all as happy as Larry. Alicia fixed a smile on her own face. If you can't beat 'em…

'Auntie Margaret, guess, just guess who visited us this afternoon!' cried Jenny, as soon as Margaret had both feet safely on the ground. Alicia sighed. Complicated times were ahead of them, she could see that coming.

'Oh um… Doctor Carter? Or was it your friend from school, what's her name, Kayleigh?' Margaret kissed Jenny and then Alicia. 'You look pale, Alicia, is Bob alright?' she asked urgently.

'He's fine,' said Alicia, trying to sound positive and energetic. 'There's nothing to worry about. We'll visit him later. Here, give me your case.'

Jenny was still standing there, her hands clasped in front of her, waiting expectantly for Margaret to guess again. Margaret laughed.

'I give up,' she said. 'Tell me who it was.'

'Daddy!' cried Jenny, and Alicia met Margaret's astonished eyes.

'Tell you later,' she mouthed as they started along the lane.

'I was worried at first because I didn't want to go to Singapore just like that,' said Jenny, skipping along beside Margaret, her great-aunt's hand firmly clasped in one of her own. 'But Daddy promised he'd organise a proper visit for me and Mummy very soon, and we're going to go up a huge skyscraper, and there's a great big zoo as well, Daddy says. He could only stay for a little while but it was a lovely visit.'

They reached the garden gate and Jenny released Conker from his lead. The two of them ran round the back, and Alicia unlocked the front door.

'Surprise, huh?' she said. 'And Paul hasn't changed a bit, still the same old sweet-talking, superficial... well, you get the idea.'

Margaret hugged her, and Alicia took a shaky breath. 'You poor thing,' said Margaret. 'What on earth brought this on? I didn't know Paul was anywhere near here.'

'You and me both,' said Alicia, depositing the suitcase at the bottom of the stairs. 'Let's be devils and have a sherry before I heat the soup. I feel I deserve it today. Paul phoned at lunchtime and calmly informed me he would come by at four o'clock, and then he rang off before I could say a word. I was so mad with him. And you know, I really do think he's just doing this to... to get up my nose.'

Margaret fetched two sherry glasses from the cupboard and sat down at the kitchen table. 'He was always good at that,' she agreed. 'Go on, love.'

Alicia poured two generous glasses of sherry and tore a piece of kitchen paper from the roll to wipe her eyes. 'Cheers and good health. Apparently Paul's here for ten days on business. He's remarried and his wife's pregnant. He says he wants proper access to Jenny, if not custody, and oh, Margaret, I don't know if he does want that or if he's just saying it to annoy me. Jen doesn't know about the custody bit and she's over the moon, he was nice as pie to her this afternoon, gave her two hundred pounds, would you believe. If he's genuine about this it'll mean a big upset in Jenny's life, trips to Singapore and so on. And if he's winding me up then she's going to get hurt.'

How petty it all sounded when she said it like that. But Margaret obviously understood, she reached over and squeezed Alicia's hand.

'Well, lovey, all you can do is be there for Jenny whatever happens,' she said. 'Maybe Paul does want to make it up to her after neglecting her all this time. And if he's paying for a trip to Singapore for you both, then you should go. A holiday will do you good.'

Alicia lifted her glass and sipped. 'Oh, I know. It'll probably work out at one visit, then when his baby's born he'll forget all about Jen again. Anyway, tell me about David and Sheila.'

Margaret smiled. 'Baby talk all the way. They've got a DVD of the last scan, it's amazing. You can actually count the toes on it.'

Alicia drained her glass and reached for the bottle. It was definitely a two-sherry day. Jenny and Conker were running round the garden, and whoops and barks filled the air. Alicia looked at Margaret and suddenly they both laughed. It was difficult to stay depressed with Jen around.

'She's a real outdoor girl, isn't she?' said Margaret.

'Yes. I'm a bit worried about that,' said Alicia, getting up to put the soup on. All this sherry was going to her head, she needed food. 'You know how she's been playing princesses in the woods? Well, last time she came back and said she'd been playing with a man who called himself Oberon and gave her chocolate biscuits. She mentioned him before once, but I thought it was a game. Now she says it's a secret, won't tell me who it was. But she said that I know him.'

Margaret looked at Alicia and smiled. 'She said something about it to me once too. I thought it was just a pretend friend. She must be lonely here. You had a fantasy friend when you were little, don't you remember? Children often do.'

Alicia shook her head. As a school nurse, she knew that eight was well past the usual age for fantasy friends. 'I know, but I don't think this is imaginary,' she said. 'She spoke about a secret once, too, but then we got distracted before I could go into it with her. And the biscuit wrapper today certainly wasn't pretend. It must be John Watson, I can't for the life of me think who else I know here that would play fairy kings in the woods with Jenny.'

Margaret leaned forward and patted her arm. 'You worry too

much, Alicia, you'll give yourself an ulcer before you're forty if you go on like this. You could always go and ask him, but think logically, lovey. I mean this is Lower Banford after all, everyone knows everyone! Either it's John, and then there's nothing to worry about, or it's a pretend friend, and that's not anything to worry about either, is it?'

Alicia stared for a moment and then grinned to herself. How true, and bless Margaret for pointing it out so clearly. 'I suppose not. Thanks, Margaret.'

She was still washing up after dinner when the doorbell rang. Eva next door had offered to take Margaret to St Joe's and Jenny had gone with them, more for the novelty of squeezing into the back of Eva's Smart car than any desire to visit her grandfather, but it meant that Alicia had a whole hour to herself. And now someone was interrupting her peace. She stomped to the front door.

'Sonja!'

'Hello!' said Sonja, pulling Alicia into an expensively perfumed embrace. 'Honey, you look like you need a long holiday and from what Frank says you're not going to get one anytime soon. This is chilled. Got a couple of glasses?'

She waved two bottles of Féchy. Alicia led her inside. Sonja was still small and plump, but she looked… prosperous, that was it. And happy. And concerned, and oh it was so good to see her, how on earth had they managed to lose touch for so long?

'I thought you wouldn't be here until tomorrow?'

'Change of plan. John's Mum's been given a date for a hip replacement in two weeks, so we're going straight on up tomorrow to have a bit more time with her before the op. We'll be back in August a few days earlier than planned. Alicia, tell me what's going on here. Frank wouldn't say anything and I can see it's something big.'

Alicia poured two glasses of wine and put the remainder in the fridge. It was difficult to know where to start. The child's voice in her head? The flashbacks? She began to speak, and Sonja sat listening, the expression on her face changing from gravity to indignation and then anger.

'Lici, I had no idea. We all just thought your parents were really old-fashioned and strict, and we knew they were into their religion.

I don't think you ever told me about any of these punishments. I've no recollection of giving you a Barbie, even.'

Alicia sighed. 'I sort of thought you wouldn't remember much, you were too young,' she said. 'Don't worry, maybe Cathal will. I meant to go online in Merton this afternoon and see if I could run him down, but Paul put a stop to that.'

'Why don't I do it for you? John's Mum's your original silver surfer, her broadband is to die for, and it would give me something to do while the kids are out with Granny.'

Alicia agreed thankfully. Maybe it was true that a problem shared was a problem halved. She certainly felt a lot more positive about her situation here.

'What did you think of Frank?' she said, remembering that Sonja had been worried about him.

'Well in one way he's a lot better because he has different stuff to think about here, with the house needing to be done up and his new patients and so on. On the other hand I can tell he's really tense, there's something he's not telling me. Sometimes when you look at him you can see he's thinking about it. His nerves are still shot to pieces.'

'I thought the very first time I saw him here that he was nervous,' said Alicia. 'But you know, everyone here likes him, he's well-respected and he's fitted right into the community. Maybe he's still grieving?'

'I don't think so. It's been over six years, and he never mentions Nell now. It was so terrible, Alicia, what happened. He found her in the garden, she must have gone out to do something and apparently it was one of those sudden adult death things, like footballers have sometimes. There was a big bash on her head where she'd fallen, and Frank was just kneeling there with her in his arms when a neighbour found them. Nell was dead and Frank was shaking like a leaf and I was in bloody Vancouver. It took me the best part of three days to get back to England and you can't imagine the state he was in.'

Alicia was silent. Life was cruel, no doubt about it. There were no guarantees of tomorrow for any one of them.

Sonja went to get the wine bottle. 'I was glad when he said he was selling their house, but I still don't know if coming back here was a good idea,' she said. 'But it's his life. I just wish he would share a bit more of what's going on in it.'

'I'll keep an eye on him for you while I'm here,' said Alicia.

They sat there sipping too much Féchy and talking about life after Lower Banford; Alicia felt her world go fuzzy at the edges. Margaret and Jenny came back, and Margaret made them garlic bread to mop up the wine. It was nearly midnight when Alicia took Conker and walked Sonja round the village to Frank's home.

'See you in two weeks or so,' she said, giggling as her friend wobbled towards the front door on her elegant Parisian heels.

The village street was deserted as she walked back. Only the one dim streetlight lit the lane, and the woods were pitch black. But tomorrow the sun would shine again, and maybe Sonja would soon find Cathal. But what if Cathal didn't remember anything either?

Chapter Fourteen
Wednesday, 19th July

The Stranger

It was time to start the serious organisation. He stood in his bedroom, looking down at the items set out there, ready for Saturday. It was difficult not to gloat, that throw was absolutely perfect. And the cord would make sure his little angel stayed put, though of course the medication he had ready would help with that too. The cord was just a precaution. He would need a white coat, to make him less conspicuous at St. Joe's, but that wouldn't be a problem. Now he should plan exactly what to do with big Helen, when the news of her daughter's… disappearance came to her.

And really, there wasn't much to plan. A shoulder to cry on was all she'd need. He would arrange that the two of them had some quality time before the event, just to ensure that his would be the shoulder she'd turn to first.

So an invitation was needed. He would ask her for a coffee or dinner or even a walk next time they met… a walk in the woods. How ironic that would be.

He smiled. He would ask and she would say yes. And it was all going to be quite, quite wonderful. Big Helen had no idea what was about to happen to her.

Alicia

'Okay, Louise, I'll hear from you next week, then.' Alicia, leaning against the telephone table in the hallway, frowned as Jenny and Conker crashed through the front door and headed for the kitchen.

She replaced the receiver and strode after them, fully intending to read the riot act to her daughter about banging around the place while other people were making important phone calls whilst still suffering the effects of drinking way too much wine the night before. But only Margaret was there, placidly washing lettuce. Alicia could see Jenny and Conker racing round the summerhouse outside. She grinned in spite of her headache and sat down.

'If I dashed about like that I'd be half dead by ten in the morning.'

'It's the energy of childhood. They should bottle it,' said Margaret, glancing out of the window. 'What did your lawyer friend have to say?'

'Quite a lot. She's going to investigate for me about alimony. Paul seems to be doing quite well for himself now so she doesn't see why he should get away with not paying anything back. And she said he definitely wouldn't get custody of Jen in Singapore and 99.9% sure not here either, in spite of the 'stable family' he has to offer. He might well get visitation rights, though, so she advises me to be cooperative about that if he wants to see her again.'

'Good. That sounds like more or less what you wanted to hear,' said Margaret. She spun the lettuce briskly. 'I'd like to spend the afternoon with Bob, lovey, how about you?'

Alicia only just managed not to pull a face. 'Not today. But I'll run you to St. Joe's, and then we'll collect you later, how's that?'

She noticed the vulnerable expression in Margaret's eyes and felt guilty all over again. Her aunt had so wanted to maintain the status quo here at home, but St Joe's *was* the best place for a dependent stroke patient. It was time for Margaret to get used to the new situation. The big change had happened, and they could enjoy a few weeks' breathing space while they decided what to do with this place. Would Margaret want to stay on here, or move closer to David and Sheila? Somewhere in between might be best. Then they could sell the house, and what a blessing that would be.

Slowly, Alicia felt something like peace settle over her. Everything was sorted, she could let the past go now. As soon as the thought entered her head the child's voice did too, screaming in terror.

Let go! I hate you!

Alicia jumped up, shivering. That was a memory now, not a flashback, she could actually remember screaming that loud. He'd been dragging her inside from the garden, and she'd been younger than Jenny was now. But why? What had happened? The little voice had been full of hatred. Alicia the child had hated her father as much as Alicia the teenager had, but Alicia the adult couldn't remember the details. She would have to find out more, and this might be a good opportunity to ask her aunt about it. She took a deep breath.

'Margaret – this is going to sound odd and please don't be upset, but – do you know if um, Bob, um, hurt me at all when I was a kid? To punish me? Ever since we came here I've been having this sort of nightmare and I'm not sure if it's something that really happened or not.'

Margaret was rummaging for salad tongs. She turned and stared at Alicia for a moment, leaning against the worktop.

'Oh Alicia love. I know he was always very strict about his principles; you didn't have an easy time. He used to smack you, yes, but I'm sure it was nothing more than other youngsters experienced back then. I've known him since the day he was born and I can't imagine he was ever cruel.'

Alicia was silent. He had been cruel. Look at what he'd done on her fifth birthday, all because she'd been given a Barbie doll.

'What about Mum?'

Margaret was clearly ill at ease. 'Well, I think she left most of the discipline to Bob, that was their way of bringing you up,' she said. 'But Alicia, love, don't worry. They were very adamant in their beliefs, let's say. But I'm sure they were doing what they honestly believed was best for you. I always felt their faith was very restrictive, but no-one can say that any one religion is better or worse than another.'

Alicia looked into her aunt's worried face and nodded. 'Okay. Thanks, Margaret,' she said slowly. It was no use asking further questions, Margaret didn't *know* the answers, she was just saying what she believed. What she wanted to believe.

Was there any point in raking it all up now, when her father could no longer be held responsible for his actions? He *was* demented, even though there were still these odd moments when he looked straight at her and laughed. Maybe they weren't quite moments of clarity but he did seem aware of who she was and that she hated him. But they never would find out how much he really understood. She couldn't prosecute him now even if she wanted to.

'Mummy? Can I take Moritz to the pet shop to see the kittens?' Jenny appeared at the back door, Moritz under one arm and Conker in his usual place at her heels.

'Not right this minute, sweetheart, but we could go this afternoon after we've dropped Aunt Margaret off at St. Joe's.'

And maybe they would see Doug while they were doing that. He would probably phone soon now that Margaret was home, and make arrangements for a proper date. Or should she phone him? A pleasurable feeling of excitement settled into Alicia's middle. Even the hassle with Paul, her father and the flashbacks wasn't enough to spoil her feelings about Doug.

Jenny was pouting. She kicked the door frame. 'That's mean, I want to go now. I can go by myself, it's not far and I'll take Conker too.'

'No,' said Alicia, then shook herself. Gut reactions were becoming positively commonplace this summer, but why did she have such strong feelings against Kenneth Taylor?

He's a creep, part of her brain said. He's... slimy. And she didn't want Jenny with him on her own, Conker or no Conker. A thought struck her and she glanced at her daughter. Could Kenneth

Taylor be Oberon? Was that possible? Had he been here during the Festival? But no, it must be John Watson. All this talk about Oberon and Titania was much more likely to come from a retired English teacher than an overweight and decidedly odd pet shop owner.

'Why can't I?' demanded Jenny, and Alicia pointed to the clock on the wall.

'Because it's nearly lunchtime, silly. Now take a cloth and wipe that door frame where you've marked it, please. We'll go to Mr Taylor's after lunch.'

Brilliant. Now she had let herself in for a long afternoon visit with Kenneth Taylor.

To Alicia's relief, Jenny accepted this reasoning, wiped the door frame with another pout and flounced back to the garden. Margaret looked round from the sink.

'What was all that about?'

Alicia explained about their visit to the pet shop and how she felt about Kenneth. Her aunt snorted.

'Fiddle faddle. The man's overweight and soft, that's all. Not your type, is he?'

Alicia grinned. 'No way.'

She paused halfway through setting the table for lunch. Maybe she wasn't doing herself any favours, raking the past up; it was only making her miserable. She should concentrate more on the few positive memories she had of her childhood. Sonja of course, and Cathal. School. And she'd been happy doing things with Mum too, she could distinctly remember them baking together, and going to the shops. It might be an idea to write everything down. The bad stuff here had undoubtedly been prominent, but maybe there were more happy memories than she realised. She should look for them.

The phone's shrill ring tone interrupted this happy train of thought. Alicia's good mood evaporated quickly when she heard Paul's voice, but she remembered Louise's advice and forced herself to sound pleasant and calm. It was difficult, though, when she heard what he had to say.

'I want to have Jen here in York for a couple of days,' he stated boldly. No 'please' or 'would that be okay?' Alicia noticed, and only just managed to bite back a snappy answer.

'When did you have in mind?' she asked sweetly, wondering if he would notice the sarcasm in her voice. He didn't, of course.

'My meetings tomorrow finish at lunchtime, then I'm free until Saturday morning.'

Alicia broke in quickly before he could make any more demands.

'Right. You can collect Jenny tomorrow at two o'clock, and I want her back here by nine at the latest on Friday evening,' she said firmly. 'One night away from home is quite enough for the first visit.' That was clever, she thought. By insinuating that there would be more visits she had softened her restrictions on this one.

'Oh... okay,' said Paul. 'See you tomorrow at two, then.'

He rang off, and Alicia trailed back through to the kitchen. Thank goodness Paul had agreed to her conditions without arguing. Though now she thought about it, she should have consulted her daughter before arranging a visit like that.

Fortunately, Jenny was delighted, and Alicia realised that all her little girl's former apprehension about Paul had vanished.

'A whole day and a half with Daddy! In a hotel!' cried Jenny, dancing round the kitchen with Moritz in her arms. 'You will take care of Conker and Moritz for me, won't you, Mummy? Oh, I wonder what we'll do in York, me and Daddy!'

'My goodness, there are lots of things to do in York,' said Margaret. 'You'll have a super time, won't she, Alicia?'

'Sure. Jen, I think we'll get you a mobile this afternoon,' said Alicia, the uncomfortable, apprehensive feeling in her stomach lifting slightly at the thought of being able to speak to Jenny whenever she felt the need. Lower Banford's precarious mobile reception permitting, of course.

'A mobile of my own?' Jenny's eyes were round as saucers.

'Yes, but only for emergencies and... and visits to Daddy,' said Alicia firmly. 'Off you go upstairs and wash your hands for lunch, you exuberant thing!' She held the door open for Jenny, meeting Margaret's eyes as the child ran past.

'You worry too much, Alicia,' said Margaret, shaking her head.

Alicia sighed, looking to see that Jenny was out of earshot. 'I know. But if she has a mobile I won't have to worry so much,' she said, and saw Margaret cast her eyes heavenwards.

'What do you think is going to happen? Paul isn't going to abduct her in the middle of a business trip. He couldn't get her out of the country even if he wanted to.'

'I don't care. I'm still buying her a mobile,' said Alicia, knowing she was being overprotective but quite unable to stop herself. 'If nothing else, it'd be useful if she loses Paul anywhere, you know how she dives about the place, and he's not used to that, is he?'

'Have it your way,' said Margaret, peering into the oven. 'Let's eat.'

Later that afternoon, Alicia drove back to St. Joe's to collect Margaret, Jenny beside her clutching the new collar that Kenneth had given her for Moritz. They had spent a fascinating – from Jenny's point of view, at least – hour playing with the kittens. Alicia knew she couldn't have denied Jen anything today, anyway. If only they had bags of money and a big house in the country, she could give her daughter the best childhood ever.

Kenneth had bumbled around the entire time they were there, asking if she wanted coffee, and if she and Jen could come again the next day, and how was she enjoying the Yorkshire weather. It was more than a little unnerving.

Five minutes later they were at St. Joe's. The afternoon had turned chilly, and the rose garden was deserted. Alicia followed Jenny up the main staircase.

'Alicia!' A voice called behind them, and Alicia turned to see Doug Patton and Frank Carter emerging from Doug's office at the bottom of the stairway. It had been Doug who'd called, and he grinned at her.

'I was just telling Frank that Bob's pretty good on his feet. He and Margaret walked right round the garden this afternoon.'

'That's good,' said Alicia, looking from one man to the other. Her two coffee invites, side by side. 'Is he okay otherwise? I thought yesterday evening that he was looking terribly tired.'

'His routine's different now,' said Frank immediately. 'He'll get used to things in a day or two. He's up at seven here, and I think he slept until later at home, didn't he?'

'Yes, eight at least,' said Alicia. 'I should have realised that. Thanks, Frank.'

He grinned at her, and she smiled back. Frank was good at making people feel better in whatever situation they were in. She should talk to him about Jenny's visit to Paul, maybe he could relieve her of some of her fears.

Doug put a hand on her shoulder and squeezed. 'I'll come upstairs with you, Alicia, and I'll get back to you about those referrals, Frank. I know you need to get back to the practice now.'

'Right,' said Frank, and Alicia could feel his gaze on her. He stared for a moment, then lifted his hand in a brief wave. 'I'll be off, then. What's that you've got, Princess Jenny?'

'A new collar for Moritz,' said Jenny, holding out the green and yellow band for him to inspect. 'Mr Taylor gave it to me.'

'That was kind,' said Frank. His eyes were bleak as he turned back to Alicia and she wondered if he was missing Sonja. 'I'll see you soon, then.' He turned away, and Alicia allowed Doug to steer her upstairs while chatting about her father's new routine.

They reached the ward door and Doug held it open, laughing as Jenny sped off down the corridor towards her grandfather, who was sitting with Margaret in one of the big bay windows overlooking the garden.

'It's nice to see youngsters about the place,' he said. 'Alicia, what about that dinner, maybe tomorrow? I'm sure Margaret would babysit.'

'Oh, Jenny's going to visit her father tomorrow, she'll be away until Friday,' said Alicia, the anticipation making her feel warm and excited. Her apprehension about Jenny going away was suddenly a great deal less. How long had it been since she'd been on a date? Months? No, years. Doug was everything she could wish for, and like herself he was a nurse, they had that in common. She should get his input on her flashbacks, too. Not that she didn't trust Frank, of course, but a second opinion might be useful. She smiled at him.

'Tomorrow would be perfect.'

'Great. Shall I pick you up at seven? There's an Indonesian restaurant just outside Upper Banford, we could go there, if you like?'

'Sounds good,' said Alicia, watching as Derek Thorpe strode up the corridor. 'See you at seven tomorrow, then.'

'I'm looking forward to it.' He squeezed her arm then turned to go downstairs again.

Derek immediately started telling her about the speech therapy assessment that was planned for the following day, and Alicia found herself agreeing to a feedback session with Derek and the speech therapist afterwards followed by a care-plan discussion with Derek alone. But what the hell, it might be interesting and if she knew Derek at all now there would be coffee and cake involved as well. Alicia sat down beside Margaret, conscious that a smile was pulling at her lips.

She had a date with Doug Patton. Who knows where that could lead? Alicia hugged herself.

She was the one with a secret now, and it was a very good feeling indeed.

The Stranger

Plan B. A wonderful plan for a wonderful day.

Everything was arranged in his head. All he had to do before Saturday was make sure he had his time with big Helen. Then he merely had to set plan B into action on Saturday morning, and everything would follow on almost automatically. Nothing could go wrong this time. How happy his love would be to have a little Helen all of her own.

He was so looking forward to his own time with his little fairy queen. She was such a darling. He would meet her at the special place in the woods and then he would bring her home, and he would hold her and tell her all about his own Helen in Paradise and the love that was waiting for her there. She would be afraid, little Helen, perhaps she would even cry, but he would hold her tight and comfort her. They would have all day together, on and off, and then in the evening he would take her back to the woods.

He looked around his living room. There wasn't much luxury here for his sweet little Helen. Luxuries just weren't an important part of his life any more. Losing Helen had made him see how insignificant earthly things were. But he had the golden throw for a robe, and the fluffy yellow blanket, and there was a lovely soft new towel somewhere, too. He would remove those horrible jeans or shorts she always seemed to be wearing and wrap her in the golden robe. Yes, how regal she would look. And he would loosen her lovely long hair and brush it out, and run his fingers through it and bury his face in the softness and oh, how much he would enjoy it all. He would massage her... or yes, oh yes, he could bath her in Helen's bath oil, the very same kind as Mummy always used, and then he would hold her and stroke her, his beautiful little fairy Helen. How happy he would make her and oh, it was almost too much, he was looking forward to it all so very, very much. He would be rich beyond his dreams. A fairy king indeed.

Alicia

The thought of Jenny spending thirty-odd hours with Paul was weighing heavily in her gut. Heart thudding, Alicia started to wash the dinner dishes. The doorbell's strident ring almost made her hit the ceiling; all this stress, she would have a stroke herself if she went on like this.

Frank was standing on the doorstep, a piece of paper in one hand. 'Alicia, are you okay? What's wrong?'

'Hi, Frank. Come in. Nothing's wrong, exactly, Jenny's going to visit her father for an overnight stay tomorrow. He's in York on business this week. It's a bit of a worry.'

He followed her into the living room. 'I can imagine. What's been happening there? Has he made any more threats about getting custody?'

'Not in so many words. My lawyer says he won't get custody, but I should be cooperative about visits. She's going to organise better child support for me too. It's just the thought of Jenny being with Paul that's bugging me.'

'What does Jenny think?'

Alicia looked at him appreciatively. She could talk it through with a neutral person now and maybe lay her fears to rest. She fetched them both a glass of Margaret's homemade elderflower cordial and sat back in the sofa. 'Oh, she's delighted. And I do know it'll be okay. She'll be with Paul in York for a day and a half and she'll be back home on Friday evening. But you know, Frank, sometimes I wonder why on earth I married him in the first place. When I speak to him now my toes just curl. What on earth did I see in him?'

'You were younger then, other things were important,' he said. 'And Paul would be different then as well. You have to accept the past, Alicia, I've learned that myself too. Accept it, take the good things out of it – Jenny, for instance – and move on. You can't beat yourself up about something you can't change.'

Alicia smiled at him warmly. Surely Sonja was worrying about nothing, Frank *was* talking about his past life. He was just a very private kind of person, that was all. Not everyone wanted to air their feelings to the whole world.

'I know. I think it's the whole situation here that's turning me into an old mother hen. At least my father is sorted now but I'll feel better when my own life settles down. I had another flashback recently so I asked Margaret if he had ever hit me. She thought no, just what counted as normal smacking, but she doesn't really know. I think I should try therapy of some kind when we're back home.'

'I think that's a really good plan, it'll help give you some perspective,' he said warmly. 'Um, Alicia, I was wondering if you'd like to go out for something to eat sometime soon? I'm on call tomorrow night but maybe Friday? We could have a proper chat then.'

Alicia sighed. A proper chat about child abuse over dinner didn't sound very relaxing, but he undoubtedly meant well and of course she would love to go for food or ice cream or whatever with Frank at some point. Just maybe not on Friday.

'Thanks, Frank, and I would like to sometime, but can I take a rain check for the moment? Jenny'll be coming home on Friday evening, and I don't want to plan beyond that until I see how her visit went. Maybe next week sometime?'

'No problem,' he said, though his voice was strained. To her relief he sounded more relaxed when he continued. 'We're friends, we can do things like that anytime. I'll see you at St. Joe's tomorrow, the speech therapist asked me to the meeting too. Derek's bringing angel cake so don't have too much lunch. Oh, and the reason I came by… ' He slid the piece of paper along the coffee table. 'Sonja's email address and mobile number, she forgot to leave it yesterday.'

'Thanks.' Alicia folded the paper and put it into her handbag. She would text Sonja later.

He left soon after, and Alicia waved him off, grinning to herself.

Her social life here was definitely better than in Bedford. When was the last time she'd been asked out to dinner twice on the same day? At least she'd be well-occupied while Jen was away. She shivered. If only it was Friday night and her daughter was safely home for the weekend.

The Stranger

He sat by the open window, watching as the moon shone silver across the dark stripe where sky and wooded hillside met. The delicate perfume of night-scented stock wafted up from the garden, reminding him again of his Helen. Her soft, sweet-smelling skin, her beautiful dark hair. Her eyes, and her mouth. Ripe, full, sensual. Perfect.

How beautiful she had been. But there had been danger, too. The closer he came to sending the first of his new Helens to Paradise the more he remembered the dark side of his own Helen. Old memories prickled in his mind, shocking, wicked memories, and he hated it because he had blanked all that out, he only wanted to remember how wonderful everything had been. Those bad memories always brought him pain, and with the pain came the anger. Rage, white rage. It had happened with Helen too. She had turned into the devil before his eyes, but this time it had been fear as much as anger that had made him act. He hadn't really wanted her to be gone.

He could barely remember the days after her death. His sister had organised the funeral for him, and the whole occasion had washed right over his head. There had been candles in the church, he knew that, he had smelled their thick warm smell and immediately been transported back to Mummy's funeral. That had been a much bigger affair. Dad had been gutted, he'd sobbed through the entire ceremony. The music was wonderful, Beethoven and Bach, and 'All things Bright and Beautiful'.

He'd been dutifully solemn, but the relief that no-one realised what he had done to Mummy was making his soul more lighthearted than it had been for years, he almost felt jubilant. Inside he was laughing at them all, how stupid they were. Of course it was a terrible, tragic thing that Mummy was gone, but his bad feelings about that were locked away now and he was almost able to enjoy the service. The anger had been gone by then, and the love he'd always had for Mummy was different now. Just a pleasant memory.

But now the anger was back and this time it was directed at little Helen, his bad little angel who was going away tomorrow. He wanted to love her but the rage was there too, and he simply couldn't help it. The way she had looked at him, with his own Helen's lovely face, with Helen's eyes, and then told him so calmly that she was going away with another man. Worse than that, she was *pleased* to be going away. It had been a struggle, keeping a pleasant expression on his face.

But he would get her, his bad little angel Helen. It would be alright in the end. She would return home and be pleased to see him, her King, and this time on Saturday evening, she would be right here with him. Then deep in the night when the coast was clear, off to the woods they would go and away she would fly to Paradise.

The moon disappeared behind a bank of cloud, and he rose from his chair to shut the window.

Just two more days to go.

Chapter Fifteen
Thursday, 20th July

Alicia

'This way, please.'

The waitress led the way across the restaurant, and Alicia looked around in pleasure. The decor was exotic, with colourful wooden Wayang Golek puppets hanging along the walls, interspersed with smaller Buddhas on shelves below them. The sound of water bubbling from a fountain just inside the door was competing with the jangly background music, and the waitress was clad in a pink and purple sarong and beaded sandals. It almost felt as though they were in a beach restaurant on a tropical holiday island.

The evening had begun with her twisting right and left in front of the too-small mirror in her bedroom, examining her reflection with some satisfaction. The black dress she'd found in a summer sale in Merton was perfect, and Margaret's jade silk shawl completed the look. Alicia settled it round her shoulders. It made the whole outfit more elegant, more subtle, too. Yes, she was attracted to Doug but she didn't want to look as if she was throwing herself at him.

It would be great to have a decent conversation with Doug at last. Away from St. Joe's and her family, they would have both time and peace to put the world right. He was such an intelligent man, it would be interesting to get his slant on things. Come to think of it, this was only the second date she'd gone on from this house. The first had been the fated cinema outing the night her father had almost scalped her.

Tyres scrunching on gravel had announced Doug's arrival, and Alicia ran downstairs. Her date was standing with one hand raised to ring the bell, and the expression on his face had her heart racing before they even spoke. She had almost forgotten how it felt going on a date like this, but she was remembering now… it was lovely, feeling that she was one of a pair again.

'You look gorgeous,' he said, taking her arm and leading her to the car.

'You're looking pretty smart yourself,' Alicia told him, sitting down carefully when he opened the car door for her. He was, too, she thought. His jacket and trousers were dark grey and unexpectedly old-fashioned, but they seemed to suit him, as did the plain white shirt and grey tie. Tonight was going to do her the world of good. Time for herself at long last.

'It was a pity the speech therapist couldn't suggest anything more for your father,' said Doug as they drove past St. Joe's.

How dedicated he was. But talk about business before pleasure, she didn't want to think about her father at all tonight. Of course, for all Doug knew she was a loving, devoted daughter.

'Well, I suppose there wasn't much chance of improvement after all this time,' she said. 'I was sorry she couldn't tell us how much he understands, though. But never mind, we tried.'

'We did,' said Doug. 'Look, here's the restaurant.'

The waitress seated them in a corner by the window. Oriental screens separated the tables, giving the illusion of privacy, and Alicia smiled at Doug as they opened their menus.

'This is fantastic. If the food's as good as the ambience it'll be wonderful,' she said, looking down the list of starters. 'What do you recommend?'

'Ah,' said Doug. 'Actually, I've never eaten here. In fact I've never eaten Indonesian food at all, but Derek Thorpe said once this was a brilliant place. He was here with someone last Christmas and I think they had one of the meals for two. I'll let you decide!'

Alicia examined the menu. It was fun, trying out a new place like this, and how good it felt to have an appreciative, attractive man sitting opposite her. She ordered a meal for two with a variety of starters and main dishes, and the choice of pineapple fritters or curry ice cream for dessert. Doug looked at her, his expression comical.

'Sushi? Curry ice cream? Maybe we should have just gone for a steak,' he whispered.

'Nonsense,' said Alicia. 'Sushi's really nice and the ice cream will be fun, you'll see.' The wine waiter came and she asked for a glass of Chardonnay and a bottle of mineral water. Doug smiled agreement.

The starters arrived, and Alicia insisted that Doug try everything. He obviously wasn't used to exotic food, which both surprised and amused her. It was appealing, the way he was looking to her for guidance. Up until now she had been the one on the receiving end of his help and advice, and it was good to know that their positions could be reversed in a different situation. It was interesting too that Doug-in-a-restaurant was quite different to what she'd imagined, not confident and knowledgeable at all, more hesitant, almost, and unsure.

'I'm more of a steak and chips bloke,' he said apologetically, when she asked. 'But Derek raved so much about this place I thought it would be fun to try it.'

'And it is, and Derek was right, the food's amazing,' said Alicia. 'Don't worry. I think most men are steak and chips blokes. It's probably your caveman instincts.'

He smiled. 'Your father was enjoying fish and chips when I left him,' he said, lifting a baby spring roll and gazing at her sympathetically. 'Sorry, you must miss having him at home.'

Alicia looked at him soberly. It wasn't exactly dinner table conversation, but this might be as good a time as any for the big confession.

'We didn't get on at all well, when I was young,' she said, blinking back sudden tears. Heavens, she mustn't cry here, in the middle of her sushi. 'I left home the minute I was sixteen. I have very mixed memories of my time here.'

'Then make sure you hang on to the good ones,' said Doug. 'Lose the bad ones, you're better off without them. I see that every day, happy memories make happy old people.'

Alicia sat struggling to control her emotions. She should never have started this. Right here was neither the time nor the place to talk about what her father had or hadn't done to her. She sipped her wine and managed to smile.

'Families, eh? Do you have any relatives nearby?'

He shook his head. 'No. My parents both died years ago and my sister lives abroad now. And I wasn't married long enough to have kids. Lena was gone just a few months after we married.'

'I'm so sorry, it must have been dreadful for you,' said Alicia, regretting her tactless question. Heavens, what kind of a start was this to a romantic evening? Dead spouses were almost as much of a passion-killer as potential child abuse.

'Don't worry. It was a long time ago, and I'm lucky to have a job that's so fulfilling. It helped me through the bad times.' Doug sipped his wine and Alicia was relieved to see that he genuinely wasn't distressed. Of course he'd be used to living with his wife's death now, but how on earth did he cope so well? Even now, thinking about her relationship with Paul could reduce her to tears of frustration and anger, and grief that it had all gone so wrong.

'Tell me about Jenny,' said Doug as the waiter removed their plates. He reached across the table and squeezed Alicia's hand.

She squeezed back, not caring if he saw how attracted she was. How tactful of him. The one 'family' subject that didn't have unfortunate undertones.

'Jenny? She's beautiful, brilliant, wonderful, amazing... need I go on? She brings so much joy to my life, and she's such fun, too. But I'll admit I may be slightly biased.'

But of course having a child alone wasn't everything she'd planned for. A loving, caring, sharing relationship, plus Jenny, that was the dream that had proved impossible. Until now, perhaps.

Doug laughed. 'She sounds just like her mother. We're all enjoying seeing her around at St. Joe's,' he said, raising his glass to her. Swallowing the sudden lump in her throat, Alicia clinked glasses and sat back as the waiters appeared with the main courses.

What was Jen doing now, far away in York with Paul? He had arrived at ten to two, and informed Alicia curtly that he was taking Jenny to the Viking museum that afternoon, and they would go out for a pizza in the evening and on to the cinema. Was Jen enjoying her favourite ham and mushroom pizza with extra cheese? Or were she and Paul in the cinema already? They probably were, and oh, was it a suitable film?

Doug was helping himself to fried rice with obvious enthusiasm. 'Children give you such a lot, don't they?' he said, and Alicia smiled in agreement. There wasn't much she could reply to this, so she concentrated on her food for a moment. It was excellent. Fortunately, Doug didn't seem to be short of things to say.

'Children must enrich your life so much,' he said, still busy with his rice. 'And you know, you'll have enriched Bob's life, too, Alicia. Even if you didn't get on well. I guess it's a sort of two way process between parent and child, a generation kind of thing. We all give and we all get, and you can keep those feelings forever. Working with older people, I get to see this more often than you'd think.' He reached out for more rice.

Alicia stared at him, chewing slowly. Heavens, that was a bit of a heavy load of well-meant nothings... on a supposedly romantic date, too. Was he nervous? Or...

A long-forgotten memory pushed its way to the front of her mind and she blinked in horror. Boyfriends. Desire. Sex. She'd been twenty, going out with Martin. He was studying philosophy and art, which was such a cool thing to be doing and he was an absolute doll, too. They couldn't get enough of each other and for weeks they had spent every free minute in bed. It was ages before she realised that they had absolutely nothing to talk about, no common interests, no shared opinions. And sex alone wasn't enough in the long run, even when you were twenty. Martin the person was a crashing bore, and he had probably thought the same about her, too, if he'd thought at all beyond the next time they slept together.

And now here was Doug, and her body was responding to him in exactly the same way it had to Martin, but Doug was... boring, too. The realisation was both unexpected and appalling.

The spicy food turned tasteless in Alicia's mouth and she laid her fork down. They had been together tonight for over an hour and it didn't matter what they started out talking about, they always ended up back at St. Joe's with the old people. Oh, Doug had asked about Jenny, answered the questions she'd asked, but it really seemed as if his job was the only thing he cared about. It was as if he defined himself by his job. There was no Doug apart from the work Doug. And all at once it just seemed terribly… superficial.

What would happen when, if, she bared her soul and told him about the flashbacks and her fears about what had happened to her young self? Would they still end up talking about some geriatric experience in Ward Two? Look how he'd responded when she told him she hadn't got on with her father. He hadn't even asked why. And what on earth was she supposed to do now?

Alicia took a deep breath and picked up her fork. Okay, try again. Broaden the conversation, give the bloke a chance.

'This is lovely, isn't it?' she said brightly, smiling as well as she could. 'A perfect night out. Did you go to *A Midsummer Night's Dream*? I hear it was great.'

'Yes, I did. We took a busful of patients from Ward Three, and they enjoyed it, though Derek said they'd enjoyed 'The Importance of Being Earnest' last year better. I suppose Shakespeare isn't for everyone.'

Alicia felt a sudden desire to laugh, and then pulled herself together. Doug had even dragged St. Joe's into a conversation about Shakespeare. And now that she was looking out for it, there wasn't any substance, any depth in the man that struck an echoing chord in her. Except the sexual attraction. For a few moments there she'd felt lonely, sitting opposite Doug in the middle of this busy little restaurant. Alone in a crowd. Or was she expecting too much here? Was this just the usual kind of man-woman Mars-Venus kind of thing?

To her relief he didn't seem to notice anything of the turmoil going on in her head. She chatted determinedly all through the remainder of the meal – the curry ice cream was a real talking point – and all the way home in the car. He didn't suggest going to his home, and Alicia decided against inviting him in for coffee. She would have to think hard about what she should do next. The eagerly-anticipated date had taken an unexpected turn in quite the wrong direction. Doug was good-looking, he was dedicated, he was attracted to her and she to him, but that wasn't enough.

'Thanks for a lovely evening, Doug,' she said warmly as the car stopped in the driveway. 'I won't ask you in, I know you have to be at St. Joe's early tomorrow morning.'

'Yes. School night tonight,' he said, smiling across the car at her in the darkness, but her heart didn't beat any faster now. 'I expect I'll see you tomorrow on the ward, then. Goodnight, Alicia. Sleep well.'

She stood in the doorway and waved as he drove off, then let herself in and collapsed on the sofa, not knowing whether to laugh or cry. Fortunately Margaret had gone to bed and Alicia, Conker and Moritz had the room to themselves. Oh, well, she consoled herself, it was a lovely meal, and you're not the first woman to think that an attractive, articulate man was automatically interesting too. Doug was… well, what was he?

He was someone she was attracted to, physically, but wasn't on the same wavelength as, emotionally. That was it exactly. The physical intimacy would probably be effortless, but she had to be able to talk to her partner too, share her feelings and know that he would understand what she was saying.

Like Frank last night. He had talked about real, personal issues, he had reacted straightaway to what she said and how she sounded, in fact he always did. Why hadn't she leapt at the chance to go out with him? Was she really superficial enough to favour an attractive man over a less good-looking one? Frank was a real, caring friend to her.

Did she care for him, she wondered suddenly. She did, she liked him a lot, he was part of her past, too, but they had never had the opportunity to have a proper personal conversation. They were either always talking about her father, or flashbacks and abuse, or else Jenny was there too.

And what about him? Did his caring extend to a wish for more than friendship? Was that why he'd been so awkward those couple of times? He was a shy man but he had asked her out, he had tried to build on their relationship, and she had put him off. What an idiot she was. It had taken a date with Doug to open her eyes to what she already had with Frank.

She leaned back on the sofa and closed her eyes. Frank *was* her friend, he had said that himself yesterday. They could go for a meal next week sometime and have a good talk. And with Frank she could be sure that they *would* talk.

But in less than an hour it would be Friday, and this time tomorrow Jenny would be fast asleep in bed upstairs, home safe and sound for the weekend. And it was high time she was in bed now too.

Chapter Sixteen
Friday, 21st July

Alicia

'Have a caramel, Alicia dear,' said Mrs Mullen, and Alicia accepted in amusement. Mrs Mullen must be single-handedly responsible for at least half of the tooth decay in Lower Banford. Nobody ever said no to a sweetie.

'Take one for Jenny, too, she'll be home today, won't she?'

Alicia nodded, chewing. Who on earth had supplied that information? The sound of choking behind her made her turn to see Kenneth Taylor spluttering into a large old-fashioned handkerchief.

'Excuse me,' he said, stuffing the hanky into his pocket. 'Frog in my throat. Would Jenny like to come and see the cats later on, Mrs Bryson?'

Alicia made herself reply pleasantly. 'She won't be home until late this evening,' she said. 'I'm sure she'll want to come tomorrow, though.'

'Super. I'm going to be stocktaking over the weekend, but just ring the bell. You and Jenny are always welcome.'

Alicia made her escape. Now to take Margaret to St. Joe's for the afternoon, then she would have some time to herself.

Half an hour later she was exiting her father's room having sat for the duty five minutes with him and Margaret. Three o'clock, and now at last she could allow herself to start counting the minutes until Jen came back – as if she hadn't been doing that since Paul's car had disappeared down the lane yesterday afternoon, but the wait was nearly over. A blessed hour to herself, then she'd pick up Margaret, and by the time they'd had dinner and cleared up, Jen would be heading back home again. A happy thought if ever there was one.

'Heard from Jenny today?' Derek was on the computer at the nurses' station.

'She phoned earlier,' said Alicia. 'Treats all the way, I gather.'

She tried to smile but her face must have told a different story because he left his work and walked towards the ward door with her.

'She'll be fine, don't worry. I'm sure she's looking forward to coming home and telling you all about her trip, and playing with her cat and dog in the woods too no doubt. She told us all about that the other day.'

Alicia grinned. The woods were one of the better things about this place. She even had her own happy memories of them.

'She loves the woods. I'm glad she has such a good distraction so near to home, she's within yelling distance all the time and God knows there isn't much else for her to do in Lower Banford.'

Except of course to visit the pet shop and Mr Taylor. There would be a big discussion about that tomorrow, but Alicia knew she would be so happy to see Jen home again that she would sit in the pet shop for hours if that was what Jen wanted.

'Say hi for me when she's home,' said Derek, opening the heavy double door for her. 'I might not see you tomorrow, I've got masses of paperwork and at weekends I can hole up in one of the offices downstairs for that. Ensures some peace and quiet.'

'I hope you get it, then. Bye.'

She ran downstairs, glad that Doug wasn't around today. Yesterday she'd have been aching to see him, how quickly things changed. And where the hell was her car key?

She stopped on the ground floor and was rummaging in her bag – she couldn't have dropped the wretched thing, could she? – when the lift door pinged open and Frank strode out, almost bumping into her.

'Alicia! Hi, you okay?'

His face was one big grin at the sight of her and she smiled back. This was her friend Frank and she was bloody glad she had him.

'Lost my car key,' she said, giving up on the bag and patting her various pockets. 'I went up with Margaret, and it's vanished off the face of the earth… '

She turned back to the lift, but it had disappeared upstairs. 'I must have put it down somewhere. Usually I just chuck it into my bag, but it's definitely not here.'

'Maybe you left it in the ignition?' he suggested, and she stared at him. The obvious answer, why hadn't she thought of that?

'Yes, of course. It was a pretty narrow space and I jumped out to stop Margaret opening her door too wide and bashing the car beside us. Heavens, my poor car could be halfway to Poland by this time.'

Frank laughed. 'Middle Banford to Poland in one afternoon? I don't think St. Joe's visitors are the car-trafficking types, somehow.' He opened the front door and gazed out over the car park. 'Yes, look, it's still there.'

He walked with her to the parking space. Alicia opened the driver's door, reached in and emerged again, key in hand.

'Excellent diagnosis, doctor!' she said. And how obvious it now was that she and Frank could have fun together like this, laughing and being silly over nothing, like up in the woods the other day.

She grinned across the roof of the car. 'Got time for a coffee? I bought some chocolate chip cookies this morning.'

For a split second his face froze and then lit up. 'I've never refused a chocolate chip cookie in all my life and I'm not going to start now.'

Alicia laughed. 'Great. See you at my place in ten.' And maybe this time they'd be able to have a normal conversation for a change. She sighed to herself as she drove the short distance back home. There were no butterflies of anticipation fluttering round in her middle at the thought of coffee with Frank, but she definitely wanted him in her life, and probably it was too soon after the Doug disaster to think about yet another potential relationship. So yes… it was another potential relationship… maybe.

He arrived in the kitchen while she was organising mugs and biscuits. The cookies were still unopened and Alicia looked at them unhappily.

'Biscuits last longer when Jen's not around. God, I'll be glad to have her back tonight.'

'I bet,' said Frank. 'How's she enjoying her break?'

'She phoned at lunchtime. I'm going to have to prise that mobile away from her, she just loves having her own phone. She's having a ball, it was Daddy this, that and the next thing. But she's okay.'

'She'll be back soon,' said Frank.

Alicia blinked back tears. She poured the coffee and sat down, sliding the biscuits across to Frank. 'When I think of how much I love Jen, it makes it even more incomprehensible what my father did to me.'

'Have you remembered anything else?' said Frank.

Alicia was silent for a moment. His voice had been apprehensive; did he really want to go into all this over coffee? She should make an appointment and see someone the usual way, this was abusing their friendship and she'd actually invited him here to talk more about him for a change. But he was leaning towards her, an encouraging expression on his face, so he must want to know, mustn't he?

She sighed. 'Sort of. I was awake in the night thinking about the two big fights I can remember when I was a teenager,' she said, cradling her coffee mug in her hands. 'The first one I would've been twelve, that was the Valentine's card thing. I only remembered about it when I was back living here. But that time he didn't hurt me. The second time was later. I was fourteen, I know that exactly, and it isn't a new memory. I've never forgotten it, it was what made me decide to leave home as soon as I could.'

She looked across at him and smiled ruefully. 'It was my own fault, I was really stupid.'

'Alicia, abuse is never the victim's fault,' Frank said firmly, and she looked at him without speaking for a moment. She knew that of course, but knowing didn't make her feel any different.

'Yeah, well. I'd told them I was revising geography at Alison's, but actually I'd gone to the cinema with Patrick Sinclair. They found out and when I got home, Mum was in the kitchen with the door shut and my father was waiting by the stairs. He pulled me up to my room and pinned me down on the floor and he cut my hair off. I was yelling but Mum didn't come, though she must have known what he was going to do… '

Frank was staring at her. 'Alicia. That's terrible. What do you mean exactly, he pinned you down?'

She rubbed her face with both hands. 'He pushed me down on my front and then he sort of knelt down with one leg across my back. I couldn't move, it was horrible, I was jerking about at first and then he nearly cut my ear off so I just had to stay still and let him get on with it. I had long hair, and he cut it off down to an inch of my scalp.'

She buried her face in her hands. For a moment Frank said nothing, she could hear him breathing hard, then he gripped her wrists so suddenly that she jumped.

'Okay. Listen. One thing that strikes me about these memories and flashbacks is that none of them are sexual abuse. Your father was sadistic, yes, cruel, definitely, and his treatment of you was damaging, there's no doubt about that. But sexual abuse is usually continued until the victim's able to remove herself, or is rescued. None of the abuse you do remember is actually sexual, so you can probably discount it... but Alicia, you might never know for sure. The important thing is you survived.'

His voice trailed off, and Alicia sat back in the hard kitchen chair and looked at him. What he'd said sounded logical, it sounded right.

'Okay. So, that might be something then. But when he was cutting my hair, he was enjoying hurting me, humiliating me. I could hear the pleasure in his voice.' She jumped up and tore a piece of kitchen paper from the roll. 'And I can feel there's still something more, but I don't know what it is, except I was much, much younger.'

'Don't think about it,' said Frank quickly. 'You'll drive it underground if you do. He was a brute and a bully, Alicia. And you were a strong kid and you're still strong, you'll get through this. Leave it for now, we'll see what Cathal can remember if Sonja finds him.'

'Right,' said Alicia. She stared at him for a moment. His face was pale, and there was a rigid set to his mouth that wasn't usually there. Suddenly she felt, well not better, exactly, but definitely relieved. She had unburdened herself to a friend and he had reassured her. Painful, but not something she'd have to do often. Maybe just talking about it, accepting it like Frank had said, was enough. And now she should do something to lighten the load she had placed on his shoulders.

'You know,' she said, sitting down again and wrapping cold hands round her lukewarm mug, 'I think I prefer our conversations when we're talking about stolen cars or diets.'

He made a face at her. 'So do I. I don't like to think of you being so unhappy.'

She smiled determinedly. 'Well, like you said, I survived, didn't I? Like you did when Nell died.'

'Sonja's been telling you I was a real mess back then, hasn't she?' he said, and Alicia nodded. 'Well, she was right. It was just so sudden, Alicia, she got up that day as usual and we did all the normal Saturday morning stuff and by dinnertime she was dead and I really don't remember too much about the next few days. It was horrible. But it's in the past. You don't grieve forever, though you do remember, of course.'

Alicia reached out and squeezed his hand. 'And because you remember, Nell's still with you inside.'

He smiled, and she could see there were tears in his eyes. Sonja definitely had nothing to worry about.

'Yup,' he said. 'Anyway, I'll let you get on, you'll have things to do before Jenny comes home.'

Alicia glanced at the clock and shot to her feet. 'Look at the time, I was supposed to pick Margaret up ten minutes ago. Frank, thanks. You're a star.' She grabbed her car key and bag, and he followed her out to the driveway.

'You'll get through this,' he said gently.

Alicia nodded. He was right. As usual. 'I know I will. In the grand scheme of things it's not important, is it? The important things are Jenny, and Margaret and her family – and my friends – like you. And none of you are going anywhere, are you?'

He stared again, then grinned without speaking, got into his car and turned the key in the ignition. Alicia watched as he turned into the lane.

She drove back to Middle Banford feeling charged. She was coping, she was a survivor. Okay, if she hadn't come back to stay in her father's house she might have lived the rest of her life in blissful ignorance about what had happened. But she would move on. And she would start the moving on by phoning Margaret when she arrived in St. Joe's car park. No way was she going back into her father's room today.

Very soon now Jenny would be home, and tomorrow she would phone Frank and ask him out to dinner and they would talk like normal people. Definitely. And she would enjoy every minute of it, wouldn't she? Of course she would.

Chapter Seventeen
Saturday, 22nd July, morning

The Stranger

The strident ring of the alarm clock blared across his bedroom, but he was awake and dressed already. It was Saturday.

His day had come. This was his hour. He was completely focussed, in fact he had never felt so calm. Plan B. And thank goodness, the weather was being cooperative; exactly as forecast, warm July sunshine was splitting the skies. A positive omen if ever he'd seen one.

He looked at the letter in his hand and smiled. How happy little Helen would be when she saw it! The very beginning of Plan B was the part he had least control over, and that was little Helen going to the woods. But they had made their arrangements and it would be terrible luck if big Helen stopped her going for some reason. There was no reason why that should happen, was there?

The idea of leaving her a note had come to him the previous evening, and he'd written a very brief one as he was unsure how much she could read. He would place it under a pretty stone, on one of the white napkins he never used, in the very centre of the ring of trees. It was exactly where he planned to send her to Paradise tonight, but of course she had no idea of that. He knew just what to write to intrigue her. 'Queen Titania, wait here until I come. I've got some baby kittens, and a *big* surprise for you! King Oberon.'

The bit about the kittens wasn't true, of course, but again, she wouldn't know that. Her sweet little face would light up like the sun when she saw a note from the fairy King himself. He chuckled as he strode towards his car.

How fitting it was that Plan B would begin in the very same place as it would end for little Helen. The Paradise trees.

Alicia

The whole house seemed brighter now that Jenny was back, fast asleep in her room with Conker on the floor by her bed. Alicia took a sliced loaf from the freezer to make toast. Margaret was in the shower, so she would get breakfast ready. Breakfast for her daughter. Lovely.

Paul had been very punctual, she had to admit. He and Jenny had arrived well before Alicia's nine o'clock deadline, and Jenny had hugged her father fondly before rushing inside to see Conker and Moritz.

'Back safe and sound, and in good time too,' he said, smiling sarcastically. 'And we both had a blast, so there's no reason not to repeat the experiment. I'll be in touch.'

Alicia managed a return smile and a brief 'thanks', but she knew the expression in her eyes would be telling him a different story. However, for the moment everything was back to normal. And Jenny had certainly enjoyed the two days with Paul. They had spent their time in museums and shops, as the weather hadn't been brilliant, and the little girl bubbled over talking about her experiences. Daddy had bought her two pink t-shirts and a Minnie Mouse watch, and the food had been wonderful too, they'd had pizza, and hamburgers, and fish and chips with a giant pickled onion.

Alicia opened a packet of bacon and glanced out over the garden. How peaceful it was here. Birdsong and fluffy white clouds, and with Jen back and her father away she could begin to enjoy herself. It was actually a really good feeling. She had achieved all she'd set out to do when she came here, and more. Her father was safe in a very good place, Margaret was realising that it was for the best, and Jenny was loving having a cat and a dog and had resumed contact with Paul, although that was a bit of a mixed blessing. And herself? Well, she wasn't proud of the way her father had landed in St. Joe's, but no harm had come of the episode. She had re-established contact with the Carters, and she had even been dating, even if that had turned out a bit complicated.

Most important of all she was coming to terms with what had happened to her as a child. Frank was right, she *was* going to get through this. She was a strong person and she had people here to help her.

Her mobile buzzed in the living room, and Alicia hurried to answer it as the clicking of claws on the wooden floorboards upstairs told her that Jen and Conker were up.

It was Frank. 'Hi Alicia. Just wanted to check you're okay after our talk yesterday, and that Jenny got home alright?'

'We're both fine, thanks. Jen loved her trip but I'm glad to have her back under the same roof. Um, Frank, how about that dinner? My treat. Are you free tomorrow night?'

There was a fraction of a second's pause, then she heard the nervous pleasure in his voice.

'Perfect,' he said. 'There's a great Italian's in Upper Banford.'

'Sounds good. I'll drive, shall I? Pick you up at seven?'

Alicia stood grilling bacon, aware that she was looking forward to dinner with Frank almost as eagerly as she'd anticipated dinner with Doug. This time she'd make very sure she got the chance to repay some of his kindness over the past couple of weeks. She would forget all about romance and prospective relationships and just be a friend.

'Mummy! What's for breakfast?'

Jenny was skipping up the hallway, her face shining and Moritz under one arm. Alicia laughed aloud. Let the weekend begin.

The Stranger

The sun was shining through the trees and spreading dappled shadows as he drove along the narrow country road to Middle Banford. The letter was waiting in the middle of the clearing, little Helen couldn't fail to see it. Now for the old man.

St. Joe's was still getting organised for the new day when he slid in a side door. There were always a couple of white coats on a stand outside the offices on the ground floor, and he shrugged into one. Really, the weekend was by far the best time for his plan. With no secretaries around the ground floor was deserted, and at this time in the morning there wouldn't be any visitors upstairs either. Sure enough, he arrived at the ward door without seeing another soul.

Getting to the old man unseen was the tricky bit, but luck was on his side. The only nurses in sight were right at the other end of the ward, clearing away breakfasts, going in and out of the rooms. He waited until no-one was in the corridor and then strode along and into Bob Logan's room. The old man was up, slumped on a chair with his cloth cap clutched to his chest; his roommate snoring away fully dressed on top of his bed. What a hellish place this was, he was doing the poor old chap a favour here. What must it be like, to end up like this? Swiftly, he produced the syringe he had filled with a sleeping drug and squirted it into Bob Logan's mouth, then held the rubbery lips closed until he swallowed. The old man hardly moved a muscle, he hadn't even realised that anything had happened.

He paused in the doorway, peering down the ward until the nurses were all in the rooms again before darting back to the stairwell. Down, down, and away. It was time for little Helen.

Alicia

Jenny licked her spoon after the last mouthful of Coco-pops had disappeared and beamed across the table at Alicia and Margaret.

'*That's* better,' she said deeply. 'They only had cornflakes and muesli at Daddy's hotel yesterday morning. And yoghurt and croissants and jam and honey and eggs and stuff. And I had pineapple juice, Mummy, it was lovely. Can we get it here too?'

Alicia's heart contracted with love. Right now she'd have bought Jenny the entire contents of the village shop, it was just so wonderful to have her back again.

'We'll look. We'll find some in Merton, if Mrs Mullen hasn't got any.'

'Yum. Can I go up to the woods with Conker?'

'Teeth first,' said Alicia, gathering the breakfast plates together. 'I'll make you a little picnic. I've got housework and washing to do first this morning, but we could go to Mr Taylor's for half an hour before lunch, if you like. And how about spag bol for tea tonight?'

'Woohoo!' Jenny dashed off upstairs, Conker in tow as usual. He hadn't let Jen out of his sight since she'd returned, thought Alicia, amused.

'Pineapple juice is expensive and sweet,' said Margaret disapprovingly, pouring herself more coffee. 'Orange juice is better for children.'

Alicia grinned at her aunt. 'I know, I know, but let me spoil her today, Margaret.'

Whistling, she spread a roll with the crunchy peanut butter Jenny loved and put it in a bag with an apple. Jen knew that Conker looked forward to his apple cores so it was an excellent way to encourage her daughter to eat the rest of the apple. Alicia grinned to herself. Being a Mum was fun, even with all the problems attached.

Jenny danced into the kitchen for her picnic, and raced up the garden towards the woods, Conker dashing ahead. Alicia looked at Margaret and they both laughed. You'd think the child had been away for a fortnight and was expecting major changes in her palace. What a cutie she was. Right. Now, before she got caught up in the fascinating ritual of changing the beds, she would just text Sonja.

'All fine here, Frank good too, how's St A's?' she keyed in.

The reply appeared within minutes: 'V. golfy, freezing, might have found C, will call tonight.' Alicia grinned. Her friend had never been the sporty kind.

She and Margaret did the beds and then began to sort through her father's clothes. It wasn't much of a fun job, thought Alicia dismally. She was emptying the washing machine when the phone rang. Margaret answered it, speaking briefly before appearing in the kitchen doorway.

'It's Douglas Patton,' she said, looking anxiously at Alicia. 'He wants to talk to you.'

Alicia stared. Was Doug going to ask her out again, so soon? Or no, of course not, how stupid she was – how conceited, too – he would be at work so this was a lot more likely to be about her father. She hurried down the hallway to the phone and grabbed the receiver.

'Doug? Is everything alright?' she said, surprised to hear how steady her voice sounded. Inside, she felt more than a little shaky. Had her carelessness last weekend affected her father after all?

'Alicia, hi. It's nothing very serious as far as we know at the moment, but Bob is very drowsy and unresponsive today,' he said.

'Should we come in?' she asked, gripping the receiver with a suddenly cold hand.

'I think that would be best,' he said, his voice warm in her ear. 'He's in no immediate danger, so don't rush. See you soon.'

Alicia slammed the phone down and turned to Margaret, who was clutching a tea towel to her chest, her face pale.

'He said it's probably nothing much, but Bob's a bit drowsy today,' said Alicia gently, rubbing Margaret's thin shoulders. 'I said we'd go in and see him now, so you get your jacket and we'll be off. I'll just give Jen a shout.'

Margaret scuttled off upstairs without a word, and Alicia stood at the back door and yelled for Jenny. Of course there was no answer. She shouted again, then pulled out her phone and rang Jenny's mobile, gritting her teeth when she heard the answering ring tone waft down from upstairs. Well, of course, the mobile was for emergencies only, she had said so herself.

She jogged down to the summerhouse and yelled again, with the same result. Nothing in this life was ever simple, she thought, turning back to the house. Jenny could be anywhere up there, and she wasn't expecting Alicia to call yet. It was only half past ten. Margaret was waiting by the door, and Alicia made a snap decision.

'Jen's not answering. I'll leave a note on the table, and I'll come back for her as soon as we've seen how Bob is,' she said, lifting the pad they used for shopping lists. 'She can phone my mobile if she comes home before that, but she probably won't. Try not to worry, Margaret, Doug said it was nothing dangerous.'

As far as we know, he had said. That didn't mean anything. Had they called Frank in? And why was she feeling so shaky about this? Her father didn't love her and she didn't love him. She pressed her lips together as she reversed into the lane.

Maybe her shakiness was because everything was suddenly different, because sitting at the back of her mind was now the thought that her father might die soon after all? And if his death was connected to his misadventure last weekend, then it would still be her fault. Of course she could be reading way too much into this, it might be something quite minor, a bit of a cold or such like.

Margaret was hunched in the passenger seat clutching her handbag with thin, trembling fingers, suddenly looking much older than her years. Her father looked much older too, but that was down to his illness. Alicia reached across and squeezed her aunt's hand.

Doug was standing in the doorway when they arrived at the ward, and Alicia hurried towards him, Margaret hanging onto her arm. Hell, this was awkward, she hadn't spoken to him since their date on Thursday. But he was a professional, he wouldn't mix his private life with his work.

'It's alright, he's stable,' he said immediately, and Alicia heard Margaret's deep sigh of relief.

'Come in and sit with him,' said Doug, moving two chairs to the bedside. Alicia bent over her father. He was breathing loudly but regularly, and he looked as if he was merely sleeping.

'What happened?' she asked, letting Margaret sit on the chair nearest the head of the bed.

Doug shook his head. 'For some reason he became very drowsy after breakfast. The nurses thought he just hadn't slept well, but they found him unresponsive in his chair a little while ago. I think it might be a reaction to his sleeping meds. Try not to worry, Alicia. His vital signs are okay, but Frank Carter's on his way in to see him anyway. Your father's a strong person, he'll get through this, I'm sure.'

His voice jarred inside Alicia's head and her gut twisted. She had been right on Thursday evening. Doug's words were superficial, impersonal nothing-phrases, things he could say to anyone at all. He would use them in his work, those phrases, they would comfort a lot of people, but now, with her, it was like a slap in the face... And she had *kissed* this man... How stupid she had been to think there had been any chance of building a relationship with him.

Alicia watched as Margaret stroked the old man's face, and realised that in less than a week his face had become fuller, healthier looking. They couldn't have been feeding him enough at home. It didn't look as if there was much wrong. But if not today, he was going to die one day soon. Margaret would be so sad, and Jenny would be too, the carefully-nurtured picture of Grandpa in an ideal world would be gone. And shit, she should get back to Lower Banford right now and organise something for Jen. Maybe Eva Campbell could take her for a few hours.

Doug's phone rang, and he left the room to answer it, passing Derek and Frank in the doorway. Alicia closed her eyes in relief. Frank would know what to do, and he would tell her exactly what was going on.

Frank smiled briefly as he strode into the room. 'Alicia, Margaret,' he said, taking out his stethoscope. 'We'll have a look at Bob now. Do you want to take Margaret to the relatives' room, Alicia? I'll come and get you in a few minutes.'

Alicia led Margaret along the corridor to the relatives' room, which was furnished with uncomfortable wooden chairs and a vending machine. Glumly, she searched through her purse for change and supplied them both with thin plastic cups of coffee. Margaret sipped hers and made a face at Alicia.

'Institutional dishwater,' she said, and Alicia smiled faintly. Her aunt had got over the shock, thank goodness.

'Not the best cup I've ever had, that's for sure,' she said, checking that her mobile was on. It was, but it might be another half hour before Jenny went back home, longer if the little monkey decided to stay in the woods until Alicia shouted for her, which was what usually happened. As soon as Frank told them what was going on she would get back and ask a neighbour to look after Jen for a bit.

She sat there, sipping her coffee and staring vacantly out of the window. This room faced the same way as Doug's office downstairs. Two swans were swimming across the pond, accompanied by the little troupe of ducks. Weren't swans supposed to bring bad luck? Or was that magpies? She couldn't remember.

It was horrible, being away from her daughter like this. Again. Alicia took a deep breath and consciously tried to relax. Jen'll be fine, she won't even have noticed that she'd been deserted, she told herself. What the hell was Frank doing all this time?

This was the room where they broke the news that someone has died. Maybe she would sit here with Margaret one day quite soon, and Frank or another doctor would come in and say, 'I'm very sorry, but...'

Or maybe she would sit by her father's bed with Margaret and watch him die, listen to him breathing, waiting and wondering which breath would be the last. Life was hard, sometimes. Dear God. Surely Frank wouldn't be much longer?

It was several minutes before he came in though, and the quick smile he gave her told her almost all she needed to know. He looked a bit hot under the collar and his shirt had a distinctly slept-in appearance about it. Had he been up half the night?

'I still can't tell you exactly what's going on,' he said, sitting down beside Margaret. 'But it's nothing neurological, it's not his heart, and his breathing is perfectly adequate at the moment. I've sent blood to get tested but we won't have the results for a bit. If I didn't know better I'd say he's been hoarding his sleeping pills and then took about three after breakfast, but that's not possible. The nurses always watch until the patients swallow their medication, and Derek gave him the pill himself last night. We'll know more when the blood tests come back. You can go and sit with him again, they're just moving him into a single room because his roommate always has masses of visitors at the weekend.'

'I'll go back in, then. Thank you, Frank,' said Margaret, going to the door. Alicia hesitated, waiting until her aunt was well out of the room.

'Do you think he'll recover from this?' she said bluntly, and he made a helpless gesture with his hands.

'I'll be honest with you, Alicia, I don't know. I wish we knew the reason for this change in his conscious level. And no matter what the reason is, it's not good for old people to lie around semi-conscious. But at the moment we can still hope it's temporary. Where's Jenny this morning?'

'In the woods,' said Alicia, anxiety twisting her gut into a tight ball again. 'She went off before Doug phoned, and I couldn't get her back. I left a note on the table, but she hasn't phoned yet.' She fished in her bag for her mobile. Still nothing. It was after eleven, Jen should have been back by this time. They were supposed to have been visiting Kenneth and his kittens, that was important, Jen wouldn't have forgotten that. Where *was* she?

Frank looked at her, and she could feel his concern. There was nothing superficial about Frank.

He took her arm and led her back to her father's new room. 'Say goodbye to Margaret, then go home and get Jenny organised,' he said. 'She'll be busy playing with Conker, don't worry. Kids have no sense of time. When you've sorted her out you'll feel better able to cope with things here. Call me if there's any problem.'

Alicia nodded. She gave Margaret a quick hug, barely registering the guttural breathing from the bed, and left, waving to Frank and Laura, the staff nurse, as she passed. Where was Jenny? Still in the woods, like Frank said, having lost all sense of time? It was quite possible. Or maybe she had tried to phone and hadn't managed for some reason. What would she do then? Jen was a sensible little soul, she would go to a neighbour and get help. No, the most likely thing was that her daughter *had* forgotten the time, in spite of her new watch, and was still playing in the woods.

The Stranger

It had worked like a dream. He simply couldn't have planned it better. The timing had been perfect, and right this minute little Helen was out for the count on his sofa, waiting for him to return home to play with her. It was almost too good to be true. He'd been so clever.

He'd arrived at the clearing after dealing with the old man and there she was, sitting on the fallen tree trunk, throwing sticks for that wretched dog. He'd decided what to do about that, though, so it wasn't a problem.

'Good morning to you, Queen Titania!' he said, putting on his friendliest face and bowing as low as he could.

She smiled up at him, a great big beaming happy-to-see-him smile, and he'd known then that his plan would succeed. This was more like the kind of behaviour he expected from his fairy Queen.

'King Oberon! You're here!'

'At your service, ma'am,' he said. 'And am I right that your Majesty would like to see my new little kittens?'

'Oh yes!' she said with that wonderful, innocent smile again. 'Where are they? What colours are they?'

A picture of Snugglepuss sprang into his mind.

'All pure white, ma'am. They're at my house. Would you like to come and see them now? We'd be back in less than half an hour.'

She looked at the watch on her wrist, where Minnie Mouse was pointing out that it was twenty past nine.

'Oh yes,' she said readily. 'I can stay out for another hour, I should think. Mummy'll call me when I have to go home.'

He led her round to the other side of the wood where he'd left his car and ushered her and the dog into the back seat. Now came another tricky part, he had to drive across the main road without being seen. Good job his car windows were tinted, it gave him just that bit more protection. Fortunately too Lower Banford wasn't big on CCTV, with all the driving back and forth he was doing today it was indeed lucky that there wasn't a camera attached to every second building like they had in Merton. The village street was deserted, and he drove over the dangerous crossing unseen. In his driveway he relaxed. He had made it.

'I think we'll leave our trusty servant Puck in the car,' he said, turning and smiling his most regal smile at her. 'My poor baby kittens might not like him very much.'

'Okay,' she said. 'Aunt Margaret always says he wouldn't hurt a fly. But we won't be here very long so he'll be fine on the back seat. I'll see you in five minutes, Conker. I mean Puck.'

He smiled when she said that. Little minx. She was well aware that she was doing something forbidden, even though she thought she knew enough about him to trust him. And what a good thing it was that she did trust him. They were going to have such a beautiful time together, just the two of them. Him and little Helen, it was beginning. Sweat trickled down his back.

He locked the dog in the car, using the tow rope from the boot to secure it to the back headrest, in case it 'tried to climb into the front and hurt himself'. Little Helen was quite happy with this arrangement and he led her inside, a positive wave of relief crashing through him when he closed the door behind them. Success. She was here, and nothing would stop him now.

He'd pulled the heavy velvet curtains across most of the window so the living room was in semi-darkness, and little Helen looked round, straining to see the kittens.

'Where are they? I can't see them,' she said.

'They're in the other room,' he told her. 'You sit down on the sofa and I'll bring their box in to you. And I'm sure you'd like something to drink too, while you're here.'

In the kitchen, he poured a small slosh of orange juice into the powerful sedative he'd prepared earlier and stirred the mixture. When he went back to the living room she jumped to her feet.

'Shhh, nice and quiet,' he said. 'The kitties are still asleep, so you have your juice first and then I'll bring them in. Here you are.'

He could see that she was uneasy now about being here. Did she sense that something wasn't quite right, or was she merely starting to feel guilty about going away without telling her mother? It didn't matter, of course. She was here, and she was going nowhere. Yet.

As soon as she raised the glass to her lips, he acted. It was child's play to hold her head in his left arm and force the bitter liquid into her mouth with his right. She struggled, but he held on, waiting until she swallowed the dose. And oh, how sweet she was and how afraid.

'It's quite alright, darling. Just some extra vitamins,' he said softly. 'You sit down and have a piece of chocolate while I fetch the kitties.'

She stumbled backwards, trying to get away from him, and fell over the coffee table, a high-pitched whimper coming from her throat. Smiling gently he lifted her to her feet and pushed her down on the sofa where she cowered into the corner, sheer horror in her eyes now. He stood in front of her, taking his time unwrapping a bar of white chocolate. He would just pop a tiny piece in her mouth, he didn't want her to choke. Her eyes, oh, this was so delicious, the sedative was working already and she was terrified, her eyes were wild and her whole body was shaking, but there was nothing she could do to resist him. Which was exactly as it should be, of course. He pulled the elastic bands from her pigtails and loosened her hair around her face and she made no move to stop him. There, that was much better. He stood and watched as she slumped into the sofa cushions, a glazed expression replacing the terror. He knelt in front of her and cupped her face with his hands.

'The kitties are still fast asleep, little Helen,' he whispered. 'They're so tired, and you're tired too, aren't you? You can have a nice little sleep, and when I get back we'll have a lovely game of Paradise.'

She didn't respond, and he pulled her down until she was lying flat. Her eyes were closed, and he stroked the hair back from her face, then ran his hands over her arms, over her flat little tummy and those long, sun-browned legs. She was nice and straight now, lying there like the beautiful princess she was. He knew she'd be right out of it for hours, there would be plenty of time for him to do everything that had to be done.

Whistling, he lifted the cord he had bought and tied her hands and feet firmly before covering her with the golden throw. His Queen. He had her here at last, and nothing must be allowed to go wrong.

A last look, a last touch, and he'd left her there to wait. He had to make sure that Plan B was still trundling along. But it would be, and oh, the anticipation of what was to come with little Helen…

Alicia

Alicia drove home as fast as she dared, feeling the car slide as she braked on the sparse gravel in front of the house. She had left both doors unlocked for Jen, but as soon as she stepped into the hallway she knew that no-one else was here. The house was deathly quiet. Then a scraping sound came from the kitchen, and she wrenched the door open. It was Moritz, chasing his ping pong balls around the tiled floor. And there on the kitchen table was the note, exactly as she'd left it. Alicia scooped the kitten up and ran outside.

'Je - enny! Jenny! Home time!' Her voice echoed round the garden. Jen must be expecting a call by now, surely she would hear a yell like that and come running up the garden.

But there was no answering shout, no sound at all from the woods. Coldness crept round Alicia's heart as the trees remained silent, stretching mutely in front of her, seemingly unending. She stood by the summerhouse, anxiety tightening in her gut.

'Je - enny! Con - ker!'

An even louder shout, and the same result. Alicia bit her lip. What should she do? Jenny could be anywhere up there.

The phone rang, making her jump, and she raced back inside. A smarmy voice inquired if she already had double glazing, and Alicia slammed the receiver down before lifting it again. She should call the neighbours in case Jen had gone there. Margaret's address book was beside the phone and Alicia fumbled for the numbers. Neither the Campbells nor the Watsons were at home, and none of the Donovans had seen Jenny that day. Tears in her eyes, Alicia went back to the kitchen, clasping and unclasping her hands.

Moritz seemed to sense that all was not well, and wound himself round her ankles as she stood in the kitchen. On a sudden impulse Alicia phoned Jenny's mobile again, but no, there it was still ringing upstairs. Then, in the distance, the church clock struck twelve.

Four chimes rang across the village, followed by twelve deep single notes. Right. She would go down to the very bottom of the garden where the woods began and shout again. Jenny *must* be able to hear that. She shut the kitchen door on Moritz's indignant little face and jogged down the overgrown garden.

'Je - enny! *Con - ker!*'

Three times she shouted, and three times the only reply was silence. No call from Jen, no deep growly bark. Nauseating dizziness gripped Alicia. If Jenny was up there she would, yes she *would* have heard her mother yelling like that. So where was she? Lying hurt somewhere? Had she fallen and banged her head? Or had she gone home, realised she'd been deserted and tried to walk to St. Joe's? Shit, shit, the river pathway…

Alicia stumbled back to the house and grabbed her mobile. She needed help with this now. Doug? No. The police? No, Frank first.

'Alicia?' His voice crackled distantly in her ear. Sobbing, she told him what had happened.

'Okay. Listen. I'll get hold of Andy and John Sykes and we'll search the woods. We'll find her, don't worry, she must be there.'

'Frank, do you think, could she have tried to get to St. Joe's by herself? Our neighbours are out… Jen knows you can walk to Middle Banford along the river pathway, suppose she tried that and fell in at the weir?'

His voice was doubtful. 'She wouldn't try to walk it, would she? She'll still be up there. We'll find her, Alicia. I'll be with you in five minutes.'

He rang off, and Alicia paced up and down the kitchen. Maybe Jenny *was* still in the woods - maybe she was pretending not to have heard all that shouting. Although that was unlikely given that they were supposed to be visiting Kenneth Taylor and his wretched kittens and… had Jen gone to the pet shop by herself? Maybe she'd come home, seen the note and decided to carry on without her mother. It wasn't quite impossible.

Her panic abating slightly, Alicia grabbed the phone book and rustled through the thin pages. Naturally, the pet shop wasn't listed yet. Directory enquiries?

The sound of Frank's car pulling up outside had her running to the front door.

'She might have gone to the pet shop. Do you… '

'I've got his mobile number, hang on.' Frank stood in the driveway manipulating his phone. 'Kenneth, is Jenny Bryson with you? No? She hasn't come home from the woods… yes, we're going up now. She must be there… no, you stay put in case she does turn up at the shop.'

Fear crashed heavily into Alicia as Frank rang off. A Landrover arrived in the driveway before either of them could speak. The farmers Frank had asked to help were burly Yorkshiremen, father and son, and both would know the area well. Alicia trotted down the garden after them. Frank had brought his doctor's bag, and John and Andy were carrying a rope and a tool box respectively. Alicia's mind had gone numb, it was impossible to stay so afraid. Oh God, they *would* find Jenny, they would.

Nightmare scenarios played through her head. What if there had been an accident… Christ. It wasn't even a week ago since searchers had been out here looking for her father, but this was incomparably worse.

'Okay,' said Frank. 'We'll walk uphill and cover as much ground as we can. What's Jenny wearing, Alicia?'

'Blue shorts and a yellow t-shirt,' said Alicia, hearing her voice tremble.

'Good, she should be fairly conspicuous among the trees. Let's go.'

They fanned out and walked about twenty yards apart, calling Jenny's name and looking into any large clusters of bushes they came across. Trees surrounded them after only a few steps, and the whole place was still. Alicia swallowed painfully. Apart from her feet thudding on the earthy pathway and the breeze stirring the tree tops, the only sounds were the myriads of insects buzzing around. Even the birds were silent. Old John stopped to examine a thicket of unripe blackberries, and then turned and looked back at Frank and then Alicia.

'I don't like the feel o' the place,' he said bluntly. 'It seems to me like there's no-one up here except the four of us.'

Alicia nodded. There was nothing to indicate that a little girl had passed this way. When they came to the circle of trees the three men stopped and looked around helplessly. Alicia sank down on the fallen tree trunk and buried her face in her hands. This was hopeless, they should phone the police. Frank yelled Jenny's name and his voice reverberated through the trees before silence fell again. Alicia moaned aloud. Nature pure and simple, that was all there was out here. John dropped his rope beside a tree stump and sat down heavily, lighting a cigarette.

'She's not here, Doc. Or if she is, she's being very quiet about it.'

'Mrs Bryson!' Andy had walked a little way across the clearing. He stooped and picked something lying beside a tall tree. Frank and John were hurrying over to see what it was, but Alicia took one look and knew.

'A sandwich and an apple,' said Andy, peering into the paper bag. 'And some rasps in a tissue.'

'It's her picnic,' said Alicia, hearing the panic in her voice. 'She hasn't eaten her picnic, she isn't here and neither's Conker... '

'Where the hell has she gone?' said Andy, his big face suddenly pale.

'We need to carry on,' said Frank heavily. 'We'll go down as far as the back road. If she's not there we'll phone the police. Come on, Alicia, it won't take five minutes, and the sooner we're through these woods the sooner we'll be doing something else to find her.'

He led the way, and they fanned out again. They weren't covering all the wood, of course, but Alicia knew Jenny wouldn't normally stray further afield than this. All she wanted now was to get to the back road and phone the police, which is what she probably should have done in the first place.

A low-pitched howling about fifty metres away made them all break into a run. Alicia stumbled and fell on the soft ground as she crashed through sparse undergrowth towards the sound. Frank hauled her to her feet and her thighs shrieked protest as she forced herself to run on through the trees.

The sound came again. But it wasn't Jenny's voice.

'It's a dog,' Andy called.

Alicia ran the last few yards. Andy was bending over a brown dog by the side of the road. There was blood on his head.

'Conker,' she said, dropping to her knees and grabbing the animal's collar. Conker was pathetically glad to see them. There was a long, bloody scratch on one ear, but he seemed otherwise unhurt.

Alicia forced herself to her feet and looked up and down the road. Andy and John were running in opposite directions, yelling Jenny's name. Frank stood beside her, one arm round her shoulders as if he was afraid she would fall, and Alicia could feel his body trembling.

Minutes later the other men returned, and they stared at Alicia, both faces grim. There was no sign whatsoever that Jenny had been anywhere near here.

'Thanks, lads, for all your help, but I think it's time we called the police,' said Frank slowly, reaching for his phone. Andy clapped his shoulder, and John stood shuffling his feet. Alicia literally couldn't move. It was difficult even to breathe.

'She's been taken, hasn't she?' said Andy heavily, and Alicia moaned. No no no no, that couldn't have happened. Jenny was here in the woods, she must be. She had gone further afield than usual and been unable to find her way back. Frank's next words showed he was thinking along the same lines. Or was he simply trying to stop her panicking?

'Alicia, she might still just be lost,' he said, grasping her elbow and giving it a little shake. 'She might have gone off somewhere by herself.'

Alicia jerked away from him. She would go mad, hanging around here waiting for the police. Frank's home was minutes away.

'Do you have a bike I could borrow?' she demanded.

'There's one in the shed,' Frank said. 'What are you... '

Alicia called back over her shoulder as she ran off down the road. 'You wait for the police. I'm going to bike the river pathway.'

All three men stared after her as she raced off in the direction of Frank's house.

Chapter Eighteen
Saturday, 22nd July, afternoon

Alicia

By the time Alicia reached Frank's garden her chest was burning and her throat felt raw. Not bothering to wipe away the tears that were mingling with the sweat on her face, she ran straight to the shed and hauled out Frank's bike. The path along the banks of the Ban was every mother's nightmare, narrow in places and with no fence separating the river from the track. Jenny knew she shouldn't go there alone, but she might have panicked if she hadn't been able to phone for some reason...

Grimly, Alicia started back through the village, heading for Woodside Lane and the river pathway. It was hard going, the bike was too big for her and the tyres were slightly flat. But it was still quicker than running.

Drawing level with the pet shop she jerked to a stop. Kenneth Taylor would have phoned Frank if Jenny had turned up at the shop... wouldn't he?

She pushed the bike across to the shop door.

'Mr Taylor! Is Jenny there?'

He called from upstairs, something unintelligible, and she waited, seething with impatience. He was moving around in the room above her, what the hell was he doing? A minute passed and Alicia shouted again.

Kenneth Taylor appeared from the back shop, wiping his hands on a threadbare towel and looking embarrassed. He must have been in the loo. 'Isn't she found yet? Oh my.'

'You haven't seen her today?'

He stared at her, face shining and hands clasped below his chin. It almost looked as if he was praying. 'Not at all. Is there anything... '

Urgency was already pulling her on towards the river. 'I don't know. Call Frank. I'm going to search the river path now. Thanks.'

She could feel his eyes on her back as she forced the bike along to Woodside Lane before jumping off. The sound of the Ban was all too apparent as she pushed Frank's bike down the steep track that led to the river pathway itself.

The Ban wasn't just flowing today, it was crashing and surging over the rocks and stones in its path and it was full, much more so than usual in July, swollen by all those heavy showers they'd had this past week. The ground was soft but Alicia could see no telling footprints. Surely Jen hadn't come this way. But the only way to find out was to go all the way along the path to Middle Banford.

Conscious that she was panting, Alicia forced herself to bike at a steady pace along the rough, muddy trail. If she went hell for leather as her soul was shrieking at her to do, she might miss something, some small sign that her daughter had passed this way. But Jenny knew the river was strictly out of bounds, and she would never have ventured so far without Conker anyway. This was a futile quest but Alicia couldn't stop herself. She had to be active, do something to find Jenny, even if it *was* futile.

If only Jen had simply wandered further than usual and was looking for blue fairy flowers. But that couldn't be right because they'd found Conker right at the other side of the wood. Could it be that Jen had lost the dog and then got lost herself while she was looking for him? This was an optimistic thought that would guarantee a happy end to the whole nightmare. Alicia took a deep breath. Frank was right, kids had no sense of time, and with Conker lost there was no reason the child would leave the wood to come along the river pathway here.

Yes, it must have happened like that, this fear was just the neurotic mother in her taking control. And even if Jen *had* gone back to the house there was no reason she would have failed to phone with Margaret's landline or her mobile. But then again she might have, in the anxiety of the moment, home alone with Conker lost and Mummy gone. The mobile was new and complicated and the landline was old-fashioned. Jen wasn't used to either of them. And if she'd been in the woods at all, wouldn't she have heard them all yelling her name? Oh God, suppose she *was* lying unconscious? The police would find her, but would they be on time? And every single one of these options was a million times better than the unthinkable. What if Jen had been taken?

Alicia arrived at the narrow bridge that spanned the river and dismounted. The pathway continued on the other side. Murky dark water was only inches below her feet as she pushed the bike to the other side. The tight knot of fear was still making her gut spasm, and she spat sour saliva into the river where it was immediately swirled away. She had never been so afraid, she would have given everything she owned just to have Jenny back where she belonged.

The path was still deserted, and here was the weir, white water crashing down before continuing along at a more sedate pace. What if Jen had fallen in...

The thought was pure torture, and Alicia sobbed aloud. Past the weir, no sign of a small girl. And there in the distance was St. Joe's, she could see the two upper storeys.

The pathway came to an end and Alicia found herself biking through an area of parkland which brought her to the main street in Middle Banford. The entrance to St. Joe's was about two hundred yards to the left. And no Jen. What was happening with the police? Why hadn't Frank phoned her yet? Legs shaking, Alicia lowered herself down on a wooden bench under an oak tree. She pulled her mobile from her pocket and was about to make the connection when it rang in her hand.

'Frank? I'm in Middle Banford, she's not here. Have you found her?'

She could hear his breathing. 'Alicia, I'm sorry, no, we haven't. The police have arrived and they're organising a full-scale search of the woods and the village too. You go to St. Joe's and tell Margaret, I'll deal with things here and then come to you as soon as I can.'

'Oh my God. Jenny. I can't lose her, Frank.'

'I know,' he said. 'I have to speak to the police again now. I'll see you very soon, Alicia.'

Her mobile cracked in her ear as he ended the call.

The Stranger

There had been no time for lunch today, but of course food was the last thing on his mind. Now he had time for a few stolen minutes to check that his little sleeping beauty was alright. He couldn't wait for the evening when he'd have hours to enjoy her, in fact he could hardly believe that this was actually happening, that his plan had worked so perfectly. He felt like a child who had wanted a toy for weeks and months on end, and then suddenly, there it was under the Christmas tree.

He closed the flat door behind him and crept into the dimness of the living room. Little Helen was still fast asleep under the golden robe, her cheeks flushed and her breathing nice and steady. What a darling she was. Life just didn't get any better than this.

Carefully, almost reverently he removed the throw and checked that she wasn't cold. Just looking at her lying there, waiting for him, made him feel warm himself, the sweat was trickling down his neck and his hands were shaking. Now that he had little Helen here, he could see how glorious it was to have a child...

Yet Mummy hadn't thought so, had she? Maybe because he'd been wicked? A bad little boy? But wouldn't a mother forgive her child any little wickednesses? He paused, staring at the child lying in front of him. Could Mummy have been *wrong* not to love him like he loved little Helen? No, Mummy had been perfect. But even if she hadn't been, he would forgive her anything. She was Mummy, and parents and children forgave each other, yes yes yes.

Slowly, he slid to the floor until he was kneeling beside little Helen and gazed at her, her face, her neck, the movement of her chest as she breathed in and out under that awful yellow t-shirt, her skinny little hips and long legs. She was completely in his power. How he wished he had more time for her now, but it was important that he behaved exactly as he would normally. No-one must know that he wasn't alone here today. He kissed her brow.

'I'll soon be back, darling,' he whispered, his voice hoarse. 'And I promise you we'll play for a long, long time before you go to Paradise.'

Little Helen slept on, and tears came to his eyes. He could hardly bear to leave her.

Alicia

Alicia sat on the bench staring at her mobile. A low-pitched humming had started somewhere in the background, or maybe it was inside her head, and she was aware that the colours of the world around her – the trees, the grass, the sky – were changing into metallic, silver-hued shades. Her whole world was moving, and the child in her head was crying *no, no,* but all Alicia could do was sit staring at her mobile on this hard wooden bench and try to hold herself together. Jenny wasn't there. The police were out searching.

It hurt even to breathe now. Alicia leaned her arms on her knees and tried to take slow, steady breaths. It was unbearable not knowing where her little girl was. Lost in the woods or lost somewhere else...

She was only eight years old.

Trembling, Alicia wheeled the bike towards St. Joe's. It was just down the road and she had to get to Margaret. Margaret was family, and oh, how she needed her family. How she needed her little girl.

Alicia's mobile rang again and her fingers were stiff as she extracted it from her pocket. It was the police inspector...

'We're still searching the wood, Mrs Bryson. Could you tell me exactly when Jenny left home this morning?'

Alicia felt slow and stupid as she struggled to think. 'Just after nine, I think.'

'And did anyone apart from yourself see her go?'

His voice was neutral but Alicia still winced. 'My aunt. We were both in the kitchen when Jen left, and we were home together until we drove to St. Joe's later on.'

There was a brief silence. 'Right. We're setting up an incident room in the village hall and Detective Superintendent Graham will be in touch with you later too. We'll take a full statement soon.'

Alicia closed her eyes. Tears spilled down her cheeks, salty warm liquid trickling down to drip off her chin, God she was so cold.

She hadn't felt this alone since... since she was sixteen and sitting on a bus driving along this same road, away from her father. She had gone to Margaret then and that was where she was going now.

She arrived at the care home, and ran through the ward door, along to her father's new room.

'Alicia? What is it? What's happened?'

It was Margaret's voice and she could feel Margaret clutching her arm, but she was quite unable to answer. The colours had gone funny again, and though she could see her father in his hospital bed and Margaret's concerned face gazing into her own, somehow she had moved right away from them. There was a humming noise in her head again and she could only clutch Margaret and stare at her helplessly.

Suddenly there were other people there too, Derek and Laura and another nurse, crowding round her, pushing her onto a chair. It took an enormous effort, but she managed to speak to them, tell them what was wrong.

'Jen's not in the woods. We found her picnic and we found Conker. Frank's there with the police now.' She pressed her hands between her knees and bent right over until her head was inches away from her thighs. The humming noise was getting louder and she could feel moist heat on her hands as her breath caught raggedly. Oh *God* she was so afraid, when had she ever been so afraid?

The child in her head was crying. *Don't, Daddy, please don't!*

She had been scared that day too. As a little, little child, surely the young voice had been that of a two or three year old this time... she had been this terrified. What had happened that day?

Margaret's face was white, she had never looked so horrified. Her voice was a mere whisper. 'Oh no, Alicia. Where can she be?'

'Careful, Margaret, let's give Alicia some space, she's had a shock. Laura, get some tea and see if you can get hold of Doug Patton. Alicia, what did Frank say?' Derek was bending over her, gripping her shoulder. She could feel the strength of his hand, thank God he was here. He sounded normal, reassuring, even, but she couldn't take any comfort from his voice.

Still shaking, she forced herself to sit straight and talk. It took a moment or two, but she managed to repeat what Frank had said as well as she could remember.

The child in her head had retreated into the background and was whimpering quietly. Laura appeared with a mug of sweet tea and Derek was holding it to her lips, making her drink it. She swallowed once and tried to push the mug away, but he wouldn't let her. After a few sips she realised it was helping, and reached out to take the mug herself.

'Good. That's better,' said Derek. 'You've got to get hold of yourself, Alicia. If Jenny's lost or hurt she might need you later. I think we should all go through to the relatives' room and wait for Frank there. Laura, you stay with Bob. Did you find Doug Patton?'

Laura was helping Margaret to her feet. 'I bleeped him.'

I don't want Doug here. The words went through Alicia's brain but she could no longer speak. All she wanted to do was scream, but that was one luxury she couldn't allow herself because Derek was right. Jenny might need her soon, and she would need a sensible, reassuring Mum, not a nervous wreck. She stood up, finding her balance on the floor that wasn't quite steady beneath her, and allowed Derek to steer her along the green corridor where old Mr French was still sitting picking a hole in his cardigan.

The door of the relatives' room was open, and Alicia winced at the sight of the wooden chairs and the drinks machine. She shouldn't be here. She should be out there searching right now.

'Derek. Listen. Please.'

She almost sounded like herself, which surprised even her because she had never felt less like Alicia in her whole life. But then, her daughter had never been missing before. For more than eight years, Alicia had always known where Jenny was and who she was with. School, Brownies, swimming club. She had worried about the swimming club at first. Would they be able to watch all the children? Suppose something happened and there weren't enough adults around? And of course nothing ever did happen and there were always plenty of adults. How futile those fears seemed now. She gripped Derek's arm.

'I should speak to the police. I have to go and help find her.'

Derek patted her shoulder. 'I know. But let's wait for Frank first. You'll want to hear what he has to say, and then we'll organise someone to take you.'

They sat in silence, Alicia clutching Margaret's hand with both her own. They weren't a touch-feely kind of family, she thought stupidly, and here she was holding on to Margaret for dear life. She couldn't ever remember holding her own mother's hand like this, and it went without saying that she had never held hands with her father. The worry over Jenny had completely eclipsed the worry over what her father had done to her. He just wasn't important, and to be quite brutal about it he was almost gone now anyway, whereas Jenny was right at the start of her life, still in that innocent magical time of childhood when the sun shone all summer.

And the worst thing of all was what no-one was saying. They all said she must be in the woods still, but what if she wasn't? Why, why had she let Jen play by herself in the woods? It might have been safe twenty-odd years ago when she and Cathal had been children, but nowadays… Guilt washed over Alicia. This whole situation was like one of those nightmares where you knew you were dreaming and you tried so hard to wake up but you just couldn't. Was Jen still playing in the woods, or had someone taken her away? Was she still alive? Her abductor, if there was one, had had plenty of time to torture her for hours and then kill her. So maybe there *would* be a funeral to arrange, dear Christ, how could she ever attend a funeral service for her daughter? A white coffin, children always had white coffins, didn't they? No, no, the thought was unbearable. Jenny might be lying somewhere, violated, broken, dead.

The child in her head suddenly screamed, banishing every other thought. *No Daddy, please don't!*

But he had. He had picked her up and thrown her across his bed in the bad room and torn off all her clothes, she had kicked and fought him but it was hopeless, he was so much bigger and stronger. She couldn't even have been as old as Jenny now. He'd forced her head down with one big, rough hand, and beaten her with his other hand. He had slapped her all over and then taken his belt with the buckle and struck her again and again. She'd been screaming *Daddy don't kill me*, but he had gone on and on until she stopped screaming because she could hardly breathe. Her head was jammed into the bed sheets and she could feel the blood running down her back, her legs, and he'd been grunting in a horrible, nauseating way. How terrified she had been, she thought she was going to die, that he was going to kill her, and then… what? What happened then? And why?

Another picture in her head, black and white and soundless this time, out in the lane quite late one evening, there was her and Mum and Cathal, as well as his Mum and Dad. Cathal's Dad had ordered him inside, but his Mum must have been going somewhere because Cathal had hugged her goodbye… and then he'd hugged little Alicia goodbye too, a big bear hug and a kiss on the cheek, same as he'd given his mum, and she could see his mouth form the words, 'Bye, 'Lici, see you in the morning, right?'

Her father had been watching them from the living room window, he had seen it, and of course this wasn't the first time Cathal had touched her like that… Her father was outraged… his face, dear God, she would never forget that face… He had beaten her half to death. And what had he done to her then?

But it didn't matter now, what did anything matter except Jenny? Had Jenny been this scared? Had Jenny begged for her life like she had that day?

Bile rose in Alicia's throat and she leapt up, both hands clamped over her mouth. She ran to the toilets opposite the relatives' room and vomited, crouching on the floor and retching, spitting hot, disgusting liquid into the bowl.

Derek was just behind her. 'Okay, Alicia, get it all out. Good girl. Here you are.'

He crouched behind her, rubbing her back, then helped her to her feet and gave her a wet paper towel. Dumbly, she wiped her face and ran water over her hands.

'That's good. Rinse your mouth. Feel better?'

'No,' she said, realising that she was shivering. 'I want my little girl.'

'I know. Come on, let's go back to Margaret.'

Alicia slumped down into the same uncomfortable chair and silently accepted a peppermint from Margaret.

Frank arrived a few minutes later, the strain apparent in his face. He was pale and the lines on his forehead looked so much deeper than usual. He sat down beside her, squeezed her arm then clasped his hands together, staring down at them before lifting his eyes back to hers. When he spoke his voice didn't sound like Frank at all.

'The police are out searching, Alicia, I waited at Bob's until they came and I told them where we'd already looked and gave them Jenny's trainers for the dogs. They're organising helicopters and they'll phone right away if, when, they find anything.'

Alicia pressed her lips together, not trusting herself to speak. If she spoke she would scream herself, like the child inside her head, and if she started she might not be able to stop.

Derek stood up. 'I'll get back to the ward now Frank's here,' he said, going to the door.

Margaret rose too. 'I'll stay with Bob,' she said. 'Alicia, you go and see to the police.'

Alicia nodded. Her poor aunt seemed to have aged ten years in one short day. What must she look like? She turned to Frank. 'Where is she, Frank? She can't have just disappeared.'

'I know,' he said heavily. 'If she's still in the woods they'll find her any time now. And if she's not, well, I don't... '

'She knows it's wrong to go away with a stranger,' said Alicia. 'And Conker was there too.'

Frank looked at her thoughtfully. 'Who would she go away with?' he said suddenly. Alicia sat down again.

'Well, neighbours, I suppose, though she's been told often enough to ask about people like that too. That's about it, though. The only other people she knows in the village are you and Kenneth Taylor and Mrs... ' She heard her voice rise at least an octave as realisation hit her. 'Oh my *God* Frank, how could I have forgotten, she's talked about a... a playmate. A man. I don't know who it is, I don't even know for sure if it's a real person or an imaginary friend, but she's talked about playing in the woods with him a couple of times at least. She said I knew him and it was alright, I thought it was John Watson but he wouldn't... take her... oh *God.*'

Panic filled her, churning her stomach into yet more punishing cramps. Who was he, this Oberon? An adult, Jenny had definitely said that much. What else had she said? Alicia hadn't been listening, she hadn't taken the time to listen because she'd been too busy worrying about her father and Paul and anyway, bad things didn't happen in Lower Banford. But they did, look at what her father had done to her... How could she have been so short-sighted? Jenny had talked about this person and she hadn't bothered to find out more. She hadn't seen the danger.

'We should tell all that to the police,' said Frank, reaching for his mobile. Suddenly he looked at her, 'Alicia, it wouldn't be your ex, would it?

'Paul? No, surely not. He's busy with meetings in York. At least that's what he told us... '

A shimmer of hope came into Alicia's head. Could Paul have persuaded Jenny to go off on a little outing somewhere? Just to frighten them? It would be cruel and senseless, but it wasn't quite impossible. He might even have told Jen that he had squared it all up with Mummy first.

'If she's with Paul, then she'll be alright,' she said, and Frank nodded, waiting for the police to answer his call. He relayed the story about the playmate in the woods, and Alicia sat listening. She would go and talk to the police herself, show them Jenny's favourite place up there. The fairy circle of tall trees.

'Does he have a name, this playmate of Jenny's?' asked Frank, still on the phone.

'Oberon,' she said, and he repeated this for the police sergeant.

'You should phone Paul too, no matter what you think,' said Frank, breaking the connection.

'Yes, I should have thought of that,' said Alicia, staring down at her mobile. Thank heavens the number was still in her phone. She made the connection and listened as Paul's mobile rang. His voice was loud in her ear.

'What is it, Alicia? I'm about to go into a meeting.'

'Is Jenny with you? Have you got her, Paul?'

'What the hell are you talking about? I can't go to important business meetings with an eight-year-old under my arm, can I?

Alicia, what's going on? Where *is* Jenny?'

'She's lost in the woods,' said Alicia, and heard his voice shouting at her, angry and accusing. And God knows she deserved it, she had left her child alone and now funny, lovable Jenny was gone, perhaps forever. It was the kind of thing you saw on the news and you wondered why the adults involved hadn't watched their children better. She had let her daughter down in the worst possible way.

Paul was speaking again, his voice low and furious. 'Well for fuck's sake what's she doing lost in the woods? Have you called the police? You wait until my lawyers hear about this, Alicia. And get out there and look for her too. I'll call you back.'

The phone went dead, and Alicia stared across at Frank. 'He hasn't got her,' she whispered. 'And if he hasn't, Frank, who has?'

She stumbled across the room towards him and felt his arms go around her.

The Stranger

Not much longer now. Sweet little Helen was waiting on the sofa, and in just an hour or so he would be enjoying a beautiful game with his darling. The whole day had gone exactly as he'd planned. The only thing he hadn't realised was how tiring it would all be, not to mention how hard it was to keep the correct expression on his face. No-one had any idea what he had done.

Things wouldn't be so difficult next time. When the time came to send big Helen to Paradise he would be able to do it quite differently. Hers would be a much more peaceful journey. He would invite her home and they could have a couple of drinks and he would comfort her, right there on the sofa where little Helen was now, then he would give her the same sedative in a drink.

But first he still had the pleasure of little Helen's last journey before him. And giving little Helen a beautiful send-off would make good what had happened with his own darling. He hadn't wanted that at all…

They had met in York. Helen hadn't been able to get her car manoeuvred out of a narrow parking space and she'd been in tears of frustration when he arrived, her helper and guide. She had looked up to him from the very start. No-one had ever felt like that about him, not even Mummy. Especially not Mummy. It had been so amazing to gaze into Helen's dark brown eyes and see her love for him shining out like a lighthouse in a storm.

They had married very quickly. With feelings like that there was no reason to wait, and for several months his life had been perfect. She had made him feel special, and it was like a drug, the more he had, the more he needed.

And then the black day, the day when he'd started to rub her back while they were sitting at home cosily watching a quiz on TV, he could even remember the contestant's name, Alexander Fowler, answering questions on London Parks. He had started to rub Helen's back and she'd wriggled away from him, smiled her beautiful smile and said, 'Later, darling.'

He hadn't let her see how shocked he'd been. And that had just been the first time. After that, she'd rejected him regularly, always kindly, but still rejection. And there had been a new look in her eyes, a look that told him she had changed. She wasn't his darling angel any more, no, somehow the very devil himself was worming his way into her soul. The hurt was starting to grow again and he knew how dangerous that could be, he knew that one day it might overwhelm him, like with Mummy and Snugglepuss. He would have to be careful because he loved Helen and she loved him. She just didn't want as much love as he needed to give her, that was all. It was nothing really. But then it happened. A few weeks later in the garden.

She'd wriggled away from him yet again, laughing up into his face, 'Goodness, darling, not out here,' and something brittle inside him had snapped. Exactly like with Mummy. He'd grabbed her arm and she'd pushed him away and then he'd pushed *her*, and though it wasn't a hard push she stumbled and hit her head on the old pear tree.

'Hey! What are you doing?' she cried, and the look on her face was exactly the same as Mummy's when she was falling down the stairs. He grabbed Helen's hair with both hands and slammed her head back against the tree. Her knees gave way, her body sagged downwards, but he held onto her head and felt bones crack. He could hear his own voice screaming.

The neighbour two gardens away heard too, but by the time she arrived to do her nosy-parkering he was lying beneath the tree, cradling Helen in his arms, shaking and distraught.

'I don't know what happened, she must have slipped, she hit her head, look, oh, help her, please help her!'

But Helen's neck was broken. The paving stones were wet and

slippery after rain in the night. Everybody knew how devoted they were. It had never entered anyone's head that he had sent Helen to Paradise himself.

Alicia

She stood there in Frank's arms, counting breaths, one, two, in, out. Tanking up strength for whatever was coming, but she couldn't stay here, she had to go back and help find her daughter, oh God please let them find Jenny soon. She pulled away and looked for her bag, but it was still on the kitchen table at home. She was here with nothing except her phone and the clothes she stood in. And Frank's bike.

'I have to get back, I... '

'I'll drive you.'

Alicia moved towards the door but before she had gone two steps it burst open and Doug stood there, looking past her to Frank.

'Frank, can you... Alicia, are you alright?'

Frank answered for her, his voice steady. 'I'm just about to drive Alicia to Lower Banford, Doug. Jenny's lost in the woods, the police are out there searching.'

Doug stared at her, then reached out and rubbed her shoulder. It was all Alicia could do not to flinch.

'Alicia, I'm so sorry. How terrible for you. But I'm sure Jenny's simply lost her way and you'll soon have her back. If I can do anything at all to help, just let me know. Frank.' He jerked his head at the corridor, and Frank followed him out. Alone in the room now, Alicia stood listening as the two men spoke on the other side of the door.

'You have to go up to Rose Buchanen, Frank. She's in agony, she needs morphine and there isn't another doctor in the house.'

Alicia closed her eyes. Frank would go, of course he had to help an old lady in pain. She would get herself back to Lower Banford, she was Jenny's Mum, it was up to her.

Frank's voice was angry. 'That's a bit of an imposition under the circumstances, Doug. I'll go up, but if this is going to take more than five minutes you'll have to phone for someone else. I'm not on call this weekend.'

'I know,' said Doug. 'On you go, Frank. I'll explain to Alicia and…'

'No, I will,' said Frank, and put his head round the door. 'Alicia, I have to go upstairs to see a patient, I won't be more than a few minutes. What do you want to do?'

She joined them in the corridor, looking for a minicab number in her phone. 'I'll take a taxi back and speak to the police. I'll be fine by myself,' she said, seeing the protest in his face. 'It's my little girl and I want to go now. Thank you, for everything you've done.'

'Christ, you don't have to thank me. Look, do you feel okay to drive? Take my car, that'll be quicker. I'll catch up with you in half an hour, max,' he said, pressing the car key into her hand and charging up the corridor.

Alicia was left holding the key. Should she drive in this condition? Probably not, but she was going to. She frowned at Doug. 'I'm going, and that's that,' she said defiantly.

He patted her shoulder again. 'I won't stop you.'

'I'll just tell Margaret.'

For the second time that day Alicia stood for a moment at her father's bedside, looking down at the still figure under the hospital blanket. There was nothing at all to feel now. He might have raped her, he might not, but he had certainly beaten her senseless for nothing at all. He was a wicked old man and she wasn't even going to exert the energy to hate him. She turned away without speaking, and Margaret rose to accompany her down to the car park.

Doug opened the door for them. 'Alicia, if you need me, just call. Let me know what's going on, anyway. I could help you look for Jenny when I get off here.'

She stared at him. He didn't care about Jenny, it was all just for show. 'Thank you, Doug. I don't know how the police will want to continue. Either she'll be in the woods or somewhere in Lower Banford or they'll have to start a much bigger search. Oh, God.'

Margaret was there, comforting her as they walked down the ward, arms round each other's waists. 'Stay calm, lovey.'

Alicia nodded. At the front door she stood for a moment, holding onto Margaret in much the same way as she'd held on to Frank, gathering strength. She knew she was almost at the end of what she could take.

The road was deserted as she drove along. She should have called the police before she left St. Joe's, now she didn't know where she should go. Home to the silence? To the pet shop? Just in case? No, no. If Jenny'd turned up there Kenneth Taylor would have called the police right away. Unless...

Was he Oberon? She flattened the accelerator and felt the car surge forwards. She would go to the pet shop and insist on going inside, she would look in every single room and if Kenneth Taylor had her daughter she would strangle him with her bare hands there and then.

A car passed going in the opposite direction, its horn blaring as it swerved to avoid Frank's car. Alicia slowed down. That was stupid, she could have caused an accident. She would be no use at all to Jen if she was in hospital herself. Soberly, she drove on, steering the car frantically onto the verge when her mobile rang. It was the police.

She listened, her mind going numb as the sergeant reported what little progress they'd made and arranged to meet her at home later. The minute he rang off her phone shrilled out again. This time it was Frank.

'They haven't found her, Frank. I'm just outside the village now.'

'I'm in a taxi, I'll be with you soon. What did the police say?'

Alicia clutched the phone to her cheek. 'They've been through the woods, they're pretty certain she's not there but they have teams out searching the whole area again. They're making enquiries in the village too, asking if anyone saw Jen or anything suspicious today. I'm going to see if Kenneth Taylor's in his shop. Jenny loves his kittens, maybe she went there and he, well, he's a bit strange, isn't he, Frank, what if he...'

'Alicia.' His voice faded and she heard him speak to the taxi driver. 'Quick as you can. Alicia. Wait in the car in front of the pet shop. Don't go in before I get there, okay? There's something I have to tell you first.'

He broke the connection, and Alicia drove on. The road was busier now, people were returning from Saturday excursions. The day was nearly over and she'd wasted a whole lot of time that could have been spent looking for her daughter. It would have been so much better if they'd called the police straightaway. But they hadn't known that then.

She parked in front of the pet shop and switched off the engine. Would Kenneth Taylor see her and come out? Surely he must notice her here, so if he didn't come out, wasn't that suspicious? Of course the shop was closed now and she didn't know if his flat above looked out over the street or towards the woods at the back. Maybe she should just go and ring the bell. But the day's events had caught up with her; she was pinned to the seat, her head leaning on the steering wheel. Jenny baby.

A taxi pulled up behind the car and Frank hurried over.

'Alicia.' He lowered himself into the seat next to her.

She blinked at him. 'I'm alright. What did you want to say about Kenneth Taylor? I need to go and make sure she isn't there.'

He reached out his hand and took hold of one of hers and she was startled to feel how warm he was. Or was she cold? He rubbed the back of her hand.

Tears welled up in Alicia's eyes as the numbness vanished completely, Christ how painful it all was. She could feel how fragile her self-control was, and she needed to keep that control to face whatever was going to happen. She would let Frank help her, he obviously wanted to. She found herself gripping his hand, squeezing his fingers and not letting go.

'The police say either Jen's gone off by herself somewhere, which I can hardly imagine, or someone's taken her. Frank. Tell me about Kenneth Taylor.'

'You sounded as if you thought Kenneth might have something to do with Jenny's disappearance,' he said, and she could hear that he was speaking carefully. 'I can't give you any details, Alicia, he's my patient and I have to keep confidentiality, but I can say I'm one hundred per cent sure that Kenneth has nothing at all to do with what's happened. If I had a child and I needed someone to look after her for a while, Kenneth would be one of the first people I'd go to. Truly.'

Alicia couldn't speak. She had to believe him. So Jenny wasn't in the woods, she wasn't with Paul and she wasn't with Kenneth Taylor.

'Then it's a stranger, if she's gone off with someone,' she said, her voice a mere whisper. 'Frank, she might have been abducted by some pervert.'

Her voice rose in pitch and then broke on the last word. Frank pressed her hand to his face.

'Alicia love, don't torture yourself until you know more. Try to keep calm, it's the only thing you can do now to help Jenny. You have to be ready to react the moment there's any news.'

But what would the news be? She felt her hand shake as she turned the key in the ignition.

'I'll go home again. The police said I should wait there.'

'Right. Alicia, is there a friend you could call to come and be with you?'

For a moment she considered calling Eva Campbell. But then she didn't know Eva well. And apart from Margaret there was no-one else she wanted to be with right now.

'My friends are all in Bedford, there's only Margaret here. I'll call David, though, he could come and be with us. Yes, that's a good idea.'

She pulled the car around and drove back up the street. If only they had never come here, if only she had listened to the child in her head that very first day, warning her about the bad place. She should have driven away with Jenny when she'd had the chance.

Back at her father's house she stood in the doorway for a moment, staring towards the kitchen. 'Shit, Frank. Why did I ever come back to this place?' She stepped inside and kicked a rubber bone to the side.

'Where's Conker, anyway?'

'Kenneth's got him.'

She sighed. 'I'll call David.'

He was hesitating at the front door, and she turned.

I don't want to be alone yet. The thought was loud in her head.

'If you've time… could you stay a while?'

He nodded slowly, then followed her into the house. Alicia made her call to David, listening to Frank making coffee in the kitchen. David promised to be there as soon as he could, and Alicia rang off, mildly comforted. She wasn't alone here. There was Margaret and Frank and soon David but oh, where was Jenny? Sobs rose in her throat and she was unable to hold them back. Again Frank was there, comforting her, holding her while she sobbed. Would she ever see her daughter again? The thought that she might not was unbearable. After several minutes, the spasm passed and she was able to blow her nose and talk again.

'David's on his way.' She accepted a mug and sat down at the kitchen table. Moritz came running up and wound himself round Frank's ankles before leaping up to Alicia's lap. Jenny's cat. Frank sipped his coffee silently and Alicia looked at him uncertainly. It was so difficult to work out what was going on between them, beside the friendship and trust there was the awkwardness of being in this terribly intimate situation and neither of them knew what the other was thinking about their sudden togetherness, which after all had only been caused by Jenny's disappearance.

She struggled to say something to fill the silence. 'The police should be reporting back soon,' she said tonelessly. 'Look, it's half past four already. I should let Doug know what's going on too, he said he would keep Margaret informed. He's good like that, isn't he?'

Frank had flinched at her words and she looked up to see real anguish on his face before he controlled his expression and replied.

'Yes. His talents are wasted in an administrative job, but I suppose it's better paid. But he seems a, a good man.'

Alicia felt her own body flinch too. 'My father always said that. A good man. He was proud of being a good man… a God-fearing man. But I think, oh God, Frank, he undressed me, and it was his belt… the buckle, right down my back and my legs… the pain… and there was blood everywhere, I thought I was going to die and I was so afraid and Mum didn't come. I could hardly breathe but… I can't remember what happened after that.'

'Alicia, can I look at your back?' His expression was unreadable.

217

She stood without a word and turned around. He lifted her top, moving her into the light. When he spoke his voice was hard with anger.

'You have masses of tiny scars, dozens of them, and a couple of bigger ones as well,' he said. 'They've healed and faded so they're not very noticeable now unless you're looking for them. But they're quite definite. You must have been beaten badly, and probably more than once. Alicia, we'll deal with this, I'll help you, but this isn't the time. We should concentrate on Jenny for the moment.'

For a few moments they sat in silence. Alicia felt the child's presence in her head again, there was still something more, she could feel that. The child still knew something that she didn't know yet. But Frank was right, now wasn't the time. She should keep herself in control, the police would be here soon.

Frank's mobile rang out in his trouser pocket and he jumped up to silence it. Alicia winced.

Was that Laura's voice she heard, far in the distance through Frank's mobile?

'I'll talk to her. Thanks, Laura. Tell Margaret her son is on his way too. But get Ian Cummings in, he's on call today. I expect I'll see you in a bit.'

Dear God. Her father was worse. Maybe he *was* going to die. Alicia pressed her hands between her knees to stop them shaking. She could feel the child inside her waiting, whimpering quietly.

Frank ended the call and turned to her. 'That was Laura. Bob's taken a turn for the worse again, his heart rate is down and his breathing isn't too good either. Margaret's still with him. Alicia, what do you want to do?'

She stood up, surprised that she was able to feel so determined. 'I'll go to St. Joe's,' she said. 'I can do that. I can't be with Jenny, but I can help Margaret if, if anything happens to my father.'

She saw Frank close his eyes. And how right he was, there was no end to all this today. When he looked at her again his voice was gentle.

'Alicia? Are you going to manage this?'

'Frank. My – the child's voice, in my head – it's crying nearly all the time now, sort of in the background. It's as if all this pain now has switched the pain from those days back on again.' And yet it was good, somehow, that one of them was able to cry. The child could do the crying and she could do the coping.

She picked up her bag. 'Will you come with me?'

'Of course I will.' He looked down at his trousers and shoes, still muddy from the trek through the woods. 'I'll take you to St. Joe's, but I'll have to leave you for a bit while I go home and change. The way I am now, they probably won't let me back on the ward.'

Chapter Nineteen
Saturday, 22nd July, evening

The Stranger

The sun had moved behind the house, and with the heavy curtains still closed his living room was in almost total darkness. He tiptoed to the window and opened the curtains halfway. That was better. Now he could see his little treasure, safe on the sofa where he'd left her, eyes still closed in her drug-induced sleep. He bent over her, stroked a couple of stray hairs back from her perfect little face and sighed happily. This was his time, right now. This was what he'd been waiting for since he'd first set eyes on her, no, he'd been waiting for this since Helen died, since Mummy died, all his life, actually. And his moment had come, here and now and safe at home, away from all the weeping and wailing that was going on in the world today. He'd been part of a lot of it, in fact he had caused it, but like the good actor he was he'd managed to play his part without anyone realising that he *was* acting. No-one had suspected that all he wanted was to be back here with little Helen, to enjoy those last few hours on Earth with her.

He moved the gold coloured throw that was covering her and lifted her into a sitting position on the sofa. She was like a rag doll, soft and floppy, but breathing so sweetly and steadily, eyes closed and her delicious little lips parted slightly. Pulling at the knots, he untied the cords from her wrists and ankles and pulled her clothes off, tossing them into the corner. Dreadful shorts and garish yellow t-shirt. White panties with tiny pink flowers, sandals and white socks. He would get rid of them later. The golden robe was all she would need to go to Paradise, and the fluffy blanket in the meantime too, to keep her warm. He wrapped the blanket round her, then cocooned her passive body in the golden throw. It wasn't easy, but at last he had her wrapped in a lovely golden parcel on the sofa.

Now for the bedroom. He would take her through and lay her on his bed.

It was awkward lifting her in his arms, her legs were longer than he'd thought and her feet were peeking out from under the robe, and she was heavier than she looked, too, how amazing that such a slight little thing should weigh so much. But he managed, and carried her to his bed where he laid her down and spread the robe out, leaving little Helen wrapped only in the blanket. A silvery thread of saliva was hanging from her mouth, and he wiped it away tenderly. His fairy queen really needed a bath, he would do that straightaway, yes, oh yes, he would even get in with her just like he used to with his own Helen. And then he would massage her while she was sweet-smelling like Helen.

Shivering with excitement at the thought of an oil bath with little Helen he hurried through to the bathroom and started to run the water. He was adding a generous slosh of Helen's bath oil when the doorbell rang. He froze. Who on earth would ring his bell at this time on a Saturday? He couldn't afford to ignore it, what if something had gone wrong with the 'outside' part of Plan B? Angrily, he turned off the tap, closed the bedroom door, strode across the hallway and jerked the door open. Two woman were standing there, and oh, God, one of them was Mary Johnstone, backbone of the Woman's Guild and busybody extraordinaire. She beamed up at him and spoke.

'Oh good, you're in. I wonder if we can have just two minutes of your time? We're collecting for the cat home in Upper Banford. You might not know...'

His eyes glazed over as the woman went on with her boring little speech, but there was no way he could shut the door in their faces. He had to be normal here, get rid of them as soon as he could without them realising anything.

Five minutes later the women were gone, a sizeable contribution to their stupid cat home in the donations box. Breathing deeply, he rushed back to little Helen. Good, good, she was still fast asleep. He stood there, feeling sweat gather again. Right. That had been close but it was alright again now. But imagine if someone else came to the door. He wouldn't get into the bath with her, it was too risky.

He went to check the bathwater and nodded when he saw the purple oil swirling round in a few inches of lovely warm water. She could just lie there, and he would wash her sweet and clean, sweet and clean. Little Helen would smell just like his own Helen. She *was* his own little Helen now.

It was awkward getting her into the tub, and for a moment he regretted his impulse to bath her. But then she was in, lying in the oily water, that wonderful hair streaming out around her. He started to rub her legs, starting at those ten perfect toes, working up over sun-browned shinbones, lovely little girl knees… and her thighs! Up and down and round and back again, oh, this was so much better than he'd ever imagined. The oil made her skin so soft and slithery, such a perfect little body. And of course her face. Little Helen couldn't go to Paradise without having her face washed first. He glanced at the bottle of shampoo on the edge of the bath, then decided against it. Now to take her back through and massage her. He pulled out the plug and waited until the water had drained away.

Lifting her out again was difficult too. She was slippery with oil, and still completely limp. In the end he wrapped her in the towel, and then he managed to pull her over the rim of the bath. Panting slightly, he lifted her and carried her through to the bedroom.

Reverently, he spread little Helen's hair in a kind of halo around her head, then fetched more oil and began to smooth it into those perfect little arms and legs, round the flat little tummy, mustn't forget her back. And her hair, yes, he could run his oily fingers through little Helen's hair, oh, this was so good, so good, so good…

How many times had he done this for his darling! She had been perfect too, more perfect in one way than little Helen, because of course she had loved him, she had lain there watching him as he bathed her, stroked her, then dried her and massaged her lovely body with sweet smelling oils. His own Helen had smiled up at him all the while, smiled her beautiful warm smile, he could drown in her smile, and he had felt like a real King. Those had been the good days.

Now he had another Helen, still waiting to go to Paradise. Just a few more hours and it would be time. Sighing with happiness, he smoothed the last of the oil through her hair, tied her hands and feet again and covered her with the fluffy blanket. There. She was ready. He glanced at the clock. He would need to be sure that all the searchers up in the woods had gone when he arrived there with little Helen, so he would go and see what was happening in the big bad world. Then he would come back and play until it was time to go.

Plan B was working out perfectly.

Alicia

Alicia didn't know how on earth she was coping. She felt as if she was staring down a tunnel, she could see blackness round the edges, and a tiny picture in the middle. A picture of St. Joe's. Here she was again, sitting beside Margaret in her father's hospital room. They had given him an oxygen mask with a humidifier attached to the tube, it was gurgling and hissing and making the most revolting noises, and there was nothing she and Margaret could say to each other that would help in any way at all.

The child in her head was still crying, quietly but persistently. Crying for her father? For Jenny? No, she was crying for herself, for Alicia, for the childhood that had passed so bleakly and the relationship that would never be saved.

Frank would be back soon.

She pictured his face and realised that the agony of the past several hours was subsiding. In its place the numbness was back, void, nothing-feeling, as if her mind knew she couldn't cope with all the horror and had switched the fear off for a while. Her breath caught in her throat and she coughed. Her mouth was dry and her tongue heavy, and she knew she must look terrible.

Was Jenny even still alive?

The thought was like a knife twisting inside her. Jenny might be dead. What would she do then? How could she go on without her little girl?

The door opened and Doug looked in. 'Alright, Alicia?' he said gently, and Alicia nodded. Trust Doug. Of course she wasn't alright. She was conscious and she wasn't going mad yet, that was all anyone could expect of her tonight.

Doug checked her father's oxygen, took his pulse and watched him breathing for a few moments. 'No change, but he's holding his own,' he said, patting Margaret's shoulder, and Alicia heard her aunt heave a shaky sigh of relief. Why was it so important to Margaret that the old man shouldn't die? His brain was gone and it would actually be a blessing if his broken old body just followed on. He would never again be the person he had been. Thank Christ. There was no way back from the strokes and the dementia caused by them. Alicia found herself trying to make some sort of bargain with fate, or was it with God? *Was* there a God?

If we give you my father, can I keep Jenny? The question seemed indecent, and she was glad she hadn't said it aloud. She knew she couldn't exchange one life for another. But she would try anything right now. She had never been in such a bad place in her life, but she knew that if Jenny was found harmed or dead this place today would be nothing in comparison to the hell she would descend to.

The tight feeling came back to her middle and the child started to cry again. Was she going mad? Schizophrenia or something? Or one of those people you read about with split personalities? Dear God. Alicia hunched herself up in her chair, hoping fervently that she wasn't going to be sick again.

The door opened again and she jerked round in her chair, anxious for Frank to come back. It was David, though, and he hugged her and Margaret both at the same time before pulling a chair up and sitting down behind them.

'Any more word from the police, Alicia?' he said in a low voice, leaning forwards.

She shook her head. 'They're still out looking. One idea is maybe Jenny tried to come to St. Joe's by herself and got lost on the way. They're searching the woods and they're out in the village too and between Lower and Middle Banford. They'll be in touch again soon anyway. It's a Superintendent Graham and Chief Inspector Wilson who're leading the search. Oh God, what will they do when it gets dark?'

David squeezed her hand, and Alicia was able to take some comfort. David was family, he was her own generation, he would be strong and take charge if necessary. She didn't have much of that kind of strength left, she realised. It was good to have someone here who did.

Family. The word meant Jenny. Jenny was all she wanted in her future family. Jenny and Frank, she suddenly realised, Frank was - what was he?

He was the man she loved. It had taken the loss of her daughter to make that clear. Frank was everything she could wish for. Look how well they could talk together, and the fun they'd had. And she knew with sudden blinding certainty that he loved her too. But maybe they would never get the chance to make a life together. If she lost Jenny she knew she would go far away from here, away from Frank and Margaret and everybody else and she would never come back.

'I should phone Paul again,' she said, taking her mobile from her handbag and noticing in dismay that the battery was low.

David reached for the phone. 'Want me to do that?'

Alicia hesitated for a moment, then handed it over. It was a relief not to have to speak to Paul. She listened to her cousin's side of the conversation. Paul was obviously not at all happy about things, and who could blame him? David was firm in a way she couldn't have been, though, and started to tell him what the police were doing. He was still on the phone when Frank came into the room, accompanied by Derek and a middle-aged man in a white coat. David took the phone out to the corridor, and Alicia stood up and reached for Frank's hand.

'This is Ian Cummings,' he said, gripping her fingers. 'Ian, Alicia is Bob's daughter and Margaret here is his sister.'

Ian shook hands with them both. 'This is dreadful for you,' he said quietly. 'I'm so sorry. I'll examine Mr Logan and then maybe we can have a quick chat, Mrs Bryson.'

Alicia took Margaret's arm as they left the room with Frank, leaving Derek and Ian to examine her father. David was in the relatives' room, a bottle of coke from the machine in one hand. He looked at Alicia.

'Extensive vocabulary, your ex has,' he said, handing the phone back. 'He's upset, but I managed to persuade him there was nothing to be gained by him thundering down here tonight. I said we'd phone again in a couple of hours. What's happening?'

Alicia told him, and introduced Frank, who was extracting beakers from the machine.

'Hot chocolate,' he said, handing one to her and another to Margaret. 'It's the only hot drink that machine makes that's fit for consumption. Drink it, Alicia. You need something.'

She sipped. What did it matter how the liquid tasted. She edged Frank away from David and Margaret, not wanting Margaret to hear what she was going to ask him, or what he would almost certainly reply.

'What does Doctor Cummings want to have a chat about?' she said in a low voice.

'He'll ask if they should let Bob go. The oxygen's keeping him comfortable, but if he stops breathing, or if his heart stops, you have to think what would be best.'

'He's been gone for a long time,' she said dismally. 'This is horrible, I'm standing here making decisions like this about my father when I should be out there looking for my little girl. I want my little girl back.'

How many times had she said that? However many it was, it would never be enough. And if Jenny didn't come back, she'd be saying it for the rest of her life.

Frank spoke quickly. 'Listen. I'll go back in and talk to Ian for you. Then we'll go and see the police. David's here for Margaret now, and you can't help your father anyway.'

Alicia felt tears welling and forced herself to swallow them back. 'And I can't help Je - Jenny or the police really, can I? I might even get in the way, or slow them down.'

He gripped her arm and shook it gently. 'Come on. You have to hold it together. We'll phone the police after I've seen Ian. Okay?'

She nodded, and he left her standing by the window. Two minutes later he was back.

'Margaret, Alicia,' he said. 'Bob's not doing so well, you should go back in if you want to be with him.'

Margaret reached for Alicia's hand, and together they walked back across the corridor. This was it, then. She was going to sit at her father's bedside and watch as he... where was Jenny?

'Bob's breathing has become very flat,' said Derek. 'Come and sit here, Mrs Cairns. Take his hand.'

Alicia stood at the other side of the bed with Frank. This whole ghastly situation was only bearable because Frank was here. Doug had appeared again too, but she could hardly stand to look at him in case he said something trite. This was exactly what she had dreaded. She was standing at her father's bedside, wondering which breath would be his last. And the guttural, throaty, disgusting breathing was exactly the same as it had been the day he'd nearly killed her with his belt.

'You vile old man!' she screamed in a whisper, seeing Margaret recoil in horror.

Alicia felt Frank's hands on her shoulders but she pushed him away and bent over her father. His eyes were half open and he was looking up at her. Just like he'd looked down on her that day.

'Why did you do it?' Her voice broke. The child in her head was howling and Jenny was gone. 'Why did you... '

Her father's breath caught in his throat. His eyes opened wide and he stared straight at her.

Blackness swirled in front of Alicia's eyes. He was still staring.

'I know what you did.'

And she hated him. Because it wasn't true, she didn't know what he'd done, but the child in her head knew because she was screaming now, screaming in pain and terror.

His breathing stopped.

The child retreated abruptly, leaving Alicia with a feeling of hollowness at the very centre of her being. She stared at the figure on the bed. His eyes were still half open and so was his mouth, but the terrible, guttural breathing had stopped; there was only the hiss of the humidifier and a dead body on the bed. Everyone in the room was rigid, staring at her.

Derek moved first. He reached out and covered Bob's eyes for a few moments, and when he moved his hand again the eyes were closed. Alicia took a deep breath. Her father was gone, there was nothing there now to hate. She looked across the bed to Margaret and David. Margaret was crying, clinging to David, and Alicia walked round the bed and put her arms round them both. She felt

Margaret's hand shake as it gripped her arm.

'Margaret, I'm so sorry,' she whispered. For a moment they stood there, the only sounds in the room being Margaret's sobs. Someone had switched the oxygen off, and the bubbling hiss of the humidifier had stopped too.

Doug came round to the same side of the bed and touched her shoulder and then Margaret's.

'Bob's found his rest and you'll help each other through this. Alicia, I'll be in touch later. This is a time you need family, first and foremost.'

He left the room, and Alicia straightened up, barely registering Doug's meaningless words.

'David, take Margaret back to York,' she whispered. 'Frank will help me with the police and Jenny, and it would be better if Margaret was safe with you.'

Margaret reached out and touched her face. 'Alicia, I want you to know that I love you.'

Tears burned in Alicia's eyes and she couldn't speak. She hugged Margaret hard then watched as David led his mother to the door.

Derek covered her father's thin chest with the hospital blanket and turned to her, his face grim. 'Can I get you anything?'

She shook her head, holding on to Frank's arm, feeling his whole body tremble as he stood there. She knew there was still hatred on her face. Her father was dead and Jenny was gone and dear God, what was she supposed to do now?

Derek patted her shoulder. More people had patted her shoulder these past few days than in her whole life. He stood for a moment, and she saw him struggle to find words. The expression on his face was a curious mixture of pity, curiosity and desire to help her.

'Alicia. I don't know what your father did, but some things just aren't forgivable.' He left the room, and Alicia leaned her head on Frank's shoulder.

'I want to go back to the house and then when, if, they find Jen, I want to go home,' she said.

'No problem. We can leave right away.'

Doctor Cummings was waiting at the nurses' station. 'I'm sorry, but there will have to be a post-mortem,' he said. 'We still haven't established the cause of his sudden decline. I can't give a death certificate because there isn't a known cause of death. I hope you understand.'

Alicia looked at him. What the hell did she care. 'That's fine, and thank you, but I have to go. I need to contact the police about my little girl.'

He squeezed her hand. 'I'll pray for her,' he said, walking to the front door with them.

Alicia stood on the steps of St. Joe's and phoned the police while Frank spoke to the other doctor. Chief Inspector Wilson informed her that there was no news, still no sign of Jenny, and the search by the river was to continue all night. In the meantime they were pursuing other lines of inquiry too, trying to find out if Jenny had been seen on CCTV in any of the surrounding towns.

The dreary feeling was back in possession of her brain again. 'Take me home, please,' she whispered when Frank reappeared, and he nodded.

The touch barrier had been broken, and they walked down to the car park with their arms around each other, like two teenagers. First love. Except it wasn't love she was feeling now because inside she only felt dead. Empty. The child in her head was gone, her own child was lost, and so were all her feelings.

Frank drove slowly back and opened the front door with her key. Alicia went into the living room. Her father's chair, Margaret's chair, Moritz asleep on the sofa, and what was she going to do? Her mobile blared out suddenly and she grabbed it, but it was only Sonja and she passed it over to Frank to deal with. She couldn't have explained to Sonja all that had happened without breaking down, but Frank managed in a few sentences and promised his sister he would call back when there was news.

'You should eat something,' he said, looking towards the kitchen. Alicia shook her head.

'I need to be alone,' she said quietly. 'I just want some, some quiet. Some space. But please understand, please come back tomorrow, please Frank.'

'You don't have to say please,' he said, and she heard the tremor in his voice.

'I know,' she said. He pulled her to him and held her tightly for a moment.

'I'll be back at six in the morning,' he said. 'Get some sleep. Take one of Bob's pills. You must rest.'

She shook her head again, and watched from the window as he drove away. So now she really was alone. And her father was dead. He was at peace now and he didn't deserve to be. The house was silent as she went and sat on the sofa. Staring at nothing.

The Stranger

The sun had set before he got back home, but it had been time well spent. There was still a lot of coming and going out there but no-one at all had any idea that little Helen was here with him. His wonderful plan was succeeding way beyond his wildest dreams and it was every bit as fulfilling as he'd known it would be. The best was still to come, of course, the absolute highlight: looking into little Helen's eyes as he sent her off to Paradise.

Feeding Bob more drugs had been child's play. The old man was an even easier target the second time, putting up no resistance to being fed another cocktail of drugs. Again, the most difficult part was making sure no-one saw him. And now he was home again, thank goodness.

He washed his hands and splashed his face, then went to see what little Helen was doing. There she was on his bed, beautiful as ever, and so fragrant. He untied her hands and feet and kissed her cheek, her neck, the lovely little dip where her navel was. How perfect she was.

She was starting to wake up, her eyes were half open and she was making little movements with her head and arms. Well, he would let her wake up a bit, they could play together, and he would see if she was going to be cooperative. If not, he would give her another dose, a very light one this time. He wanted her awake in the woods.

'Little Helen darling, it's playtime,' he whispered, rubbing her cheek, his fingers sliding over the oily skin. He turned little Helen on her front and started to massage her back, rubbing rhythmically, circling and stroking round her shoulders, down her back, that smell, over her hips… She was as skinny as a rake, puberty was a long way off. Skinny was the wrong word, though, she was… lithe, that was it. Oh, it was almost too much.

Her eyes were wide open now, but they were unfocused, he could tell she wasn't registering what was happening to her. He turned her on her back again and stroked her face.

'Wake up, darling,' he said softly. 'It's alright, you weren't well, but you'll be better soon. It's playtime.'

She was quiet for a moment, then to his dismay she started to wail, a high-pitched, wordless keening sound that completely destroyed his sensual atmosphere. No, oh no. It would never do if any of the neighbours heard her and came to see what was going on, and of course the whole village knew that a child was missing. He would have to put her under again.

He poured the drugs mixture into her mouth, taking care not to give her too much, and then he held her, muffling her wails with the fluffy blanket. In a few minutes she was quiet again, lying in his arms like a little golden goddess. He looked down at her. He was going to lie with her, that was a promise he'd made to himself. He would have something to eat now, and then they could go straight on up to the woods and play some more. It wouldn't matter if she wailed there, no-one would hear her. The searchers were still out by the river, he could see their lights from the bedroom window. But up at the clearing where everything was in darkness he could do whatever he wanted.

Humming to himself, he whisked up eggs for an omelette and added cheese and a shake of dried parsley. There was some lettuce left over from earlier, too. A nice little meal. He would allow himself a glass of white wine, after all, tonight was going to be a celebration. Little Helen was going to Paradise.

When the food was ready, he carried the tray back to his bedroom. He could feast his eyes on little Helen as he ate. And then it would be time.

Playtime and Paradise. What a wonderful end to the day.

Alicia

Alicia slumped down on the sofa. Frank was gone and the whole house was silent as the grave.

She shivered. She'd wanted to be alone, but now that she was, it was almost more than she could bear. Even the child in her head had deserted her, and she found herself wondering if she would ever hear her own young voice again. Maybe it was enough for the child that their father was dead. The child could rest, it was Alicia the adult's job to find out what had happened. Did she really want to know more than she did already?

He had whipped her. Beaten her with his belt, and here in the silence of this house she was able to think about it almost neutrally. He had beaten her for being a normal, affectionate little girl whose friend had hugged her goodbye. How terrified she had been that day. And other days too. She had been afraid for her life several times.

What had the fear done to her? It had forced her to forget the beatings, and maybe they were best forgotten. Forgiven? No. Like Derek said, some things weren't forgivable, her father had abused his child with *pleasure*, his little girl who had only wanted a normal childhood with a normal Mum and Dad and normal fun and who quite simply hadn't understood.

Awful memories of her father's ill-treatment and her mother's indifference. Mum had been such a quiet, shadowy kind of person. Why hadn't she come to Alicia's aid? Could she have *agreed* with what her husband was doing? Or maybe she had known that to stick up for her daughter would mean a punishment for herself too.

If that had been the case, what terrible memories her mother must have taken to her grave. And now this day had its own terrible memories. Jenny was gone, and so many people's lives had been affected by what had happened. The searchers, the people at St. Joe's, Margaret, David. They were all going to remember it forever. The day a child went missing and her mother made such a scene at an old man's deathbed. Had her father realised? Had he heard her, had he understood? What did it matter now?

Alicia felt her shoulders slump. The horror of her own child's disappearance was completely eclipsing any feelings she might have had about her own childhood suffering.

Legs shaking, she stood up and went through to the kitchen, Moritz following after her. At least she wasn't quite alone, Moritz was here too. Mechanically, she spooned cat food into his bowl and set it by the back door. He tucked in, obviously ravenous.

The numbness was beginning to wear off. Again. Jenny's pink cardigan was hooked on the back of a kitchen chair, and Alicia grabbed it and held it to her face. She felt the lump at the back of her throat grow and thicken, and she made no effort to control the sobs that forced their painful way from the core of her being. For long minutes she leaned over the kitchen table, her body shaking with sobs. This was the worst day, the worst hour of all, things just couldn't get any worse than this.

Oh yes they could, her head told her brutally, a policeman could come by any minute and tell you they've found a crumpled little body in a ditch somewhere. Now she was going to have to organise a funeral for an old man and maybe one for a little girl too, a double funeral. Words floated across her mind: *Dearly beloved, we are gathered here today.* Or was that weddings? Or both? She could never go to Jenny's wedding if the funeral came first. *Ashes to ashes, dust to dust…* An oak coffin for her father, the white one for Jenny. But no. No way could she have them together even in death.

What could have happened? The idea of Jenny setting off for St. Joe's all by herself didn't ring true, somehow. If Jenny had seen the note and for some reason been unable to phone, she would have gone to a neighbour. Definitely. And even if she hadn't seen the note, if she'd arrived home and found the house empty and the car gone, surely, *surely* she'd have gone to a neighbour then too. The

Donovans had been at home. So Jen must have gone away with someone, either voluntarily or against her will.

The crying fit had passed, and her brain was sharp and clear again. Adrenalin was pumping through her. Think it through, Alicia, reason it out, maybe you'll be able to work something out.

If an absolute stranger had taken Jen, there was nothing she could do. No amount of reasoning or thinking would help, it would just be one of those awful, hideous coincidences that happen in life. Other little girls had been abducted, raped and killed because they were in the wrong place at the wrong time. It happened. But right now she should focus on the other possibility, because there she might be able to think something out.

Who would Jenny go away with? Well, start nearest home. Paul was already ruled out. The neighbours and quite a few others too; the search for her father had introduced them to a whole set of villagers they hadn't known until then. But the police had ruled these people out too and there was no reason to think they'd make a mistake.

Kenneth Taylor from the pet shop. Suspect number one, as far as Alicia was concerned. There was definitely something strange about him. On the other hand he'd been kind to them, look at the way he had taken the time to tell Jenny all about the kittens, and that collar he'd given her for Moritz was an expensive one. But then if he was a paedophile grooming his next victim, he would be kind, wouldn't he? Alicia paused in her thoughts. There was something wrong with that. Kenneth Taylor a paedophile? She closed her eyes and pictured him, working in his shop, talking in his strange high voice, his smarmy manner. Then she knew. The man wasn't a paedophile, he was gay, that was what he was, gay, yes of course, and think of those times he had acted strangely, snatching his hand back from Jen's grasp when he was bleeding, touching her then jumping back. HIV. He was gay and he had HIV, that was it. So there was no reason in the world to think that he would take Jenny and harm her. And Frank had given him a good character.

That left Frank himself, Jesus Christ, what was she thinking, this was the man she had decided she was in love with. Except that right this minute the feelings part of her brain wasn't working properly so it was difficult to tell. Jenny liked Frank, she would trust him. As for the timing, well, he'd been back and forward all day, it wasn't impossible. But dear God no, she couldn't think like this. Frank was the only person she had left to trust here. So push that thought right away.

But who else was there? People like Mrs Mullen at the shop. Well. That couldn't possibly be true. Then there was the handful of people from St. Joe's who were known to Jenny, she would trust Derek, for instance, or Doug, or Laura. But was it really within the bounds of possibility that one of them had actually taken her? Not Laura, because Oberon was definitely a man. Derek? He hadn't been around in the morning, paperwork, he'd said, but he'd been there some of the time in the afternoon. And like Frank, Doug had been back and forward all day. Working in a hospital was like that, you were in and out of the rooms and then you went to pick up some meds or take a patient somewhere and then you were back again.

This was no use. She was too tired to think straight and she wasn't going to get any sleep, she could tell, the constant, gnawing fear would make sure of that. What could she do, what could she do….

The landline shrilled in the hallway and she stumbled in her haste to grab the receiver.

'Lici, I'm so sorry, what can I do?'

A man's voice, and in spite of the crackling line she knew at once whose it was.

'Cathal.'

'Sonja just called, she told me what you're going through. Lici, I want to help but I don't think I can. The only thing I remember about your Dad is that I was scared stiff of him. But your little girl, that must be all you can think of right now.'

'It is. Cathal, I, if I lose Jenny I think I'll go mad.'

'You won't. You're strong, look what you've already come through. Your father and all. And Frank will help you.'

Was there any way to tell him that she didn't even know that it wasn't Frank who had taken Jen?

'We'll keep in touch now, Cathal.'

'We will. Hang on in there, Lici, they could find her any time. I'll call tomorrow.'

The line buzzed in her ear and she stood clutching the receiver. If only Cathal was here. Or Sonja. She could trust them. But she was alone, and it was suddenly unbearable.

She would go back to St. Joe's. Laura was on duty, she could talk to Laura. Yes.

The sky was darkening rapidly, lights were on all over the village. Lower Banford was getting ready for the night. Alicia could see the woods, a thick black shadow on the hillside. The moon was out, casting eerie, ghostly shadows across the garden, but dark clouds were gathering too. If Jenny was lying injured outside somewhere and rain started, it might well make the difference between life and death for her. But then everything pointed to her having been abducted.

Chapter Twenty

Alicia

There was little traffic about as she crossed the belt of fields between Lower and Middle Banford. By daylight this was such a pretty place, but now everything seemed sinister and threatening. Jenny was missing, and Alicia knew she was going through every mother's hell on earth, not knowing what had happened to her child. She had read somewhere that the police reckoned that if you don't find a missing child within six hours, then you probably won't find them alive. Jenny had been missing for what, twelve hours? They didn't know the exact time she had vanished from the woods. Was she going to lose her despised father and then her beloved daughter, all in the space of a weekend?

The care home was in almost total darkness when she pushed the front door open and walked into the echoing hallway. Most of the old people would be asleep by this time and the night staff would be tiptoeing about getting the last of them settled. She blinked as a figure came towards her from the cloakroom on the ground floor, his face pale in the dim light.

'Frank!'

'I didn't know where else to go,' he said, taking her arm with a hand that was as cold as her own. 'Alicia, please let me help. What are you doing here?'

'I wanted to talk to Laura. Cathal phoned, and I just couldn't be alone any more, I was going over and over everything in my head and I needed someone… '

Alicia found herself clutching Frank's hand. Oh God, surely he hadn't taken Jenny. Not Frank.

'Let's go upstairs,' he said. 'Derek's car is here so he must have come back for some reason, maybe they've found out something about your father.'

Frank pushed the ward door open and they crept along the semi-darkness of the corridor to the nursing station. One of the staff nurses came towards them, sympathy on her face.

'I expect you want Derek.'

'I didn't think he'd be here,' said Frank.

The nurse made a face. 'Harry French lost his illicit stash of lager this evening and had a massive tantrum, insisting that Derek had put it away somewhere. I phoned him just in case he had, and you know Derek, back he came with more lager to help settle Harry. He was still doing that when Jim Slater upset Lily Buchanen again, and she started screaming blue murder, so poor Derek ended up in the middle of that one too.'

Life and times in a geriatric hospital, thought Alicia. It would be funny in any other situation.

Frank knocked on the office door and pushed it open. Derek was sitting in front of the computer, tapping at the keyboard with a glum face and Alicia saw that he was filling out an accident report. He jumped to his feet.

'Alicia! Here, sit down.'

'We're just here to talk to someone,' said Frank, leaning against the desk. 'I hear you've had an interesting evening off.'

'I have,' he said, raising his eyebrows and falling back into his chair again. 'But never mind that, you haven't come to help us look for Harry's lager, I'm sure. Is there anything I can do for you?' He looked from Frank to Alicia.

'I'm sorry I made such a scene when Bob died,' said Alicia. 'He was terrible to me when I was a kid and with Jen missing I just couldn't… '

'You've done nothing to apologise for,' said Derek. 'Hold on, Alicia, don't give up hope.'

He was right, there was no proof that Jenny was dead. But how hard it was to keep hoping and hoping, knowing that with every passing minute the likelihood that Jen would be found safe was decreasing. It was an agony that was too painful not to suppress.

Frank spoke. 'Did Ian have any more thoughts on the cause of Bob's death?'

Derek looked at Alicia, seemingly considering before he spoke. She nodded at him, and he sighed.

'No. I'll tell you something, Frank, I don't like it. I know it's impossible, but it looks to me very much like an overdose of his sleeping pills. That's *not* possible, though. He couldn't have hoarded any, he simply didn't have the wits to do that, and whatever it was, it happened twice today. Ian's put through an urgent post-mortem and I'm going to be very interested in the results.'

Alicia closed her eyes. What did any of this matter?

Frank moved towards the door. 'Me too,' he said. He reached for Alicia's hand and she stood up. Time to go and, what? There was nothing left to do now. She listened drearily as Frank spoke.

'Thanks, Derek. We'll leave you to your report. What happened there?'

Derek shrugged, smiling grimly. 'Jim Slater had ructions with old Lily, who flounced off into her room and slammed the door so hard a picture fell off the wall resulting in broken glass on the floor, which she promptly cut herself on. Jim, of course, feels himself completely innocent. He could get a churchful of cardinals fighting, that one. Doug Patton called him Puck yesterday afternoon and you know, he's not far wrong. I think... Alicia? Are you okay?'

She was motionless, the hand that had already been stretching out to grasp the door now frozen in mid-air. Ice cold clarity swept through her and suddenly it was difficult to breathe.

'Doug Patton called him... Puck...'

'Frank.' She could only mouth his name. It was another of those moments when the world seems to move round and round in slow motion, blurring at the edges, and only the very centre of her vision was left in focus. Shakespeare. The Festival. *A Midsummer Night's Dream.* Oberon, Titania. Puck the jester, Puck the malevolent... Oberon. But dear God, that couldn't be. She was aware of Frank standing rigid beside her, and Derek staring, then rising to his feet, alarm written all over his face.

'What's wrong, Alicia? Frank! What is it? You both look as if you've seen a ghost.'

It was difficult to talk but Alicia knew they had to tell Derek, then she had to act as fast as she could. Her voice was hoarse. 'Derek, Jenny has a playmate she meets in the woods, a man, and most probably it's him who's taken her. He calls himself Oberon.'

'We have to call the police,' said Frank.

Derek was staring, his face white. 'Ober... oh, *shit*. Frank, wait. That can't be, Alicia. It must be a coincidence. There's been so much about that play around here this year. And Doug is... well, he's Doug. It's *not* possible, it must... '

His voice broke off.

Alicia felt herself sway. Dear God... she had kissed... and what had he done to her daughter?

Frank pushed her back down on the chair and reached for his phone.

'I don't know if it's right, Derek, but it is possible,' he said grimly. 'And I'd rather make a mistake and look like a fool than risk a child's life by not acting. Get me Doug's address, would you?'

Alicia was fighting dizziness. The whole room was swirling around her and she bit down painfully on the inside of her cheek, listening as Frank spoke into his phone.

'This is Doctor Frank Carter. Jenny Bryson may be with a Douglas Patton who lives at... ' He glanced at the computer screen where Derek had accessed a list of St. Joe's employees. '... 9 Fairweather Court, Lower Banford. Would you please check this, I'm going over there with Jenny's mother now too.'

He disconnected and Alicia grabbed his hand.

'Come *on!*' she cried wildly, pulling him to the door. They had to go, they had to get to Jenny.

'Arrange an ambulance!' Frank shouted at Derek, and then they were running down the ward, down the stairs and outside into the darkness.

The road back had never seemed so long, stretching endlessly in front of them. Alicia forced herself to concentrate on keeping calm, sitting in Frank's car as he drove. In the distance, she could see lights down by the river where the search parties were still out looking for Jenny. If Doug had her they had undertaken a pointless task.

The Stranger

He placed his plate and glass in the sink and ran the hot water. So mundane, and yet the very fact that he was doing the last, the very last couple of things before the culmination of his plans was so wonderful. Expectation was making him sweat more than ever and the shivery feeling was building inside him, just another hour and then he would be watching little Helen's eyes glaze like Mummy's had, like Helen's had, feeling her delicious little body go limp... knowing that his own darling wasn't alone in Paradise any more. And then tomorrow, or the next day, it would be big Helen's turn.

It was time to go. What did he need to take with him? Little Helen herself, of course, and her golden robe. And the cords for her neck, he wasn't going to be angry this time so he might not be able to send her off to Paradise with his bare hands. And the fluffy blanket, too, in case he wanted to smother her voice if she wailed at the wrong time. That was all.

He went back to the bedroom and gazed down at little Helen. Her eyes were half-closed and her breath was coming in enchanting little pants. She was more awake than she'd been earlier, so the timing was working out well, perfectly, in fact.

Swiftly, he bound the little girl's hands and feet. Reef knots were best. They wouldn't come undone even if little Helen started to struggle. He'd learned that at Boy Scouts when he was ten or eleven. He had hated going, but Mummy made him. She had made him do so many things he hadn't wanted to. Well, these days he could do what he liked, and soon he'd be cuddling up to little Helen in the circle of trees, the Paradise trees, under the midsummer night sky.

He would lie with her on the golden robe and it would be perfect. The thought was terrifying and wonderful all at the same time.

Carefully, he wrapped little Helen in the blanket and robe before lifting her, noticing proudly that he was used to carrying her now. He had the feel of her body. He opened the flat door, and held her against his chest with one arm while he locked it again behind him. Now for the dangerous part, though he already knew that it was unlikely that either of the other flats in the building would be occupied at this time on Saturday night. Down the stairs, quickly, quietly, don't drop anything, and out to the waiting car, parked right by the front door in preparation. Little Helen could lie on the back seat and he would cover her completely with the golden robe.

He drove the back roads to the far side of the woods. It was better not to drive through the village, you never know, there might be policemen still around. The back road was deserted, and he arrived at the grassy verge where he'd kicked the dog out earlier.

It was dark up there, though. He hadn't thought of that. Never mind, there was a torch in the boot, if he balanced it on little Helen there would be enough light to see by. Oh, he was so looking forward to this.

Slowly, slowly, carefully up through the trees. Don't stumble, it would never do if he dropped little Helen or bumped her against a tree. He looked down at the child in his arms. Her eyelids were flickering, and the keening sounds were coming once again from her little throat, how very fortunate that no-one was around to hear her. It was more difficult than he'd anticipated, walking up through the trees. He was a fit man, but he could feel his thigh muscles begin to ache.

Almost there. The circle of trees, there it was, dark and magical. And it was different in the darkness, too, much better, for the little clearing had a moonstruck eeriness in the light of the stars. Here he was, right in the middle of the circle. He had arrived.

Panting, he laid little Helen on the mossy ground and tugged at the golden robe until it was straightened out nicely underneath her. She was quiet now, eyelids half open, yes, she was waking up, how perfect.

He stretched her arms above her head and spread her legs. His star-shaped little Helen. He was going to have such a beautiful time with her now.

Alicia

'Stop, we should leave the car here,' said Alicia, as Frank drove past the village shop and hesitated at the crossroads. 'If he's in the house with her we don't want to just drive up and park outside, that would warn him.'

Had Doug taken Jenny? Was that even remotely possible? It might have been pure coincidence, the mention of Puck after the mention of Oberon. But even allowing for that year's theatre production, 'Puck' wasn't exactly a name anyone would call someone else unless they'd been thinking about the play. Troublemaker, mischief-maker, agitator, stirrer - these were the words that would have sprung to her own mind if she'd been complaining about Jim Slater. So it couldn't be coincidence. Doug must be Oberon. Dear God, to think she had once been attracted to this man, she had been out for dinner with him, sat opposite him and eaten curry ice cream for Christ's sake, and now she was quite prepared to believe that he had abducted her daughter. But tonight she would be prepared to believe anything at all, if it meant she would get Jenny back. But if Doug had taken Jenny for any reason at all, then surely he wouldn't have *hurt* her. The whole village liked Doug, everyone at St Joe's too, they couldn't all have been so completely mistaken about him, could they? But of course they could, just look how mistaken such a lot of people had been about her father.

Frank parked opposite the pub and they jogged up Doug's road, peering at the house numbers to find the right one. Alicia could feel her heart thumping in her chest. She grabbed Frank's arm. There it was, number nine, right in the middle. A tall house, and it had been split into three flats, one on each floor. The whole place was in darkness. Was he asleep? Or away somewhere? Was Jenny with him?

Alicia realised in dismay that Doug's car was nowhere to be seen. Where would he be at this time on a Saturday evening after working all day? The pub was only five hundred yards away and he wouldn't take the car there anyway. Was he out visiting someone? Or had he taken Jen away to some other place? Not speaking, she and Frank crept up to the house, walking on the narrow strip of grass to prevent their feet crunching on the gravel.

Frank pushed the front door. Rather to Alicia's surprise it opened, revealing a dim communal staircase. She followed on up six steps and arrived at the front door of the ground floor flat. Carson, the nameplate above the doorbell informed her. Not Doug's flat. She continued up the stairs, trying to ignore the dryness in her mouth.

'I'm not sure we should be doing this,' muttered Frank.

Alicia gripped his hand. 'The police'll be here any minute. We won't put the light on. Quick!'

The moon was sending ghostly shafts of silver through the stairway windows, providing just enough light to see by. A pewter umbrella stand and a large wooden giraffe flanked the doorway on the first floor. Not Doug's flat again. So the top one was his, just one floor up now. There it was, a large, old-fashioned door with frosted glass panels; yellow, red and green in alternating squares of colour.

Alicia put her ear to the door and listened. Silence. Frank indicated the doorbell, looking at her with raised eyebrows. She rang the doorbell loud and long.

Silence again. But maybe he was in bed, asleep. Again she leaned on the bell, again it shrilled out in the silence. Two seconds, three, four, five. Yet more silence.

'He's not here,' she whispered. Where was he? And where was Jenny?

'Or he's not answering,' said Frank. He tried the door, but it was locked.

Alicia began to shiver. Jenny might be in there. Should they hammer on the door? She raised clenched fists to her mouth, staring at the door. Footsteps and voices on the ground floor spurred her into action. The police had arrived. Alicia turned and ran down to the middle floor, meeting Chief Inspector Wilson on the way up with two policemen.

'He's not here,' she said, standing back to let the Chief Inspector's bulky frame charge past.

'And neither should you be,' he said, battering on the door of Doug's flat. 'Police! Open the door!'

'He's not here,' said Alicia again.

The Inspector looked at her grimly. 'We'll get in, but I want you both to stay put here until we're certain it's safe,' he said, nodding to one of his colleagues, who stepped forward with a metal device which he slammed against the lock. The wooden frame cracked and the door swung open. Alicia watched as Chief Inspector Wilson disappeared inside the flat, his men following on. Her heart was really thumping now, it was as if someone was wielding a hammer right inside her chest, the blows reverberating round her ribcage, and there was a rushing noise in her ears too. She felt horribly dizzy.

'No-one,' said the Chief Inspector from the top end of the hallway. 'Come in, Mrs Bryson, and see if you notice anything that would tell us if Jenny's been here.'

The hallway was painted a rather dingy beige colour; old, flaky beige paint, and Alicia felt a quick jolt of surprise. This didn't seem at all like the kind of place immaculate Doug would have chosen to live. It was a rather sinister indication of how little they really knew him. The living room was dingy too, with heavy dark red velvet curtains drawn across the window, shutting the night out. One of the policemen clicked the overhead light on and Alicia and Frank moved into the room. Two threadbare armchairs stood left and right of the disused fireplace and a sofa that didn't match them was up against the opposite wall. A door at the far end probably led into the kitchen.

'Alicia.'

Frank was right beside her, holding her close to him with one hand while the other pointed. She turned her head, and there in the corner, beside the sofa, she saw a pathetic little pile of clothes. Jenny's clothes. All of them. Blue shorts, yellow t-shirt, socks, knickers. Minnie Mouse watch. New summer sandals. Every single thing Jenny had been wearing that morning was lying there.

'Boss!' One of the policemen was in the hallway, looking into another room. Alicia wrenched herself away from Frank and ran to the bathroom doorway. She found herself staring at an ancient bathtub, partially filled with clouded, oily water.

'Okay, I want everyone out of here right now, please,' ordered the Chief Inspector. 'This flat is a crime scene.'

He pushed Alicia back out to the stairwell, where she clutched at Frank with both hands. The buzzing in her ears was so loud she could barely hear Chief Inspector Wilson on his radio, organising backup, more search parties, road blocks. Frank held her, but she could feel his heart beating wildly too. Doug Patton had Jenny. He had undressed her. And what else? She couldn't bear to think. It was the worst, the absolute worst thing she had imagined since Jenny went missing. A pervert. A paedophile. Doug was Oberon. This was a man she had trusted, and now such betrayal. The pain was excruciating, for a moment she literally couldn't breathe.

The Chief Inspector joined them on the landing. 'There's no sign of a struggle,' he said. 'Try not to think the worst before we know what went on here. We'll start an immediate search through the whole village, barns, outhouses, the lot. Mrs Bryson, if he's here we'll find him.'

'It might be too late,' she whispered, knowing there was nothing anyone could say to this. It might be too late. Jenny, beautiful Jenny, what had Doug done to her? And why? Why had he picked out Jenny, Jenny who loved life and animals and playing in the woods, why had he…

'The woods!' she said suddenly. 'The special place in the woods, where they met and played… '

The Chief Inspector stared at her for a split second before marching to the stairs. 'Come on, we're going.' He spoke into his radio as he went, reporting the new details. 'The Super's meeting us there.'

They ran down, Frank almost yanking Alicia off her feet and the Chief Inspector thundering ahead at a speed that belied his size. Two police cars were parked in the front drive, and Frank pushed Alicia into the back seat of the first one and got in after her.

'We can go up through the woods from the bottom of Alicia's garden,' he said to the Inspector. 'It's nearer the clearing than going up from the back road.'

The Inspector looked at him, his face grim. 'You know it too, then?' he said, nodding when Frank confirmed this.

The brakes squealed as they rounded the corner by the hotel. Alicia winced. She should have phoned Paul long ago. He could have been trying to reach her for ages, she had left her mobile on the kitchen table.

'I should phone Paul,' she said to Frank. 'Have you got your phone? He's at the King's Hotel in York.'

Frank fumbled with his phone, looking for the hotel's website. His voice shook when he spoke but the connection was quickly made.

'It's ringing in his room,' he said, handing the phone to Alicia.

'Yes?' Paul's voice sounded sleepy. Alicia felt as if she'd been slapped hard in the face.

'I'm sorry to interrupt your beauty sleep, but you might remember I told you our daughter is missing,' she hissed, suddenly furious, more furious than she had ever been in her life before, as if being angry with Paul was going to help Jenny. She knew that Doug was the person who deserved her rage, but for the moment it was easier to let it out on Paul.

'Well, we know now that she's been abducted by a psychopath and they're searching the woods again to see if they can find her alive. But don't bother yourself about it, I'll phone you again in the morning when you've had your sleep and tell you if you'll need a black tie to come and see her next time.' She broke the connection.

'That told him,' said the Chief Inspector, and Alicia nodded grimly.

'He's never been much of a father,' she said, and tears poured down her cheeks.

Another police car was parked in the lane when they arrived there, and the waiting Superintendent spoke briefly to his colleagues before turning back to Frank and Alicia.

'Doctor, you're with us,' he said, striding up the back garden. 'Mrs Bryson, I'd like you to wait here.'

'No!' she cried. 'I must... '

'Wait at the bottom of the garden,' said Frank firmly. 'It's better you don't come up, Alicia. If Jenny's there I promise I'll take care of her until we can bring her down to you.'

'No,' said Alicia again. She knew there was no way she could simply stand and watch while the men went off to look for her Jenny. If there was the slightest chance that Doug had Jen up in the woods she wanted to be right there to help her daughter at the very first opportunity.

The Superintendent looked at her and she could see frustration and understanding mingling on his face.

'Okay,' he said. 'You can come, but if Patton is there with her I want you to promise you'll stay back until I call you on. You do exactly as I say. Clear?'

'Okay, clear,' said Alicia, relief flooding through her. 'Thank you.'

She followed the five policemen up the woodland path, treading where they were treading, making as little noise as she could. Frank was up at the head of the procession, showing the way, and a young policewoman had appeared and walked behind Alicia. Chief Inspector Wilson and one of the others were carrying torches, which they shone on the ground before them, but it was still too dark to see properly. She knew they didn't want Doug – if he was here – to get wind of their arrival.

What would she do if Jenny was dead up there? Alicia felt sick with fear at the thought. Jen was only eight years old. Would she cope without her? Would Margaret? The thought was appalling. She would give up everything, she would do anything and go anywhere at all, if she could have Jenny back unharmed. How unlikely that seemed right now. Christ, how she wanted her old life back.

The woods were dark but not cold, and somehow not as sinister as she'd have thought. It felt as if the trees and bushes were merely waiting for dawn and sunshine and the warmth of another day.

Frank and the first policeman stopped to confer in a low mutter that Alicia couldn't understand, and she strained her ears to hear something from the direction of the clearing. They were only about halfway there, walking quietly like this was maddeningly slow.

Frank pointed out the way they should take, and the policeman stood back to let him go first before the procession started off again. They went on in silence for another twenty yards or so before the Inspector's large shape appeared beside her.

'Wait here, Mrs Bryson,' he murmured. 'We'll call you as soon as we're able. Marjorie'll stay with you.'

Alicia stopped immediately. This was no time to argue. She watched as they disappeared into the darkness, six men. Moving carefully, not wanting to disturb Doug if he was there, in case there was any chance of getting Jenny back alive. The young policewoman stood beside Alicia with a large torch, sharing the wait.

'She's my only child,' whispered Alicia, and the younger woman nodded, making no attempt to offer consolation or false hope.

After a moment there was no sound from the men. Alicia stood motionless, staring into the darkness. In a few short minutes she might know what had happened to Jenny. What would the police do if Jen was dead? Lying in a heap in the woods where she had once played so happily. Didn't they have to leave bodies where they were found, and take measurements and photos and footprints? When would they let her go and see her dead daughter? Tonight? Tomorrow? Alicia raised clenched fists to her mouth, and the policewoman put a hand on her arm.

'Steady now,' she said. 'Just keep it together, they won't be much longer.'

And still silence in the woods.

The Stranger

He looked down at little Helen, lying there on her cloth of gold, her arms and legs spread to the heavens. Beautiful, a little star waiting for her lord and master to send her off to Paradise. His own angel. But look, there were goose bumps all over the child's body. She needed warmth, and what better way to give her that than to lie down beside her and take her in his arms? He lowered himself to the ground, gathering little Helen to him with one hand and pulling the golden covering over them both with the other. There, that was better. And how delicious it felt, holding her close like this in the holy place. Her head fitted snugly under his chin, and he could feel the movement of her chest as she breathed. She was still pretty much out of it, though she had stopped making the keening sounds and her eyes were now open. He arched his body against her, then winced as something sharp on the ground beneath him jabbed into his side. Lovely as it was, it had been a whole lot more comfortable on his bed at home. And lying with a child like this... it was sweet, but forbidden-sweet. Lying with big Helen tomorrow, on the other hand, would be completely natural, she was larger, softer, much more comfortable to hold and squeeze. Just like his own darling Helen, in fact. And it was time to finish up here, he was too impatient now to play more with little Helen, he wanted her to be where she belonged. Then he could go home and dream of his own two girls playing together. Riches indeed. How happy his darlings would be.

He scrambled to his feet again and bent to brush a few twigs from the golden robe. A moan came from little Helen's mouth, and he looked at her critically. She was nearly ready. A few more minutes and she'd be conscious enough to understand what he was going to do with her. He wanted to see the fear in her eyes fade away and be replaced by the silence and emptiness of eternity. He reached into his pocket and fingered the cord.

She was looking at him now, and yes, oh yes, there it was, there was recognition on her face, apprehension too, she was afraid, she was ready.

Alicia

Alicia turned and looked back the way they had come. The streetlights of Lower Banford were glowing in a faded kind of way below the night sky, she could make out the nearest lamp at the end of the lane where her father's house was. She would sell it, she knew. No matter what happened tonight she could never live in that house again, knowing the anguish she had endured here. That had started when she was a very young child, and the past few days had merely been an extension of the horror. Multiplied a million times because now she wasn't the one in danger, it was her daughter. And if Jenny was dead she would lose her chance of happiness with Frank. She would never think of him or of this place without feeling the grief and the dread.

The events of the day suddenly caught up with her, and Alicia sank to the ground on her knees. The policewoman crouched beside her, and gripped her arm.

'Look, Mrs Bryson. Alicia. There's a stump over here. You can sit on that.'

Alicia allowed herself to be led over to the tree stump. It was a relief to sit down, her legs were aching, but the moment she did sit her knees started to tremble and the shivering started again. It was the most horrible thing she had ever lived through, this waiting, not having any constructive role to play herself.

And still there was nothing. It was so cold, oh God how cold she was.

A rustling sound came from several yards further up the path, and Alicia leapt to her feet and strained to see who was coming.

'Mrs Bryson!' It was a deep male whisper, and she stumbled towards it, recognising it as the youngest policeman's, the one who had been there when her father went missing too. Her heart went into double time. Frank and the senior men were still up there, so that must mean Doug was up there too. With Jenny.

'He's there. With Jenny. We can't tell yet if she's hurt or not. Keep very quiet and follow me.'

Alicia pushed him back the way he had come and followed close on his heels. She still had no idea what had happened to Jen, but within minutes she'd be with her daughter, and she would know the worst.

'No talking,' murmured the young policeman, gripping her arm. 'He has no idea we're here.'

Alicia saw that Frank and the other men were in pairs, crouching behind sturdy trees around the clearing, and she followed the policeman to a tree of their own. Cautiously, she peered out from behind the tree and found herself looking at Doug from the side. He was about twenty yards away, bent almost double and arranging some kind of cloth over a light coloured bundle on the ground.

Alicia's head swam as she stared, blinking back tears of impatience and frustration and straining to see if the bundle was moving because that must be Jenny. But oh no, no, the bundle wasn't moving and it wasn't making a sound either. It was only the policeman's hand gripping her arm that prevented her from running to her daughter herself. Doug stood up, dusting his hands and looking satisfied. Alicia winced. It was Doug, but the man's whole posture was different, the set of his head looked awkward and he had a satisfied, sinister grin across his face. She had never seen him look like that.

'Helen's waiting for you in Paradise,' said Doug conversationally. 'When you get there you'll see her. She's just as lovely as you are, little Helen. And Big Helen will join you very soon. It'll all be perfect, you'll see. And now it's time for you to go.' He produced a length of cord from his pocket and started to wind it round his hands.

The Superintendent stepped forward and Alicia saw with a stomach-lurching shock that there was a gun in the policeman's hand. 'Police!' he yelled. 'Hands over your head!'

Doug started wildly, glared round at them and then made a leap for the bundle on the ground. With appalling suddenness a single shot rang out, and birds in the trees screamed skywards. Alicia's ears rang and Doug crumpled over the small figure at his feet. The Inspector moved forward.

'Wait there, Doc,' he shouted, but Frank was right behind him, in front of the other policemen. Alicia forced her legs into action and ran across the clearing to Jenny while Frank helped the Superintendent and Chief Inspector Wilson pull Doug away. Alicia put trembling hands on Jenny's face and felt warmth. Jenny's eyes were half open and she was breathing, she *was* breathing. Alicia's heart felt as if it would burst. Jen was alive. They could help her now. Frank was kneeling beside her too.

'She's alive,' he said to the others, then bent over the child again. 'Jenny? Jenny darling, it's Frank, sweetie, we've got you safe, everything's going to be alright. Mummy's right here too.'

He nodded to Alicia, but her throat had closed and no sound came from her mouth when she tried to speak. She put her head close to Jenny's instead, smelling the heavy perfume and feeling oily slickness on the child's skin.

Frank put a hand on Jenny's brow. 'Temp's okay,' he said, and motioned to one of the policemen to bring a torch over. Alicia blinked as a sudden ring of light swayed over them, and saw Frank dash tears from his eyes before bending over Jenny again, shining the light into her face.

Jenny's breathing was ragged and Alicia saw that in spite of the torchlight, the child's pupils were dilated. She must have been drugged, good, she might not have realised the full horror of what had happened to her. Alicia forced herself to speak.

'Jenny? Does anything hurt, darling?'

Jenny was staring at her, trying to focus. Frank took out his stethoscope and Alicia loosened the covering from Jen's thin chest, her gut cramping when she saw that the oil was all over the child's body.

'Heartbeat's strong and steady,' said Frank reassuringly, brushing back the strands of greasy hair that were sticking to Jenny's forehead, half-covering one eye. Alicia found a tissue in her jeans and started to wipe Jenny's oily face. The child frowned up at them, and Alicia saw she was trying to assemble something to say.

'Jen? Where does it hurt, lovey?'

Jenny's voice was a drunken whisper, 'M - m - my head feels - fu - funny,' she said, and tears rushed into Alicia's eyes again.

'I think you've had medicine to make you sleep, you know, like Grandpa gets,' said Frank, putting his stethoscope back into his pocket. 'Don't worry, Jen, you'll feel better very soon.' He turned to the Superintendent who was bending over Doug Patton.

'Unconscious but alive,' he said, in answer to Frank's look. 'The bullet's in his shoulder. Don't worry about him, the police doc will be here any minute. Is Jenny going to be alright?'

'Yes, she's going to be just fine.' Frank had uncovered Jenny completely and was checking for broken bones. Alicia leaned towards him and gazed at her daughter's oily body in the light of the torch. There was no blood, thank God, no blood.

'All in one piece. I want to take her back down now,' said Frank. He was smiling at Jenny but Alicia could hear the strain in his voice. It was only now that they had Jenny back that Alicia could allow herself to acknowledge just how terrible the past twelve hours had been.

She knew that Frank's 'just fine' and 'all in one piece' had been for Jenny's ears too. They wouldn't know until later how badly she'd been hurt.

'There'll be an ambulance waiting in the lane,' said the Superintendent, moving aside as the police doctor arrived. 'Young Joe over there'll go with you. I'll wait for our doc to finish here and give a hand with this one.' He jerked his head at Doug.

Frank rolled Jenny up in the blanket again and lifted her. 'I'll carry you, Jen, and Mummy's right beside us,' he said, and Jenny reached for Alicia's hand and then wriggled until her head was tucked into Frank's shoulder. Alicia took a deep breath. Jenny's eyes were fixed on her face, and she kissed the oily wrist.

'It'll all be okay in the end, lovey, you'll see,' she said. Please God she hoped it would be.

The policeman called Joe went in front with the torch, lighting the way, and Frank walked slowly and carefully behind him.

Alicia almost crept along beside them, as if she was afraid Jenny would disappear again if she moved too quickly. She put her free hand round Frank's shoulder and walked down through the woods with Frank and Jen encircled in her arms, and really she didn't care where she was as long as they were both there with her.

Chapter Twenty-One

Alicia

Two paramedics were running up the garden with a stretcher.

'We're okay, she's quite comfortable like this, let's get her into the ambulance and have a proper look,' said Frank, striding towards the vehicle parked in the lane.

Alicia stumbled along beside him, still clutching Jenny's hand and Frank's shoulder. Thinking about what Frank might find when he examined Jenny made her feel as if she would throw up any minute. How quickly things change. Jenny was here, she had her daughter back alive, and already that wasn't enough. What had her child been forced to endure today? And how horrific it was that ever since they'd arrived in Lower Banford, Alicia had been wondering and worrying about the abuse her father had inflicted on her, and now the same hurt might have been happening to her daughter. Here and today. At Doug's flat.

Frank stepped nimbly up into the back of the ambulance and laid Jenny on the trolley there. The paramedics followed, and Alicia remained standing on the step because there was no room for her in the back too.

'I'm right here, Jen,' she said thickly, reaching out and squeezing Jenny's foot. 'Frank's going to check you over. Don't worry, darling.'

Any second now Frank would be able to tell her what Doug had done. Shit, if she could have two minutes alone with Doug Patton, what wouldn't she do to him. She could kill for her daughter, she knew. Mother's instinct, maybe. She had never felt such apprehension; it was more than torture. Her breath was coming in painful, shallow gasps.

Frank jumped down from the back of the ambulance and walked her a few steps away. Alicia pressed both hands to her chest, bracing herself for bad news.

'Has she been… ' She couldn't bring herself to say it out loud. He shook his head.

'I don't think so but I can't tell without a full examination,' he said. 'There's no blood, but that might have been washed off. There are no obvious signs that she's been sexually assaulted but there's bruising on her thighs, her back, her ankles and wrists – looks like he tied her up – and she's definitely been drugged, too. We'll have to go to hospital, Alicia, she needs a full examination and a police doctor, but you'll be able to stay with her the whole time. I don't think she remembers much of what happened, so don't let her see you're so upset, okay? It's not time for her to start dealing with this yet. We'll get her on her feet again, see what she remembers and take it from there.'

Alicia sighed, feeling her breath shake. She could still hope.

Fixing a calm expression on her face, Alicia got into the back of the ambulance. She couldn't reach Jenny's hand from where she was sitting, she couldn't touch her daughter. Jenny had an oxygen mask over her face and her eyes were closed. 'I'm right here, darling,' said Alicia, but the child's face remained oblivious.

'She's still pretty out of it,' said the paramedic. 'But she's quite stable, don't worry. Right, Pete, off we go.'

The ambulance sped off towards Merton and the general hospital there. Alicia fought back a sob. Nothing in her life until now had prepared her for this, speeding along in an ambulance, blue light flashing and siren wailing as they drove through Saturday night revellers in Merton, and her child, *her child* lying there unconscious and helpless. It was almost more than she could cope with. She gripped her seat with both hands, forcing herself to breathe slowly. She was getting good at that now.

At the hospital, Jenny was trolleyed swiftly into the A&E Unit. Alicia jogged alongside, never letting go of Jenny's hand, relieved to see that the paediatrician who came to meet them was a woman around the same age as herself. They took a few blood samples, and countless swabs from various parts of Jenny's oily little body. Alicia didn't watch exactly what they did; Jenny had roused up again and needed constant reassurance. There was a policewoman in the room too, but she made no attempt to ask Jenny any questions. Hopefully that could wait until much later, thought Alicia. After all, they'd caught Doug red-handed.

When the examination was finished she was allowed to help wash Jenny at last, and get rid of some of the oil. There wasn't much they could do about the little girl's hair, though.

'Let's leave it until the morning when she's properly awake,' said the nurse. 'Don't worry, Mrs Bryson. I know you must want it all off right this minute, but she's almost asleep again. She can have a nice hot bath with plenty of shampoo first thing.'

Alicia wiped a wet hand over her face. 'I just want her back home in her own bed,' she said, hearing her voice shake.

'I know. It's been a dreadful ordeal for you. She'll have to stay here until the drugs wear off, but you can probably take her home tomorrow,' said the nurse, inserting Jenny's unresisting body into a hospital gown and covering her with a pink blanket. 'She can go up to the ward now, and you'll be able to stay with her, of course.'

She left the room with her trolley of utensils, and Frank put his head in the door. Alicia held out her arms. More than anything else now she needed reassurance, she needed someone to tell her that the horror was over and they were all safe. They stood beside Jenny's trolley, looking down at the sleeping child. Her Jenny, and yet not at all the Jenny who had woken up that morning and looked forward to a beautiful, shining summer day.

'She has to stay in,' Alicia said, sniffing.

He handed her a tissue. 'I spoke to the doctor,' he said. 'Jen wasn't damaged physically, but unless she can tell us later, there's no way to know exactly what he did to her. However there are no injuries other than the bruises, the doctor thinks she may have fallen. And she was drugged, of course. We'll see what she remembers in the morning.'

He was silent for a moment, and Alicia could feel tension in his body still. She stepped back and looked at him.

'What is it? There's something you're not telling me.'

'Nothing about Jenny,' he said quickly. 'Oh Alicia, I went up to the lab to see if I could find anything out about your father's blood test, the one I took this morning. It came to the lab here. Alicia, it looks like he *was* given an overdose of his sleeping pills.'

Alicia cringed. 'Doug? Frank, did Doug Patton kill my father?'

He hugged her tightly. 'It seems likely. I suppose he was trying to keep you otherwise occupied while he took Jenny. I'm sorry, Alicia, I didn't want to tell you until tomorrow.'

She pressed her lips together for a moment before speaking. 'No. It's better to know things like that straightaway,' she told him. 'Then there's no secrets. Jenny's going to be home again tomorrow, and we're damn well going to start the rest of our lives.'

'Together,' he said, reaching out and lifting one of Jenny's hands from the trolley. 'You, me and Jenny. Together.'

Alicia sighed. It sounded like everything she had ever wanted. They were going to get through this. She almost managed a smile and leaned her head against his neck. He was warm and he smelled of… coming home.

'Of course, together,' she said.

Chapter Twenty-Two
Six months later

Alicia

The road sign for Merton swooped by, and Alicia felt her shoulders relax. They were nearly home. She'd almost forgotten what a long drive north it was from Bedford. It had been great to spend New Year with their old friends, of course, but being there had assured Alicia that Lower Banford really was home now.

'Are we nearly there?'

Jenny's voice from the back seat was bored, and Alicia grimaced. Shades of last summer. This was almost exactly the spot where she'd told Jen that Margaret had a dog called Conker. And Jen had started looking forward to a wonderful summer that had never happened.

'Ten more minutes,' said Frank, steering left off the motorway. 'Got Conker's present ready for him?'

Jenny rummaged in her rucksack and produced a garish pink and yellow rubber bone with a slot for edible treats.

'I'll fill it with his biscuits before I give it to him. Does Kenneth know we're nearly home?'

'Text him and tell him,' said Alicia, handing over Jenny's precious mobile.

'Woohoo!' Jenny sank down into the back seat and Alicia turned her face towards the window, blinking hard. The relief when Jenny reacted like a normal eight-year-old still caught in her throat every time. The child who had danced so happily into the woods that

July morning was only now beginning to reappear. Even though Jenny hadn't been physically injured by her ordeal at Doug Patton's hands, the mental scars were taking longer to heal. Maybe they never would heal completely. Jen could remember going to Doug's flat that Saturday morning, and that he had promised to show her some kittens. She thought he had given her something to drink, but she wasn't sure about that, and the next thing she could remember was waking up in hospital the next morning and eating beans on toast for breakfast. She did sense, however, that something bad had happened to her, something she didn't understand, and the fact that she couldn't remember what it was distressed her greatly.

Even now, six months later, she hadn't remembered much more, and the psychologist she still saw regularly thought it might stay that way.

Frank stopped at the traffic lights in front of Merton Infirmary and Alicia stared at the A&E department. Not only did they not know what, exactly, Doug had subjected Jenny to while she had been unconscious, they had never found out why, either. There didn't seem to be anything about his past that would explain behaviour like that; his sister had no idea and there was no-one else to ask. He had been taken to a prison with a psychiatric wing and he was still there, refusing to speak about what he had done. Alicia didn't want to hear what psychosis had prompted him to act the way he had, and she didn't really want to know what was going to happen to him either. The important thing was that he was out of their lives forever.

And life as a proper family was working out well, she thought, grinning as Jenny's mobile rang and was promptly answered. How good of Kenneth to call back when he got the text. Jenny had a brief but upbeat conversation about Conker and the holidays before saying goodbye and relaxing into the back seat again.

'Kenneth's going to bring Conker to meet us at home,' she announced.

'He'll have to be quick, then. ETA three minutes,' said Frank. Alicia glanced up Woodside Lane as they passed. A young family lived in her father's house now. She and Jenny had moved in with Frank as soon as they'd come home from hospital the day after Jenny's abduction. And for the first time she'd had a proper home, filled with love in Lower Banford. Frank looked across and grinned as they passed Mrs Mullen's, and Alicia felt warm all over.

As soon as the car stopped in the driveway Jenny was out, hugging Conker, who had been lodging at the pet shop while they'd been away. Max and Moritz the cats came to wind themselves round Alicia's ankles and she stooped to scratch soft heads. She'd had quite a job dissuading Kenneth from giving Jen all four of his kittens after her rescue. How wrong she'd been about him. What she'd considered strangeness had simply been nerves. It wasn't easy being in his situation. Homosexuality and HIV didn't really go with life in a quaint and conservative Yorkshire village. But he was making it work. He had guts, did Kenneth, and Frank had been right. Kenneth was often the first person they called on to babysit.

So on the face of it her life had returned to normal. Or not quite. Some shadows would stay forever. The important thing was to find happiness in today, and now she knew how fragile happiness was. The next event was to be their wedding at the beginning of March, a small affair to go with their small families. There was to be just Margaret, David and Sheila with baby Meret, Sonja and Cathal and their families, and a few close friends, including Kenneth as best man and Jenny as bridesmaid, of course, complete with a traditional pink frilly dress even though the bride would be wearing a non-frilly sage green dress and coat. It would be a mixed-up higgledy-piggledy kind of wedding and it would suit them all perfectly.

Alicia watched as Frank and Kenneth settled down on the sofa with bottles of beer, and Jenny pulled on wellies and her old jacket and ran out to the garden with Conker.

So what now? Time would tell. And they had all the time in the world again.

Come and visit us at
www.legendpress.co.uk

Follow us
@legend_press

Lightning Source UK Ltd.
Milton Keynes UK
UKOW05f0142071113

220549UK00002B/5/P